Rebellious Young Ladies

Finishing school was meant to turn them into perfect aristocratic ladies...but these four friends can never be contained by Society's expectations!

To conform to what Society deemed correct for females of their class, Amelia Lambourne, Irene Fairfax, Georgina Hayward and Emily Beaumont were sent by their families to Halliwell's Finishing School for Refined Young Ladies—which they soon dubbed "Hell's Final Sentence for Rebellious Young Ladies"!

Instead, the four found strength in their mutual support to become themselves and a lifelong friendship was formed...one they'll need to lean on when each young woman faces the one thing they swore never to succumb to—a good match!

Read Amelia's story in
Lady Amelia's Scandalous Secret

Read Irene's story in
Miss Fairfax's Notorious Duke

And watch for Georgina's and Emily's stories, coming soon from Harlequin Historical.

Author Note

Miss Fairfax's Notorious Duke is the second book in the Rebellious Young Ladies series, featuring four friends who meet at Halliwell's Finishing School for Refined Young Ladies, which they call Hell's Final Sentence for Rebellious Young Ladies.

Irene Fairfax is a talented artist but is thwarted in developing her talent, first by her parents and then by the art school she attends.

Female artists in Victorian England faced an uphill battle to be taken seriously. They were often denied entry to art schools and, when they were admitted, were not allowed to attend life drawing classes as it was seen as far too risqué for the gentler sex.

As a rebellious young lady, Irene fights against these prejudices and finds an unlikely champion in notorious Joshua Huntingdon, the Duke of Redcliff.

I hope you enjoy *Miss Fairfax's Notorious Duke*. I love hearing from my readers and can be reached at evashepherd.com and Facebook.com/evashepherdromancewriter.

EVA SHEPHERD

—

Miss Fairfax's Notorious Duke

HARLEQUIN®
HISTORICAL™

Recycling programs for this product may not exist in your area.

ISBN-13: 978-1-335-59566-9

Miss Fairfax's Notorious Duke

Copyright © 2023 by Eva Shepherd

For questions and comments about the quality of this book, please contact us at CustomerService@Harlequin.com.

Harlequin Enterprises ULC
22 Adelaide St. West, 41st Floor
Toronto, Ontario M5H 4E3, Canada
www.Harlequin.com

Printed in U.S.A.

After graduating with degrees in history and political science, **Eva Shepherd** worked in journalism and as an advertising copywriter. She began writing historical romances because it combined her love of a happy ending with her passion for history. She lives in Christchurch, New Zealand, but spends her days immersed in the world of late Victorian England. Eva loves hearing from readers and can be reached via her website, evashepherd.com, and her Facebook page, Facebook.com/evashepherdromancewriter.

Books by Eva Shepherd

Harlequin Historical

Rebellious Young Ladies

Lady Amelia's Scandalous Secret
Miss Fairfax's Notorious Duke

Those Roguish Rosemonts

A Dance to Save the Debutante
Tempting the Sensible Lady Violet
Falling for the Forbidden Duke

Young Victorian Ladies

Wagering on the Wallflower
Stranded with the Reclusive Earl
The Duke's Rebellious Lady

Breaking the Marriage Rules

Beguiling the Duke
Awakening the Duchess
Aspirations of a Lady's Maid
How to Avoid the Marriage Mart

Visit the Author Profile page
at Harlequin.com.

To the talented writers at Word X Word—
you're always a fabulous source of
inspiration and great ideas.

Chapter One

Joshua Huntingdon, the Duke of Redcliff, frowned at his reflection in the tarnished mirror, then laughed. Whatever had happened to him last night was sure to make an interesting tale. Unfortunately, he would not be the one doing the telling as he had absolutely no idea what had occurred and how he had come to be dressed in this curious attire.

He had left home wearing his black evening suit, with its swallowtail jacket, white shirt, white tie and a maroon waistcoat with embroidered gold thread. Somehow, during the evening he had changed into worn, brown moleskin trousers, scuffed leather boots and a faded, collarless shirt that had probably once been brown but was now an insipid, washed-out shade of puce.

On many a night he had lost his shirt at gambling, but never before had he literally done so. Perhaps some lucky workman was now either dressed as inappropriately as himself or had exchanged his clothing for a tidy sum at the nearest pawnshop.

Or maybe his clothing got mixed up as a result of an encounter of a more amorous kind. He did have a vague recollection of a rather comely lass offering some interesting suggestions to him on the many and varied ways she could make the night a particularly memorable one. If he had agreed to her offer, then he was afraid she had failed in her promise, as he had no memory of what had occurred. However, it would explain why he had taken off his clothes, although not why he had dressed himself in some other man's.

He looked around the empty gambling house, still bearing the signs of last night's revelries. Chairs and glasses were overturned, and the air carried the stale fug of cigar, cigarette and pipe smoke and spilt alcohol. A few snoring men were slumped in corners, and an elderly woman was slopping water on the floor from a grey metal bucket, in an attempt to bring some semblance of order to the disarray.

Moments earlier he had been one of those snoring men adding to the discordant sounds, and he suspected he might have contributed in no small way to the overturned chairs, spilt drinks and abandoned empty bottles that littered the room.

He decided to let his fellow former revellers sleep it off rather than wake them to see if they could explain what had happened to him. They looked even the worse for wear than himself and could probably not recall how *they* had got into that state, never mind explain what had happened to anyone else. Instead, he picked up what was presumably now his flat cap, placed it on his head and smiled one more time at his incongruous reflection.

Passing the charlady he reached into his pockets, found a few coins and placed them in her hand.

She stared at the coins, then tried to hand them back to him. 'That's kind of you, but are you sure you've got enough to get yourself to work? I wouldn't want to see you go short on my account.'

'Don't worry about that. I'm afraid I might be partially responsible for some of this mayhem you're clearing up, and after last night I could do with a walk in the fresh air to clear my head.'

She sent him a gap-toothed smile. 'Bless you.'

Her smile warmed his heart and was worth far more than the few pence he had tipped her, especially as she thought he was a working man about to start his day's labour, and not a worthless aristocrat who was ending his night of carousing. A man whose only plan for the day was to get some sleep before he repeated the whole thing the next night. He scowled quickly, somewhat ashamed of his pointless life, then doffed his hat to the hard-working woman, who had gone back to her cleaning and left the gambling house.

The light hit him like a punch to the head. Was the sun always this bright? Even in the narrow alleyway it burned into his eyes and reflected painfully off the red bricks and cobblestones. Blinking, he looked up and down the back street and tried to orientate himself.

Last night he had started out at one or other of his clubs. That much he was sure of. He had a hazy recollection of climbing into someone's packed carriage and travelling across London, with a young lady on his lap, if he remembered correctly. What was her name again? Minnie? Maisie? Whoever she was, she must have been a beauty because he had a vague idea he might have invited her, along with her equally beauteous friends, to his estate in Devon. Then what? He could recall spilling out onto the pavement in front of another drinking establishment, but after that, nothing.

He looked up at the sign hanging above the door of the gambling house. The Queen Victoria. The sign meant nothing to him. There were many such establishments in London named after the reigning queen, although he suspected none were as lacking in majestic dignity as the one he'd just left.

It seemed for now, last night and the reason why he was dressed in such a manner was to remain a mystery. He wandered up the alleyway and turned into a busy commercial area, where businesses were already open, women carrying wicker baskets were doing their daily shop, horses and carts laden with goods were making deliveries and people with a purpose in life were getting on with whatever it was that people with a purpose in life did.

A few hansom cabs rattled past, but none of the drivers bothered to try to get his attention. That was novel. Usually an aristocrat walking home would be an irresistible fare not to be missed. Perhaps he should take it as a sign that he really did need to walk off the excesses of last night, whatever they might be, and attempt to clear his head.

By the time he arrived in Piccadilly he was none the wiser on how he'd come to be dressed in workman's clothing, but the morning air had revived him somewhat and he was looking forward to the hearty breakfast Cook always provided for him after one of his more raucous nights.

Eggs, sausages, bacon… Joshua could almost taste them and it was exactly what he needed to soak up the remaining effects of the night before.

That sense of well-being died as he approached his town house. A familiar carriage glided down the tree-lined road and came to a halt at his doorstep. Aunt Prudence.

Thankfully, she had driven straight past him and had not noticed that the rather scruffy workman who was incongruously walking down the quiet, immaculate street was none other than her reprobate nephew.

Joshua watched from the corner as the footman opened the carriage door and lowered the steps, and his imperious aunt disembarked. The last thing he felt like right now was a lecture from Aunt P. In fact, there was never a time when he felt like a lecture from that formidable lady. He'd been receiving the same lecture for the last ten years, since he acquired the Dukedom at the age of twenty, and the crux of it never changed. He needed to find a wife. He needed to change his ways. He needed a duchess to sort him out. He needed to settle down and produce an heir.

His shoulders slumped as he continued walking. The sooner he got the lecture over and done with, the sooner he could have his breakfast and get some sleep. Then, fully refreshed, he could repeat last night all over again, and again the following night. He released a dejected sigh, then forced himself to straighten up. Partying was what he did best and was hardly reason to feel jaded. It must be the effect of whatever happened last night, or his reaction to seeing Aunt P so early in the morning.

His walking came to another abrupt halt. Lady Gwendolyn Stanhope stepped down from the carriage and followed his aunt up the path. Joshua did an about turn and walked off in the other direction. 'I'm doing this for your sake, Lady Gwendolyn,' he muttered to himself as he increased his pace and rushed around the corner.

His pace accelerated until he found himself running. He needed to put as much distance between himself and what awaited him inside his home as humanly possible. It was not a selfish action. Well, it *was* a selfish action, but not entirely. He was saving Lady Gwendolyn and all the other debutantes who pursued him from a fate that none of them deserved.

Like so many other young women, Lady Gwendolyn thought marriage to a duke would be a dream come true. How these young ladies could be so deluded never failed to amaze Joshua. He was quite obviously not good marriage material, and the state of him this morning was proof of that. And yet the matchmaking mothers and his aunt kept foisting these innocent young things on him, hoping one would stick. And the innocent young things were just as bad. They were happy to turn a blind eye to all his excesses simply because of his title.

But he knew better. He had seen how his father had treated his mother. As everyone kept reminding him, he was as much a rogue as his father, so the least he could do was save some poor woman from the life his mother had endured.

Joshua slowed down and resumed walking, albeit at

a brisk pace. If Lady Gwendolyn and those other young ladies knew the future he was saving them from they would be thanking him from the bottom of their hearts. Instead, the mothers of overlooked daughters scorned him and Aunt P chastised him for not taking a wife, rather than admiring him, as she should, for his integrity in protecting the young ladies from a life of misery.

A hansom cab came to a halt beside him, not to ask if Joshua needed a ride, but to drop off a somewhat shamefaced young man who proceeded to sneak up the pathway to his home, his shoes in his hands, his tie and top hat askew.

'To Paddington Station, thank you, my man,' Joshua called up to the driver as he climbed into the cab.

'I'll be seeing the colour of your money first,' the driver said, gripping his whip in what was presumably a threatening manner.

Joshua reached into his trouser pockets, turned them out and found them empty. He looked over his shoulder. Should he run back to the house, sneak in the back way to get some money, maybe a change of clothes, all the while avoiding Aunt P and Lady Gwendolyn, and the spies he was sure his aunt had placed among his servants? Just the thought of doing so was causing his head to ache.

The driver turned in his seat and flicked the reins.

'Wait, wait,' Joshua called out, patting the pockets of his jacket and coming up with a few coins in answer to his prayers. 'I have money.'

The driver pulled up the horse and reached down to take the coins. 'All right then, mate, 'op in.'

A few days at his Devon estate was just what Joshua

needed to recover from whatever had happened last night and to escape from his aunt and Lady Gwendolyn. The social season was over, thank goodness, so his aunt would no longer be trying to force him to attend balls and various soirées. But it seemed now she was going to start dragging the unmarried young ladies to the sanctuary of his town house. Yes, what he needed was a day or two in the country to recover and gather his wits so he could continue his war of resistance against his aunt. And maybe Maisie, or Minnie—or was it Marjorie?—and her friends would accept his invitation and make his time in the countryside that little bit more enjoyable. Those young ladies were most certainly not marriage-seeking debutantes and he loved them all the more for being so.

He arrived at the bustling Paddington Station, where the pandemonium of raised voices, hissing steam trains, wailing children, busy porters and constant movement assaulted his senses. The sooner he got out of this noisy confusion and to the quiet of the countryside the better.

He removed the last of his coins, handed them to the ticket agent and bought a seat in third class. Entering the train, he paused at the doorway of the carriage, which was packed to the gills with people and luggage. It was a short distance from the spacious first-class compartments he was used to, but it was as if he had entered a different world.

His fellow travellers moved along to make room for him on the hard wooden bench. After an exchange of polite greetings, he attempted to get comfortable, to block out the sound of babies crying, children making those noises that children inevitably made and the crush of bodies in the cramped carriage so he could get a bit of much-needed sleep.

Irene Fairfax waited anxiously on the wooden platform as the train pulled into the Seaton station, filling the area with gushing steam. Doors flew open and the almost empty station was immediately full of people, noise and activity. First-class passengers strolled down the station while porters rushed around them, organising their trunks to be taken to waiting carriages. Second-class passengers retrieved their cases from the luggage carriage, while third-class passengers hauled their bags out of the train.

She spotted a man who looked like Joshua. Madeline had described him as tall, clean-shaven, with tousled blond hair and brown eyes. She'd also said he was exactly what Irene needed. She watched as he lifted a small girl down from the carriage then chatted with her parents. Irene doubted she had ever seen a more sublime example of masculine beauty. Madeline was right. He was perfect.

He tipped his cloth cap to the couple and strolled down the platform. Despite his workman's clothes and dishevelled appearance, he had a noble bearing and a swaggering confidence that made him stand out from the milling crowd. Oh, yes, Madeline was certainly right. He was exactly what she needed for what she had in mind.

Under normal circumstances she would avoid handsome, confident men as if they carried the plague. Which to her mind they almost did. They were cer-

tainly capable of causing destruction and acute emotional damage to young ladies foolish enough to fall for
their well-tested flattery and flirtation. That was a lesson she had learned in the first social season and one
she now heeded well. But right now, only a man who
was the epitome of masculine beauty would do.

'Joshua,' she called out, drawing his attention.

He turned in her direction, and looking over the
heads of the crowd, frowned in confusion.

'Allow me to introduce myself,' she said, pushing
through the mass of people and extending her hand in
what she hoped was a professional manner. 'I'm Irene,
Miss Irene Fairfax.'

He raised his eyebrows as if requiring further explanation.

'Madeline's friend. She told me to meet you at the
station.'

'Madeline,' he exclaimed, nodding thoughtfully as if
she had just revealed one of life's mysteries. Irene had
no time to contemplate this odd reaction especially as
her attention was diverted by the smile that followed.

A glorious smile that caused her heart to foolishly
skip a beat. What was wrong with her? It was obviously a well-practised smile, designed to enchant. Well,
he was about to learn such tactics had the opposite effect on her.

'I've a cab waiting outside and it's not far to my cottage.'

'Your cottage?'

'Yes, my cottage.'

He might be as handsome as Adonis, but it seemed
Madeline's brother was a bit dim. Not that that mat-

tered. She had asked for a man who looked good, not one who was intellectually stimulating.

'Yes. Didn't Madeline tell you? That's where I'm living at the moment.'

'Hmm. Sorry, I've had what was probably a decidedly peculiar evening and today has been no better. It has made me a bit forgetful. But lead on, Miss Irene Fairfax. Take me to your cottage.'

He gave a small laugh as if this was all a jolly good jape. It was rather strange behaviour, but Madeline did say her brother was a bit of a bohemian who lived a decidedly outlandish lifestyle. Such odd behaviour was perhaps to be expected. You would hardly expect a conventional man to agree to do what she wanted, so she would just have to accept a bit of eccentricity.

They walked towards a waiting Hansom cab and he began patting his pockets, but Irene held up her hands. 'The cab is paid for and it's only a short trip.'

'Thank you,' he said, taking her hand and helping her up the steps to the cab. 'I'm afraid I'm a bit short of funds but I will repay you as soon as I can.'

'There's no need,' she said, frowning. Of course she would pay for the cab and intended to compensate him well for his time and for agreeing to do what so many men would be horrified by, even insulted, if she dared to ask them.

They drove in silence and he appeared to be about to doze off. She frowned. She needed a man who was alert and energetic. At the thought of what she was about to ask him to do, the churning in her stomach increased. As they drove through the quiet village she swallowed repeatedly to try to relieve the tightness in her throat and reminded herself of why she had to take this extreme action.

She had no choice. She had to do this. And if she was to get the most out of their time together she needed to be calm and composed.

There is no need to be nervous. No need at all. Men do this sort of thing every day and nobody thinks there is anything wrong with it.

She looked out the window, at the respectable people going about their daily activities, people who would be scandalised if they knew what she was up to.

No, she would not care about that. If it wasn't for society's appalling prejudices she wouldn't have had to pay for her friend's brother to come all the way from London. She wouldn't have to behave in such a furtive way but could be completely open.

She sat up straighter and lifted her chin. She had no need to be nervous. Society should not treat women the way she was being treated. She should be able to behave just like a man and no one should judge her for it.

They were brave words. It was just a shame her churning stomach did not appear to be taking heed of them.

The cab pulled up in front of her cottage. He climbed out and took her hand once more and helped her down. He really was handsome. Perhaps too handsome. If he wasn't so damn good-looking then she was sure she wouldn't be quite so nervous. But then, a handsome man was what she needed, and Madeline had assured her he would do as she asked him and give her what she needed.

She opened the door to her cottage and he followed her into the parlour.

Feeling too uncomfortable to make eye contact, she pointed to the silk screen in the corner. 'You can undress over there. Please let me know when you're completely naked.'

Chapter Two

Was Joshua now losing his hearing along with his memory? 'I can what?'

'You can get undressed behind the screen. I've left a robe there, but you will have to take that off before we start.'

She wasn't the first woman to tell him to get his clothes off, but usually it was done after a sufficient level of amorous preliminaries, and was said with much giggling and suggestive pouting, not in such a matter-of-fact manner. But if she wanted him naked, who was he to say no? After all, wouldn't it be impolite to refuse? Yes, it most certainly would, and as a gentleman he was expected to display impeccable manners at all times. So there was nothing for it. He unbuttoned his jacket and placed it on a chair.

'Are you going to get undressed here?' she said with a shocked gasp. 'In front of me?'

It was an unexpected display of modesty under the circumstances, but then, everything about this encounter was decidedly unexpected. If he could recall his conversation with Madeline, who he now knew was not

Maisie, Minnie or Marjorie, it might make more sense.
It must have been a very interesting conversation, but
unfortunately it remained beyond his recall.

Perhaps if he *could* recall it he'd know how Madeline knew he was coming down to Devon before he did,
and how he came to be dressed in workman's clothes.
These were mysteries that would probably remain un-
solved for now. In the meantime, he was expected to
get naked, so that was what he would do.

'If you're going to see me naked anyway, why would
I want to take my clothes off in private and why put on
a robe only to take it off again?' he asked, a perfectly
reasonably question to his mind.

She stared at him, her brow furrowing into deeper
creases. Not the expression he would expect from a
woman who had just asked him to strip off his clothes.

'Yes, I suppose you're right,' she said, seemingly not
sure if he was right or not. 'It's just that usually…' She
looked towards the screen, still frowning.

He pulled off his trousers and threw them onto the
chair with a flourish, hoping she'd enjoy his exuberance,
but she was looking down, as if this situation, which
was entirely of her making, was rather uncomfortable.

Once stripped of his clothing, he raised his hands,
palm upwards, in a display of *Here I am in all my naked
glory. Do with me as you wish.*

She didn't look up.

'Where do you want to do this?' he finally asked,
sounding as unromantic and businesslike as she had
moments ago. Whatever she wanted and wherever she
wanted it, he was more than happy to oblige. He only
hoped after a night of overindulgence, which he had

undoubtedly had if only he could remember, that he would be up for the task.

She looked at him as if he was an imbecile. 'Here of course, in my studio, and would you please stand back from the easel and move into the light.'

He looked around the room and laughed. It was all now making sense. Why had he not noticed that he was in an artist's studio when he came in? The canvases piled up against the walls, the easel propped up in the corner, the shelves full of paint tubes were all obvious clues. And the room held a distinctive smell of linseed oil, charcoal pencils and oil paints. Miss Fairfax had covered her dress with an artist's smock, and now that she had removed her gloves, he could see her hands were flecked with paint. This woman was an artist and she wanted to paint him.

He laughed again at his understandable and completely forgivable mistake. After all, when a young lady invites you back to her cottage and asks you to take off your clothes, there were few men alive who would take the time to notice the décor.

She moved behind the easel and picked up a pencil. 'Please adopt the pose of Michelangelo's *David*.'

Joshua cast his mind back to when he saw the famous statue in Florence. He placed his weight on one leg, lifted up his arm as if cradling a rock that he was about to hurl at Goliath and looked over his shoulder at the approaching imaginary giant.

'That's good,' she murmured. He smiled to himself. She wasn't the first young woman who had murmured words of appreciation when observing his naked body, although usually they were in the same state of undress as himself and were expecting him to do a lot more than just stand still in the middle of the room looking off into the distance.

He shook his head to drive out that thought, to drive out all thoughts of what would usually be expected of him when he was with a woman and in a state of undress. A few moments ago, he had hoped last night's damage would not prevent him from being up to the task; now he hoped that it had. The last thing he wanted to do was to expose the effect having an attractive young woman staring at your naked body could have on a man.

'How long have you been drawing naked men?' he asked, hoping a little light conversation would divert him from any thoughts of the woman observing him, of her long brown hair, which was casually piled on top of her head, of those big blue eyes surrounded by long, dark eyelashes or that rather enticing, curvaceous womanly body.

He coughed, reminding himself not to, under any circumstances, think of that curvaceous womanly body.

'You're my first.'

'I'm honoured,' he said, fighting not to put an inappropriate connotation on her admission. 'Why is that? I would have thought you'd have men lining up to take their clothes off for you.'

She gave a small, humourless laugh. 'I thought Madeline told you why I need to do my life classes in private.'

He shrugged.

'Please don't do that, I'm sketching your shoulders.'

'Sorry,' he said, forcing himself to stay still. 'Madeline might have told me. I forget.' Along with so much else. Apparently, last night, he had promised Madeline he would pose naked for her friend. It certainly sounded like the sort of thing he might do. 'Remind me, why do you have to do life classes in private?'

'Because I'm a woman.' She sighed loudly. 'The art academy in which I was enrolled said it was inappropriate for a woman to attend their life classes. That's despite the fact the models were women and the tutors had no problems with the single men attending.' He could hear the anger rising in her voice. 'They also don't seem to care that I need to be able to draw the human form if I am ever to progress as an artist. But then I suppose that's the whole idea. It's as much about keeping women in their place as it is about any stupid sense of morality.'

He looked over at her. She had stopped sketching and was glaring at the canvas, her pretty lips tightly pinched, her forehead once again deeply furrowed.

'I'm sorry,' he said, unsure what he was apologising for: the way women were treated, the injustice that she had experienced, for being a man, for all the men who had treated women badly, including his father, including himself.

'It's hardly your fault and I do appreciate you helping me out this way.'

'Happy to do so. Any time you want me to take my clothes off for you, all you have to do is ask.'

She continued to frown at him, obviously not amused by his attempt to lighten the mood.

'Please resume the pose.'

Once again, he looked over his shoulder at his imaginary foe as her pencil resumed scratching on the canvas.

'I take it you're not the sort of woman who is happy with painting watercolours of flowers and trees,' he said. Wasn't that what young ladies were expected to do, partake in the gentle art forms? He had been informed by many a matchmaking mother of her daughter's simply divine watercolours, as if that would make him abandon his cherished bachelor status and chain himself to a wife.

She snorted her disapproval. 'That's another reason why I'm hiding down in Devon. My mother thinks it is deeply shameful for a woman to work in oils. *"Your hands, your hands, how will you ever get a husband with paint-splattered hands,"'* she said in an older woman's outraged voice. 'She even sent me away to finishing school in an attempt to turn me into a proper young lady.'

'Well, I'm pleased she failed.'

She snorted again; this time, he hoped it was in amusement.

'Not that you're not a proper young lady,' he added, turning to look at her.

'Don't move your head,' she snapped in a manner no proper young lady ever would use. But then, no proper young lady would ask a complete stranger to take off his clothes. He had to admit, he rather admired her lack of propriety.

'I'm not a proper young lady, never have been and hope never to be.'

'Good for you. I'm sure the world would be a better place if more young ladies were improper.'

The sound of the drawing pencil halted and he hoped his flippant comment had not offended her.

'The world would be a better place if men allowed women to be and behave how they wanted, not in a manner that makes them good wives.' The derision she placed on the word *good* seemed to hang in the air like an accusation.

That too was a statement with which he could only wholeheartedly agree. Surely his lovely, kind mother would have been much happier if she hadn't been trained from birth for one purpose only, to make a *good* wife. She should have been free to live the way she wanted, with a man she loved, and not married off to a man chosen for her by her family, a family that only cared about his father's status and his wealth and turned a blind eye to his philandering, gambling and other excesses.

'I'm sorry,' he repeated, apologising for what had happened to his mother and every woman who had suffered in a similar manner.

'It's hardly your fault,' she said.

It wasn't, but he couldn't help but feel responsible for the fate of women like his mother, for debutantes like Lady Gwendolyn who would sacrifice everything to become a duchess, and for all those other young women who had chased him, season after season, oblivious to the miserable life that would await them if they actually did catch him.

'Please stand up straighter,' she commanded.

He did so, unaware that such maudlin thoughts had caused him to slouch. 'I take it you have no intention of becoming a good wife yourself.'

She merely sniffed her disapproval.

Not moving his head, he looked at her out of the corner of his eye. That sniff held something more than disapproval and he suspected there was a story behind this young lady's cynicism.

'No, I have no intention of becoming a wife, good or otherwise,' she said, a note of bitterness in her statement.

He hoped that no man had hurt her and caused her to become cynical, but something had presumably opened her eyes to what marriage could be like. He only wished all young women were as sensible, if for no other reason than it would make his life a lot easier.

'Madeline said that you live a rather unconventional life yourself,' she continued.

He was about to nod but remembered that she did not like him moving.

'I wouldn't call it unconventional. I just like to enjoy myself and try to avoid responsibility whenever possible.' It sounded like a sad indictment on his life, but when you've got immense wealth, a title and nothing to do, what else is there left except indulging in endless, pointless pleasure?

'I'm surprised you describe your life like that. It's not what Madeline said. She described you in glowing terms, but that's to be expected, I suppose.'

Joshua was surprised that anyone who knew him would describe him in terms that were anywhere close to glowing. Perhaps, somehow, he had made an unwarranted good impression on the lady on his lap. He had no idea how she had passed on this inaccurate information to her friend, but it had to be corrected. After all, he had no desire to fool anyone, least of all this young lady.

'I'm sorry. My recollection of last night is somewhat hazy and I'd hate for you or Madeline to get the wrong impression. The fact that I can't really even remember who Madeline is or what I said to her proves that I'm not the man she thinks I am.'

The movement of her scratching pencil stopped. The room went silent. He sent her a sideways look. She was staring at him and did not look happy. In fact, her scowling face contained more emotions than he could name.

'Madeline is your sister,' she said quietly. 'She arranged for you to travel to Devon and pose for me.'

'Ah,' was all he could reply. This was all making sense now. He was the wrong Joshua. He had made no arrangement with the forgotten Madeline. This young woman had not invited *him* into his home and asked *him* to take off his clothes. She wanted this other Joshua to do so. Really, when he thought about it, that also made perfect sense. But after the night he'd just experienced, the one he couldn't remember, nothing much was making sense and such a mistake was surely understandable.

He dropped his pose and turned towards her, smiling. 'I believe a rather amusing misunderstanding has just occurred which I'm sure will make you laugh.' He was sure of no such thing but could only hope she had a rollicking sense of humour.

'Who are you?' she said through clenched teeth.

It would appear she had no sense of humour, rollicking or otherwise.

He stepped forward, hand extended. 'I'm Joshua

Huntingdon, the Duke of Redcliff, and I'm very pleased to make your acquaintance, Miss Fairfax.'

'Get out,' she said, those teeth still clamped tightly together. 'Get out,' she repeated, grabbing at everything she could within arm's reach.

Joshua had seen that look on a woman's face before and knew now was not the time to try to reason with her. Instead, he bundled up his clothing and, moving as quickly as he could, he pulled on his trousers, but not before a hail of sharp pencils, paintbrushes, wooden palettes and heaven knows what else came flying in his direction.

Chapter Three

Irene stared at the door through which the Duke had hastily departed. How on earth had that happened? She cast her frazzled mind back to the meeting at the railway station. Had he introduced himself? Told her his name was Joshua? She was sure that he had.

She couldn't recall him saying he was the Duke of Redcliff. If he had, her mistake would have been immediate. And why on earth was a duke dressed in such a manner? Was he in disguise? Was he hiding from someone? Whatever his reasons for such subterfuge she was sure they would be disreputable.

Everything about him was disreputable. Only a disreputable man would allow a woman he had never met before take him home without asking any questions.

Her hands flew to her burning cheeks. And only a man who was worse than disreputable would actually take off his clothes and pose naked in front of her without a single question. He must have known at that stage a mistake had been made. Or did he often get accosted by women at railway stations, invited back to their home and asked to strip naked?

The heat of her cheeks spread to her entire body. What must he have thought she wanted from him when she asked him to undress? It was all too mortifying.

She drew in a deep breath, her hands clasping her stomach. She had done nothing wrong. That was all that mattered. She had made a genuine mistake, one that anyone could make. He was dressed exactly as she would expect a poor art student to dress. He was travelling third class and he met the description that Madeline had given her: tall, good-looking, with blond hair and brown eyes. And to make matters worse, his name actually *was* Joshua.

No, she had done nothing wrong. She had nothing worthy of reproach. Except, perhaps, for asking a complete stranger home and telling him to strip naked for her.

She cringed again and looked at the painting. But he did make a sublime David. With that tousled hair, those full lips and that defined musculature, he had been a dream to sketch. And, if she was being honest, a dream to look at.

She continued staring at the sketch and failed to hear her maid of all works, Hetty, until she entered the studio.

'Morning, miss,' she trilled. 'I just saw the oddest thing. The Duke of Redcliff, strolling up the road in the oddest get-up, like some down-on-his-luck labourer.'

Irene attempted to throw a cover over her sketch but was too late. Hetty was behind her, excited to see the latest work.

Usually, Irene was happy to show the maid what she'd drawn, but not today.

'Oh, my. My, oh, my,' Hetty said, and gave a low whistle. 'I've often wondered what he looked like without his clobber on. I'm probably one of the few women that haven't seen him in his birthday suit. And now I know what I've been missing. It's actually even better than I imagined.'

'I believe I told you I needed some life drawings for my portfolio,' Irene garbled, wishing the burning on her cheeks would settle down. 'And the Duke kindly agreed to help.'

'It doesn't surprise me he would be agree to pose for you. He's a bit of a one, I can tell you.'

As she stared at the painting, Hetty's expression changed to the one she adopted just before she was about to have a good gossip. Irene rarely indulged her maid as she had neither the time nor the interest in the latest goings-on in the village, but today she couldn't help herself. She wanted to hear about the man who had entered her house under false pretences and happily stripped off in front of her.

'What do you mean?' she asked, trying to keep her voice as neutral as possible.

'Well, he's a bit of a chip off the old block. The old duke was a right one, I can tell you.' Hetty shook her head as if in disapproval, although it was contradicted by her gleeful smile. 'I'm too well brought up to go into details, but let me just say there's been quite a few children born in this village that bear a striking resemblance to the Duke's father, if you get my drift,' Hetty said, getting into her stride. 'And the tales some of the

maids have told about what went on up at the big house
and at his town house in London, it would make your
hair curl. And that poor duchess.' She frowned theat-
rically and shook her head. 'She was a lovely woman
and such a martyr to the old sod, if you don't mind my
saying.'

'What about the son?' Irene was unsure why she
was bothering to ask. The mere fact that he went to the
cottage of a woman he didn't know and took off his
clothes without blinking an eye spoke volumes about
his character.

'Well, the servants don't have a bad word to say about
this one, not in terms of him being an employer any-
ways,' she said, looking back at the painting. 'He always
pays well, and no one is overworked the way they are
in some of them grand houses, and he certainly doesn't
chase after the maids the way the old duke did. But they
do have some interesting tales about his behaviour up
in London and the young ladies he entertains. They say
there's no point trying to remember the name of the
latest lady in his life because they change so quickly.'

Hetty smiled, still staring at the sketch. 'Can't help
envying those young ladies in some ways, can you?'
She sent Irene a quick wink. 'Looks like you've had a
bit of a nice time yourself.'

'It's art,' she said in a voice that sounded decidedly
pompous. 'He's merely a combination of light, shape
and form. When you're doing a life sketch you hardly
see the person at all.' *Liar.* She could see from the unsteady lines on her sketch how she had most definitely
seen the naked man before her and had fought hard to

keep her reactions under control. 'It's no different than painting a bowl of fruit.'

'And very nice fruit they are too,' Hetty said with a laugh.

Irene sent her a disapproving glare. She had always been on easy terms with her maid of all works, disliking the high-handed manner in which employers treated their servants and wanting their relationship to be more one of equals. Now she was wondering whether that had been a mistake.

'Begging your pardon, miss,' Hetty said, sensing the change in Irene's mood. 'I'll get on with me work then.'

A twinge of guilt ripped through Irene. 'Thank you, Hetty. Oh, and perhaps it might be best if you don't tell anyone about the Duke posing for me.'

'Right you are, miss,' Hetty said, as she departed for the kitchen.

Irene was unsure if Hetty really would be able to contain herself from sharing such a juicy bit of gossip, but she could only hope. She had little to do with the villagers but would prefer it if they didn't think she was yet another of the Duke's women who were in his life for such a short time there was little point anyone trying to remember their name.

As she continued to stare at the painting, she cast her mind back, trying to remember if she had ever met the Duke before. Over the last five seasons she had attended more balls and social events than she wished to remember but had never met the Duke of Redcliff. She could, however, vaguely remember his name being mentioned as one of those elusive dukes that every matchmaking mother and ambitious debutante was determined to catch. It was chatter she rarely paid attention to. Why should she? She was not seeking a husband, and most certainly had no interest in joining the ranks of young women in search of a man with a title.

Why women should chase after such dissolute men she would never understand. She released a long, slow sigh. Who was she trying to fool? She knew exactly why. Because they were wide-eyed innocents and refused to see the evidence before their eyes. Just as she had been, until Edwin Fitzgibbon had opened her eyes.

Until then, she had not only been blind, but stupid as well. It was hard to believe that she had ever been that naive, that she could have been dazzled by a man's good looks, charm and position in society and oblivious to the dark character underneath. Until it was too late.

A small shudder rippled through her. And the Duke of Redcliff was just like Edwin. But she was no longer that innocent young woman attending her first season. She would never again be flattered by a man's attention and gullible to his sweet-talking lies.

When Hetty described his behaviour she could just as easily have been describing Edwin. He too lived a disreputable life, one about which she had known nothing.

At least the Duke appeared not to hide his dissolute side, unlike Edwin, who pretended to be oh, so respectable while ruining reputations and wreaking havoc with young girls' hearts.

She removed the sketch from the easel. Yes, it was one point in his favour, but only one. From what Hetty had said, and from what she had observed herself, being an honest rake hardly made him a man of upstanding character, so while he remained in Seaton he was a man best avoided.

She turned the painting towards the wall and a terrible thought occurred to her. If the Duke was the wrong Joshua, what had happened to the right Joshua? Had she left the poor man, who had kindly offered to give up his time to help her, abandoned at the train station?

Rushing towards the door, she grabbed her hat and coat and called to Hetty that she was going out for a few minutes.

Just as she reached the door, the knocker sounded, and she pulled it open, hoping to see the right Joshua, her excuses and apologies already forming in her mind.

Standing at the door was a young man dressed smartly in the uniform of the telegram delivery service, his shiny black bicycle held with one hand, the other stretched out and clasping an envelope.

'Telegram for Miss Irene Fairfax,' he said self-importantly.

Irene thanked him and quickly opened the telegram and scanned the words. The mystery was solved. The right Joshua had not left London. The expense of such a method of communication meant Madeline did not go into detail, merely apologised without explanation.

Irene tipped the telegram boy and released a sigh of relief. At least she would not have to explain her embarrassing mistake to Madeline or her brother, but it did mean she no longer had a model for her life classes.

Returning to her studio, she picked up the sketch and placed it back on the easel. As annoying as it was, he did make a perfect David.

Perhaps she should put aside the unfortunate manner in which he came to pose for her. After all, she was a serious artist and serious artists focused on their art. They were not distracted by the triviality of life, and that was what the Duke was, a triviality, a mere prop. He had said he was happy to pose for her and she did need a model. Her gaze scanned down his body. As she had told Hetty, it mattered not who the model was; he was just a composition of shape, light and form, no different to a bowl of fruit. But if she did ask him to pose for her, would she be able to ignore what Hetty had said in response, that he was very nice fruit indeed?

He shouldn't have done it. He absolutely should not have done it. Deep down he must have known she was making a mistake. He should not have ignored the signs. Unlike Madeline, who was once again possibly Maisie or Minnie, Miss Fairfax was obviously not the sort of woman to casually ask a man to take off his clothes. Despite knowing it was wrong, Joshua couldn't help but smile to himself as he walked along the country road that would take him to his estate.

It had certainly been an interesting and entertaining day and he whistled a tune he had heard somewhere, perhaps at a music hall, as he strolled beside the hedgerows and continued to think about the lovely Miss Irene Fairfax.

She was not his type. In fact, despite her somewhat unconventional lifestyle, and today's rather extraordinary interaction, she was exactly the sort of woman he avoided. Those missiles that had come flying his way when she discovered her mistake were a pointed reminder of that. His type of woman loved a good time as much as he did. No ties, no expectations, and a complete disregard for the rules of polite society—that was the sort of woman he was attracted to.

Artists had a reputation for living as free spirits, and one or two had featured in his past, but Miss Irene Fairfax was quite obviously not like them. She was not a young woman to be trifled with. Far too passionate, far too intense and, fortunately, sensible enough to have thrown him out of her cottage the moment she realised what sort of man he was.

She might be tempting—in fact, she *was* tempting— but sometimes temptation was best avoided. If Miss Fairfax was in need of a man in her life, it would be a serious man, one with a purpose in life, one with as much passion as she herself possessed. Not a man like Joshua.

His father's voice suddenly echoed in his ears. 'You and I are lucky, son,' he had said more times than Joshua could remember, often with a hearty slap on the back. 'We have money, we have status, and all that is expected of us is to enjoy ourselves.' That was usually followed by a lascivious wink. 'Even if we were as ugly as trolls and as stupid as asses, the ladies would still love us and be more than eager to do whatever we want. You'll discover for yourself when you become duke just how much fun those young ladies can be.'

When it came to his life, only one thing was expected of Joshua: to have as much fun as possible. And when it came to women, his father actively encouraged him to sow his wild oats as often and as far as he wished. Then he was expected to find himself a sweet, innocent young lady from a good family to be the next duchess so he could sire an heir.

That was it. That was Joshua's life, and so far he had met his father's expectations of him and his oats had been sown throughout the land. There was only one way in which he would disappoint the old duke. No innocent young woman would be sacrificed on the marriage altar and become the next Duchess of Redcliff.

He stopped walking and his jaw tensed, as it often did when he thought of his father. Other memories of conversations with the old duke tumbled through his mind. Ones where the old man boasted that once that deed had been done and a son had been born, Joshua need never have anything more to do with his bride.

Never for a moment had his father thought that Joshua would be offended to hear him talk in such a way about his mother. Nor had the old man seen anything wrong with the way he treated his wife, thinking she should be happy enough being a duchess, and content to be abandoned in the country and neglected while her husband was seen about London with an endless stream of mistresses.

If the former duke was alive, he'd be horrified with his son's behaviour. Not for his carousing, not for his womanising, all of which was expected, but for his vow that he would never subject any young woman to the life his mother had experienced. He would never marry, never sire the requisite heir. When he died the Dukedom would pass to his cousin and the world would carry on none the worse for it.

He continued walking and resumed his whistling. He need not think of that now. He had escaped another season. All he had to do was continue to fend off his Aunt Prudence and only mix with women who didn't want marriage, women who also wanted to spend their endless free time indulging themselves in pleasures of all descriptions. Pleasures he was more than happy to provide.

A horse and cart rounded the corner and came to a halt beside Joshua. 'Want a lift, mate?' the driver called out. 'I'm delivering some goods up to Redcliff Estate if you're going that way.'

Joshua turned around and the man's smile turned to a look of confusion, then he quickly doffed his cap and clasped it tightly in his large hands. 'Beggin' your pardon, Your Grace.'

'Thank you. A ride is just what I need.' He climbed up beside the man at the front of his cart.

'Sorry about that, Your Grace. I didn't recognise you at first,' the man mumbled, not making eye contact.

'Nothing to be sorry for, my man, and I'm very grateful for the ride.'

They drove through the countryside, then turned into his estate and drove down the long gravel pathway that led to his country home. It was a place that held many happy memories, growing up with his mother and the servants for company. Occasionally the Duke would pay a visit, usually accompanied by a rowdy group of friends. The household would be thrown into turmoil and his mother would take on a strained appearance. Even as a small boy he could see how unhappy his father made his sweet, mild-mannered mother. At the time he had wished he could do something to make her happier, but there was nothing he could do.

The cart pulled up in front of the house and Joshua

jumped down, then the driver continued on around the back of the house to deliver the goods to the kitchen.

Joshua strode up the stone stairs and announced his arrival to the servants, none of whom seemed the slightest bit surprised to see him dressed as a labourer.

'Shall I prepare a bath and arrange a change of clothes, Your Grace?' the head footman asked.

Despite starting to feel comfortable in his present garb, Joshua knew it was time to go back to being the Duke of Redcliff. Miss Irene Fairfax flitted back into his mind. He would not have thought it possible, but he had caused even more havoc than usual when dressed as a labourer than he ever did as a duke, and that had to stop.

'Yes, a bath and some suitable clothes is exactly what I need,' he said over his shoulder as he headed up the stairs to his bedroom. After a good night's sleep, or full day's sleep, he would return to London, back to his life and back to causing mayhem with people who actually appreciated such behaviour.

Chapter Four

The next day Irene awoke with a strong sense of resolve. After a previous day of achieving very little she needed to focus. It was time she settled down and finished her sketch of David. Once her life drawing was complete, she could put behind her all that had happened the day before. The entire incident with the Duke could be consigned to the past along with all thoughts of that irritating man.

Working hard to keep her mind free of all distractions, she picked up her pencil and turned to the canvas. Her resolve evaporated. How could she call herself an artist when every time she looked at that sketch she lost the ability to draw a straight line? It was merely a line drawing and yet it was enough to cause a series of peculiar reactions to erupt inside her. Her gaze moved along the breadth of his shoulders, and the musculature of his chest, arms and legs. Heat rushed to her cheeks and she could almost feel the coiled strength under the smooth skin. In her mind's eye she could imagine running her hands over those beautifully defined muscles.

She stepped back, shocked by the direction in which her thoughts had travelled. It was ridiculous. She was ridiculous. Men like the Duke of Redcliff did not attract her. In fact, she abhorred such men. Given that she wanted nothing to do with the subject matter of the sketch, she should have no trouble separating the man from the drawing.

It's all just light and form, she reminded herself, *no different than a bowl of fruit.*

She tentatively approached the canvas and raised her pencil, lowered it and sighed. This was impossible. If she was to ever master drawing the human form, she had to get over these absurd feelings and remain detached.

This uncharacteristic behaviour had to be the lasting effects of yesterday's upsetting encounter. That was all. A brisk walk in the fresh air was what she needed. That would clear her mind and settle her nerves. Then she could return to her work refreshed and ready to concentrate.

With a display of fortitude she did not feel she briskly turned from the canvas, strode to the front door and removed her hat and coat from the hooks. As always, she took with her a sketch book and pencils. She could leave the house without a hat or her gloves, but her sketch pad and pencils were accessories she rarely travelled without.

Striding down the village street, she smiled and greeted the locals, scanning their faces to see if they were looking at her any differently.

As a single woman living alone in a rented cottage during the off season, the villagers already thought her a bit peculiar. She did not need them to think of her as a woman of ill repute as well. Hetty had no doubt informed them that she was an artist. That would merely confirm their belief that she was eccentric. But if anyone had seen a half-dressed duke running out of her cottage her reputation would descend from somewhat unconventional to somewhat loose. From what Hetty had said, seeing the Duke leaving a woman's house would not surprise the villagers, but she did not want to be thought of as yet another of his conquests.

She walked down the quaint street, passed small cottages surrounded by white picket fences and pretty gardens and detected no sign that her reputation had been totally destroyed. The villagers returned her greetings in their usual cordial yet reserved manner. Thank goodness for that.

Although they kept to themselves, the villagers were used to strangers, albeit not usually at this time of year. In the summer they hosted a stream of visitors all keen to take in the sea air. The more adventurous even took to sea bathing, with the beach divided into sections for men and women.

Women used bathing machines, which were wheeled down to the sea, allowing them to enter the water discreetly, dressed in a bathing costume that covered them from neck to ankle. While the men were free to swim in a less cumbersome costume, or even, rumour had it, in nothing at all.

The bathing machines had now all been rolled away and put in storage, but in the summer season, the visitors provided a good income for the village. Their invasion had led to the opening of a variety of new shops and tea rooms in the main street to cater for the passing trade. It brought in money, but it was obvious that in the off season the villagers gave a collective sigh of relief to have their hometown back to themselves.

It was this departure of the holidaymakers that meant Irene was able to stay in her little cottage. Georgina, one of her closest friends from finishing school, had a father who was a savvy businessman. He had seen the potential of Seaton as a desirable seaside destination long before anyone else and had bought up as many houses as possible in the previously sleepy village to rent out to the summer trade. The houses often remained empty during the off season and Georgina had somehow cajoled her father into allowing Irene to stay there. Georgina had her otherwise stern father wrapped around her little finger, and there was no one better at coming up with plots and plans so she could get exactly what she wanted. For that, and so much more, Irene was eternally grateful to her friend.

Leaving the village behind, she took the coastal track and tried to let the gentle sea breeze blow away her jitters and still her whirling thoughts. Even before she could see the ocean, she was able to smell its fresh salty scent, and she paused in her walking to breathe in its reviving qualities.

The sea worked its magic and with renewed vigour she strode up the hillside to a path that took her along the top of the cliffs. When she reached the highest point she paused again and looked out at the ocean. It was a sight that always enchanted her. Every day it was different and a constant source of inspiration. It could be dramatic, even violent, with the sea crashing on the craggy rocks below, or it could be as it was today, calm and tranquil, with small waves lapping the sand.

Capturing this dramatic seascape, with its ever-changing shades of the ocean and the surrounding emerald green grass and trees, had been one of her greatest pleasures since arriving in Devon.

Reaching her favourite cove, she climbed down to the spot she called her own. It was as if it had been designed for her, with a small, flattened area between two hillsides providing an ideal place to sit while she remained hidden from anyone walking on the track. She looked out at the gently swelling ocean, then up at the sky. The calmness was a temporary respite. Grey tumbling clouds were moving in from the southeast, threatening a storm for later in the day.

Irene flicked open her sketchbook, determined to capture this transformative scene of a tranquil ocean threatened by a coming tempest, before it disappeared.

As hoped, surrendering herself fully to her art drove all other thoughts out of her head, and she was soon in that glorious meditative state where she forgot everything other than the movement of her pencil on the paper. Smudging the pencil outline with her thumb, she tried to replicate the ominous clouds above the gently rippling shore. She looked at her sketch, then up at the ocean, then back at her sketch. She hadn't quite caught it. She looked up again. In those few seconds the scene had altered.

A man was swimming around the edge of the cliff and heading towards the sandy beach. Irene quickly closed her sketchbook and gathered up her pencils to make a hasty departure. She looked up again. The swimmer had emerged from the water, moved behind a low rock and was pulling on his clothing.

It was him. The Duke. Did this man take off his clothes at every opportunity? But now Irene had a dilemma. If she stood up and started climbing the hill, would she draw his attention? But if she stayed, and he saw her, would he think she was spying on him? Perplexed by indecision, she remained immobile. *Flee now*, she told herself while still watching him. It would be terrible if he caught her, if he thought she was deliberately watching him dress.

He looked up in her direction. She crouched down. Could he see her? She was sitting in a small gully. She wasn't visible from the pathway. Was she equally invisible from the shore? Did the long grass and the contours of the hillside hide her?

She peeked up above the grass. His smile answered that question.

Damn, damn and damn it again. This could not be happening. She looked around. What would be less embarrassing? To remain where she was or to make a run for it? While she continued to debate these equally embarrassing options, he had picked up his shirt and, still bare chested, was climbing the hill.

She now had no choice. To run would make her look ridiculous. She was going to have to act as if seeing him naked, again, had no effect on her whatsoever. Unfortunately, what she was asking of herself seemed a monumental task, especially as her agitated body was still desperate to escape.

Stay calm, act nonchalant, remain composed, she recited as he climbed closer and closer.

'I wasn't spying on you,' she blurted out the moment he reached her, in a manner that was neither calm nor composed.

His smile grew wider. 'I'm sure you weren't, Miss Fairfax. After all, you wouldn't be seeing anything you haven't already seen before and studied in minute detail.'

Heat exploded onto her cheeks, destroying any vestiges of nonchalance. 'I was…' She held up her sketchbook, unable to form the words to prove to him that she was engaged in the innocent pursuit of sketching the cove, a cove that had been free of naked swimmers when she had sat down.

He took the sketchbook as if she had offered it to him and flicked it open. His face became serious as he looked at each drawing, many of which were of the cove over which they were now looking. He turned and looked out towards the ocean, then back at the sketchbook, then at her. 'These are wonderful,' he said, his voice quiet, almost reverential. 'You have a rare talent.'

She reached out for her sketchbook, and stayed silent waiting for him to add the inevitable *for a woman*, but he ignored her outstretched hand and continued to look through her work, finally stopping at the one she had been working on.

She braced herself. Her work was so important to her. It was her life, and she had learned to be armour-plated in the face of critics so the condescending comments and outright insults no longer penetrated.

He looked from the ocean to the sketch. 'I love the way, in a few strokes of your pencil, you've caught how the ocean is calm at present but it is all about to change, as if something foreboding is on the horizon.' He turned to face her. 'That's why I went for a swim before the weather changed. You've captured it perfectly. It's as if something threatening is behind this beautiful, supposedly calm scenery, as if everything is just about to be completely disrupted.'

Irene stared at him, unsure what to say. It was exactly what she was hoping to express, and it wasn't just about the scenery. She had also been trying to draw her own turbulent emotions and he had seemingly sensed that.

'Don't look so surprised,' he said, that disconcerting smile returning as he flipped shut her sketchbook and handed it back to her. 'I am capable of a bit of art appreciation. I'm more than just a man who likes to take his clothes off.'

Irene pinched her lips tightly together, reminding herself and hopefully him that she was not like other women. His good looks and easy charm had no effect on her. Hetty had told her of his reputation, one that often involved him taking his clothes off and doing a lot more besides. That made him exactly the sort of man she most despised.

As if under a will of their own, her eyes moved to his naked chest, still sleek from the seawater. He might be despicable, but damn it all, he was magnificent, with a body like a marble statue of a Greek god, all hard muscle and defined sinew.

He laughed lightly and pulled on his shirt. 'Is that better?'

Damn, damn, damn. Stop this. Act nonchalant. Remember.

'No one usually lingers at this cove,' he continued,

doing up his shirt buttons and slowly removing more of his chest from her view. 'It's not as traditionally picturesque as some of the other parts of the coastline so it doesn't attract the holidaymakers, and it's not the route the villagers usually take so I didn't expect anyone to see me. But now that I know you're a frequent visitor I promise I'll be more discreet in future and avoid exposing myself to you, yet again.'

The last of the buttons closed. Irene's gaze rose to meet his and she realised she hadn't stopped staring at his chest, and what was worse, his smile seemed to be saying he knew exactly what she had been thinking and what effect he was having on her.

He reached out his hand to help her walk up the hill but she ignored it. She did not need the touch of his skin to further unnerve her. Instead, she busied herself with brushing down her skirt to remove the dry grass that had attached itself to the fabric while she fought to regain some composure.

This encounter was becoming increasingly mortifying. She had to make him see that unlike all those other women in his life, whose names Hetty said nobody bothered to remember, she was not in the slightest bit attracted to him and she was most certainly not chasing after him. It was vital he know this meeting was entirely by accident and was unwanted.

She lifted her chin high and held his gaze. 'I hope you are not under the misconception that I'm here deliberately.' Good, she sounded unruffled, even if that was not how she felt. 'The cove was empty when I sat down. I wasn't…'

That slow, appealing smile returned. The one that

made his eyes sparkle. That damnable smile that caused the corners of his eyes to crinkle. The one she just knew he used on all those women he had reputedly had in his life.

'You weren't…' She tried to continue but had lost the thread of what she was attempting to say. 'I meant to leave as soon as you swum into sight but…' She looked over her shoulder and up the hill to where escape had beckoned, wishing she had taken the option to flee the moment she had seen him. 'Anyway, I need to return home now.'

He held out his arm once more. She looked at it as if unsure what it was and why he was offering it to her, causing him to send her another of those irritating, knowing smiles.

'Allow me to escort you.'

She paused, then placed her arm through his, determined to prove she was not at all intimidated by him. He led her back up the hill and they walked along the path.

Pull yourself together and do not think about him naked, Irene recited to herself, even though she knew that telling yourself not to think of something invariably caused you to do exactly that.

'Was it the dramatic landscape that brought you to Devon?' he asked, breaking the silence between them.

'What?' she blurted out, trying to rein in her inappropriate thoughts. 'No.'

He waited for her to explain further and she wondered how much she should reveal to him. But what did it really matter? And at least it would keep the conversation and her thoughts away from more awkward subjects.

'Yes, I do love the landscape, but that wasn't the only reason I chose to live in Devon. My friend Georgina told me of an empty cottage her family owns. They rent it out in summer but it's empty the rest of the year so she organised for me to stay there.'

He gave her an assessing look. 'It's unusual for a young lady to be given such freedom. Your parents must be quite progressive to allow you to live on your own. Or is it that they are art lovers and wish for you to develop your talent?'

Irene stifled a snort of disparaging laughter. 'No, we told everyone I was poorly and needed the sea air to help me recover. That was Georgina's idea. She told her father that once I made a full recovery, he could use it to convince wealthy people that Seaton was the perfect winter health spa.'

She gave a little laugh at the memory of Georgina's scheming. 'I told my mother my nerves were fragile after another failed season and I needed a nice long break to repair for the next one. My mother thinks Georgina is staying with me for the same reason, along with her lady's maid and several of the family's servants. The last few weeks on my own have been glorious and I'm so looking forward to spending the entire winter here.'

He gave her a sideways look.

'But I'm not alone,' she rushed on. 'I have a maid of all works, Hetty, who practically lives with me, and Georgina and my other friends visit regularly.'

'I'm pleased to hear it. Seaton can be a lonely place in winter.'

She wanted to say she doubted that he was ever alone and could not possibly know what loneliness felt like,

but she neither wanted to raise the topic of his womanising nor draw attention to her own inner state.

'And are your parents proud of your art?'

She laughed, although her laughter contained no
amusement. 'My mother can't understand why any
young woman would indulge in anything that takes
them away from finding a husband,' she said, failing
to keep a note of bitterness out of her voice. 'My father, alas, does as my mother commands, although as
a young man he did show talent himself, a talent that
was also not encouraged by the family.'

'Families can be a trial,' he said quietly. 'And so you
escaped to Devon where you can be yourself?'

'Yes.'

'Good for you.' They walked for a few moments in
silence.

'I too do my best to avoid living the life others expect of me.'

'Yes, so I've heard, but it's all so easy for you, isn't
it? Men have choices. Women do not.'

He raised his eyebrows in question, clearly taken
aback by her terse tone.

'I'm sorry. I didn't mean to snap.'

'No apology necessary. If you could choose the life
you wanted, what would it be?'

Irene hardly knew how to answer that. Her life had
never been about making free choices but trying to
gain what she could with the limited options available.
'Well, I wouldn't waste time attending all those tedious
balls and soirées in London.' She had fought to keep
the bitterness out of her voice but had failed. After that
first disastrous season, each successive season was an

increasing torment for her, and she was grateful that at the age of twenty-three she would soon be free and would officially be classed as a spinster.

'I take it you too do not enjoy all that rampant match-making and angling for the best catch,' he said. 'It's something I've managed to avoid season after season and intend to keep doing so and remain single right up to my dotage.'

She merely nodded her agreement.

'Although, despite what you say about women having no choices, it seems you have managed to make a few choices in your life,' he said, nodding towards her sketchbook.

'I don't know if that is a choice. It's almost as if I would die inside if I couldn't paint. It's my love and my refuge,' she said quietly, then smiled to try to make light of such a personal confession. He did not return her smile but gazed back at her, his eyes staring deep into hers, capturing her attention and making it all but impossible to look away.

'It must be wonderful to have a purpose, for your life to contain such passion,' he said quietly.

She continued to gaze at him, hardly hearing his words, only seeing his eyes, those dark brown eyes staring intently into hers.

'You really are a unique woman,' he said, as if to himself. 'A unique, admirable, passionate woman.'

As if breaking a spell that had woven itself around them, she looked down and gave a little laugh. 'My mother wouldn't agree with you on that. Or perhaps she would, but would not see it as a good thing. She has devoted her life to trying to turn me into a conventional young lady.' Once again, she gave a forced laugh, as if they were merely having a polite conversation and that unsettling, intense look had not occurred.

'She decided that I had an unhealthy obsession with painting and sent me away to finishing school to turn me into a proper young lady.' She knew she was burbling but she'd prefer to burble than think about what that look might mean. 'It was called Halliwell's Finishing School for Refined Young Ladies, but my friends and I always referred to it as Hell's Final Sentence for Rebellious Young Ladies.'

He gave an appreciative laugh.

'That's where I met Georgina, another rebellious young lady, and my other closest friends, Amelia and Emily.' She smiled in memory of the happy times they had shared. If it hadn't been for their friendship Irene doubted she would have survived the misery of the finishing school.

'I take it the school didn't succeed in finishing you off.'

'No, not at all. I continued painting, much to my mother's consternation. She says painting will be the ruin of me and I'll never get a husband with hands like these.' She held up her hands, with their chipped nails and cracked skin from the constant use of turpentine and from stretching canvases.

He took her hand and lightly kissed the back. 'They are hands that create beauty,' he said. 'Therefore, they are beautiful and let no one tell you otherwise.'

Her breath caught in her throat at the gentle touch of his lips on her skin. Ripples of awareness coursed through her body, causing her heart to beat wildly as if trying to escape her chest. What on earth was happening to her? Whatever it was, it was something over which she appeared to have no control.

She leaned towards him, holding his gaze as he turned over her hand and gently kissed the palm. Her pulses throbbed wildly. Her tingling lips parted, as if willing him to do more than kiss her hand.

Lowering her gaze, she focused on her hand, still encased in his, still held to his lips. She took in the splatters of paint, the broken nails, the roughened skin. That was who she was. An artist. Not some flibbertigibbet seeking a man's attention.

She snatched her hand away and clutched her sketchbook tighter to her chest, as if protecting her vulnerable core. It was unbelievable. After all the painful lessons she had learned in her first season, she was once again succumbing to the charms of a flirtatious man.

She resumed walking at a brisker pace and he matched her, step for step.

'It appears we have a lot in common,' he said, his voice once more jovial, that exchange that had so unsettled her obviously having no effect on him. But then, why would it? After all, he was a womaniser, and one doesn't become a womaniser without knowing how to seduce women. That was another harsh lesson Edwin had taught her.

'I said, we appear to have a lot in common.'

She chose to make no reply.

'I too have escaped to Devon and am hiding myself away.'

She sniffed her disapproval and wondered which of the endless stream of women he was escaping from.

'Although in my case the woman I have escaped from is not my mother,' he added, causing Irene to roll her eyes.

'My Aunt Prudence is one of the most formidable women I have ever met. I love her dearly but when she's on a mission I find it best to avoid her. So I have fled to my Devon estate.'

'And what mission is she on?'

To stop your womanising?

'Let's just say that, as with your mother, my aunt would like me to conform to society's expectations.' He smiled at her as if they were co-conspirators, which they most certainly were not.

She did not return his smile. A man like him would never understand the constraints placed on a woman. He was free to live however he wanted, do whatever he wanted and have as many women in his life as he wished.

He reputedly transgressed society's rules on countless occasions and no one condemned him for it. In fact, she suspected he was admired for such behaviour. But she had slipped just once, and a scandal had only just been avoided by the exchange of a sizeable amount of money.

If he did decide to marry, being a duke, he could have his pick, but she would always be the slightly peculiar woman that no man was really interested in, unless they were a man like Edwin, and were merely playing with her.

'No, we have nothing in common,' she said emphatically.

'Yes, we're both escapees. I've hidden myself away

in Devon to escape a determined aunt, and you've hidden yourself away to indulge in the vice of painting?' That slow smile returned. 'And on occasion paint naked men.'

'I told you why I had to do that,' she said, her voice louder than necessary. 'I was excluded from the life-painting classes and I need practise in drawing the human form.'

'And I ruined it all. I am sorry.'

She merely hmphed at his apology, preferring not to discuss anything that reminded her of him standing naked in her studio.

'And did the real Joshua ever arrive and disrobe for you?'

'No.' She could hear the petulance in her voice and did not want to sound like that. The mistake was hardly his fault, or at least, not entirely his fault. And she did overreact somewhat, was still overreacting, but didn't seem capable of not doing so.

'I'm sorry for throwing things at you,' she said, her voice not sounding sorry at all.

He laughed. A rather pleasant laugh. Damn him.

'No need to apologise. You're not the first woman who has thrown things at me or sent me on my way with some colourful words ringing in my ears, and I suspect you won't be the last.'

Irene had no doubts about the veracity of *that* statement.

'But I meant what I said. I admire you for having a dream and pursuing it,' he continued. 'Perhaps you should have told your mother you needed to escape to Paris rather than Devon for the sake of your health. I believe over there the women painters and sculptors have formed a union to promote their art.'

She stopped walking and looked at him in surprise, causing him to laugh again.

'I do have a brain, you know, as well as a body. I've spent a lot of time in Paris and am a great admirer of the new art movements. During my time there I saw many exciting works by women artists.'

She continued to stare at him, hardly believing that a man like him would have any interest in anything other than having a good time.

Then a loud warning bell sounded deep inside her. Hadn't Edwin also claimed to support her dreams of becoming an artist? And hadn't it been all part of his seduction technique? In reality, he had cared as little about art as she suspected the Duke did.

Edwin had known that complimenting her looks, the way he might with most women, would fall on deaf ears but complimenting her art and claiming to support her dreams had caused her to fall in love with him and ignore all those warning bells that had kept trying to tell her that he was nothing other than a lothario.

Just as they were ringing out their warning now. She had ignored them once and would not ignore them again. History would not repeat itself. Once Edwin had what he wanted, his true colours came out, and he had been heard boasting to friends that he had deflowered his first debutante of the season, but certainly not his last. It was only quick action by her father, and a payment to Edwin as generous as her dowry, that had nipped that scandal in the bud and saved her reputation.

She had learned her lesson the painful way, and she did not need to be taught it again.

'We're approaching the village and I would prefer not to be seen walking with you,' she said, not at all ashamed that her voice sounded prim and proper. 'Goodbye, Your Grace.'

With that she strode off down the path at an accelerated pace, leaving that sweet-talking rake behind, where he belonged.

Joshua watched her retreating back and tried not to focus on the sway of her hips. He was unsure what he had done or said that had caused her to be so upset with him. But upsetting Miss Irene Fairfax seemed to be his forte.

He shouldn't care, but strangely he did. He did not want this interesting, passionate woman to dislike him. Although causing Miss Fairfax to dislike him was something else he seemed to be very good at doing.

He turned and retraced his steps, back up the hillside, along the coastal path to the roadway, where his patient driver was waiting with his coach.

Driving home, he had to admit it was all for the best that she was so dismissive of him. She was not for him and thank goodness she at least was aware of that fact. For one fatal moment, he had almost forgotten that he did not dally with innocent young ladies, and despite her unconventional lifestyle, innocent she obviously was.

He only had to remember her blushes, her awkward movements, her embarrassment at once again catching him naked to reinforce the fact that she was not the type of woman to associate with a man like him.

But then there was the other side of Miss Fairfax, the one he was determined to forget all about. As if to torture him, the image of her lips parting as she gently sighed when he kissed her hand appeared before his eyes. He moved uncomfortably on the leather seat, desperate not to think of that sigh or those inviting lips.

He knew that look well, had seen it countless times before. For one, brief moment she had let down her guard and exposed her attraction to him. And by God, loath as he was to admit it, he was also attracted to her, more than he could remember being attracted to any woman. She wasn't conventionally beautiful as the women in his life always were, but she seemed to shine with an inner light that was decidedly alluring. And how could he not admire her passion and her talent?

But he had his rules. He was not his father. If he was, he'd be doing everything he could to get the lovely Miss Fairfax into his bed. He would not just be imagining what that curvaceous body looked like without its layers of clothing but taking his time to observe, caress and kiss every lovely inch. He would not just be remembering those parted lips, but would know what they tasted like, what they felt like and how she reacted when he took her in his arms and kissed her.

He coughed, as if that would drive away that improper image, and stared out at the passing scenery. He was not his father. His father cared nothing for the women he hurt. If he saw a woman he wanted, he relentlessly pursued her until she succumbed, and used whatever means he could to get what he wanted. Once he had caught his quarry, he inevitably lost interest and moved on to the next pretty face and luscious body that caught his eye. No, he was not his father. And even if he was, the no-nonsense Miss Fairfax would be far too intelligent to fall for any man's seduction techniques. Hadn't her guard come back up just as quickly as it had been lowered?

And unlike the debutantes he spent his life dodging, she was far too sensible to chase after a duke. She had said she despised the season and had hidden herself away in Devon. Those was not the actions of a woman in search of a husband.

He just wished all those other debutantes and their mothers were as sensible as Miss Fairfax. It would make his life so much easier.

The carriage crunched to a halt on the gravel driveway outside the entranceway to his home. He opened the door and climbed out before the driver had a chance to jump down and open the door for him. As he entered his home a few splatters of rain darkened the gravel path, signalling the storm that was to come.

Yes, Miss Fairfax was certainly not like the other young ladies who attended society events, but she was still an unmarried young lady and she was still out of bounds to men like him.

Although, if the unmarried young ladies who attended society events were all as interesting and enchanting as Miss Fairfax, he might be more tempted to attend a ball or two during the season. He sat down on the bench in the hallway and lifted his foot onto his knee to remove his boot, then laughed at the absurdity of his thoughts. Of course he would not be attending any balls, even if they were full of young ladies as fascinating as Miss Fairfax. Such behaviour led in only one direction, towards the wedding altar.

He looked out the door at the dark sky, remembering the way she had caught the coming tempest with a few strokes of her pencil. It was hard to imagine what it would be like to have such passion and drive, to have something all-consuming in your life, to have a purpose.

A footman rushed towards him. 'Allow me, Your Grace,' he said indicating the boots.

Joshua waved him away. While Miss Fairfax was devoting her life to creating works of beauty, he wasn't even expected to take off his own boots.

He looked back out at the forlorn weather, which seemed to mirror the change in his mood. What was he doing, staying down here, away from his friends, away from all the fun and pleasure London had to offer? It had been a hoot to flee from Aunt Prudence and his behaviour was sure to have irked her, something he always enjoyed doing, but he had never stayed alone at his country estate for more than a day or two.

Yesterday he had resolved to return to London immediately, but like the fickle man he was, he had changed his mind this morning and decided to remain. Now it really was time to return. He looked out at the rain, which was now falling more persistently, and hoped Miss Fairfax had made it home before the deluge set in.

His boots off, he squelched down the entranceway and up the stairs to his bedchamber to change out of his damp clothing.

He stripped off and climbed into a warm bath a servant had thoughtfully prepared for him. He lay back and smiled, remembering the array of expressions that had passed over her face during their brief time together. It seemed Miss Fairfax was just as turbulent and changeable as the weather.

As the warm water lapped at his skin he made a decision. He would stay in Devon. Just for a few more days. After all, there was no urgency to return to London.

Chapter Five

Irene took a long, circuitous route home. She had set off with the intention of clearing her mind of the Duke; instead he had imposed himself even more on her thoughts. Although she wanted a diversion, as she strolled through the village, she didn't look at the hats, ribbons and gloves displayed in the shop windows as most young ladies would. She didn't enter the tea rooms to join the local women taking tea and cake, and time out for a good gossip. Rather, she walked as if in a glazed state, trying and failing not to think about the tumult that had raged inside her during her latest encounter with the Duke.

Again and again, she told herself that the expression on his face was merely proof that he was a practised seducer. That look in his eyes when he took her hand to her lips meant nothing. It was what men like him did. They tricked women into thinking they meant more than they did, that they were special.

That was why men like the Duke had an endless stream of women in and out of their bed. But for a moment he had actually fooled her. She *had* thought she was special, that he wanted *her*, just her and no one else. For one reckless moment she had hoped he would kiss her. If he had taken her in his arms, she would have put up no objections. Even now, she was still regretting that she had not experienced what it was like to be held in those strong arms, to have his lips on hers.

She touched her lips and sighed. There was no denying it; despite everything she knew, she had still almost succumbed. She knew exactly what he was like. Knew precisely what would have happened if she had kissed him. And knew how he would react when he had finished with her. It was not as though she was still a naive young woman full of romantic illusions. Edwin had ended any such fanciful ideas. He had taught her what men could be like and how rakes treated women. And yet, she had still fallen so easily for his charms.

Hopefully, she had not revealed any of this to the Duke. It would be mortifying if he actually thought she was attracted to him. She would hate it if he thought she was yet another woman who was his for the taking. Because, despite that one lapse in good sense, she most certainly was not. She could not deny that he was attractive. And yes, there was something exciting and tantalising about him, but he wouldn't be any good as a rake if he wasn't attractive to women. But should they meet again, he would learn that she most emphatically was not his for the taking.

She turned and walked towards her cottage, determined to stick to that resolve, and hoping that the Duke would soon leave Devon and her resolve would not be put to the test.

Rain splattered the pathway just as Irene entered her cottage. She threw off her cloak, hung it back on the hook and placed her hat on the hall table. Hetty had left, as she often did during the times when Irene did not require her, so she could thankfully disappear into her studio and concentrate on her work without any further distractions.

That had been the entire reason for going for a walk: so she could focus. But instead of clearing her head of any thought of the Duke, all that had happened was she had wasted more time and energy thinking about him. That was not why she was in Devon. She most certainly had not come to be distracted by handsome, charming men with seductive smiles, but to paint, and that was what she would do.

She entered the studio and froze in the doorway. Her breath caught in her throat. Her body went rigid.

Forcing herself to move forward, she plastered a smile on her face. 'Mother, what a pleasant surprise. The maid is presently absent but I'm sure I could make tea. I've become quite resourceful since I arrived in Seaton.' Still staring at her mother, she gestured towards the kitchen where this tea making would occur, her smile held painfully in place.

'What on earth is this?' Her mother all but squawked, turning from the easel and fixing Irene with an accusatory stare.

Irene placed her hand on her stomach, drew in a long, slow breath and released it equally, slowly, fighting to come up with an explanation, but all eluded her.

'While I'm recovering from my illness I thought I'd draw—'

'What have you done, Irene? My God, what have you done?' Her mother's shrill voice cracked through the air as she turned back to the easel.

Irene fought to remain calm as she walked around the back of her mother to look over her shoulder. There was Joshua Huntingdon, the Duke of Redcliff, in all his naked glory, standing in the pose of *David*.

'It's a life drawing, a depiction of Michelangelo's *David*,' Irene said, her voice steadier than her nerves.

'It's a naked man,' her mother gasped. 'An obscenity.' She turned from the drawing, as if no longer able to look at the abomination, and all but staggered over to the nearest chair.

'It's no different than all those nude paintings and statues you have seen in the national gallery,' Irene said, knowing she was grasping at straws. Her mother would not see it like that. It was one thing to look at statues created in days of antiquity and quite another to know that your daughter had been gazing at the body of a naked man.

'What will your father think when he hears?' Her mother clasped her head and shook it slowly, while Irene stood in the middle of the room, feeling like a young child about to receive a serious reprimand.

'We'll have to keep this secret,' her mother rushed on. 'You'll have to destroy it. I hope you haven't shown anyone. Tell me you haven't shown anyone.'

Well, Hetty has seen it and she's a bit of a gossip.

Irene cringed, knowing her mother did not want to hear that.

'And what of that man?' her mother demanded, not waiting for Irene's reply and sending a disgusted look in the direction of the easel. 'Who is he? Can he be bought off? If we pay him, will he forget all about this?' She sighed loudly. 'Oh, Irene, I didn't think we'd have to pay off another man. I would have thought you would have learned how to behave yourself. Instead, you lie to me and say you're coming down to Devon for the sake of your health.' Her mother pulled at the neck of her blouse as if struggling to breathe. 'And then you demean yourself by indulging in this decadent immorality with some unknown man.'

Anger started to well up inside Irene. She had done nothing wrong with Edwin other than trust an unworthy man. He was the one who had harmed her, the one who had behaved abominably and yet she was the one who was blamed. And she had done nothing wrong now, other than draw a naked form, something male artists had been doing for countless generations. But she knew from bitter experience there was no point saying this to her mother, so she swallowed down her anger.

'And where is Georgina? Where is her lady's maid? Where are the servants?' She looked around the room, as if expecting them to pop up from behind the furniture. 'Did you lie to me? Have you been living here alone, and entertaining men and… Oh, Irene. How could you?'

Irene had thought her mother would be happy with regular letters with updates on her improving health. Now she realised that of course she would visit. She needed to think quick to explain herself.

'Georgina has made a brief trip up to return to London and—'

'And you *have* been here, all on your own, entertaining naked men and… Oh, Irene, have you no shame? What sort of daughter have I raised? You shamed us once, but this—' she gestured towards the easel '—this is worse, so much worse.'

'It's not like that… We didn't… I was just—'

'Stop lying to me. Tell me the truth. Who is he and how much is it going to cost your father this time?'

'It won't cost anything. I'm sure the man in the painting is capable of discretion.' Irene wasn't entirely sure of that but she could only hope.

'Who is he?' her mother repeated, narrowing her eyes.

'Just an art lover who posed for me so I could practise drawing the human form. As you know, they wouldn't let me do so in the art classes I attended, so I had to—'

'And quite right too.' She stood up and began pacing the room. 'I should never have allowed you to attend those classes in the first place, mixing with all those artists and whatnot. They've turned you into some sort of bohemian who no longer knows right from wrong.'

That was not Irene's recollection. Her mother had been set against the classes. It had been her father who had relented and paid for the lessons. And those other artists were as conservative as the men she met at society balls. At least, they were when it came to their attitude to women artists. Particularly when they discovered she wasn't just a lady who was dabbling but took her art seriously.

Her mother stopped in her pacing and turned to face Irene. 'But you still haven't answered my question. Who is he?'

'He's just one of the locals.'

That was not entirely a lie.

'Good.' She nodded and resumed pacing. 'If we pay him off, we might be able to keep this secret. No one in society is ever likely to know. Your father will have saved your reputation, yet again. And that—' she stopped and scowled again at the easel '—can be put on the fire. You can come back to London with me on the evening train. Your father can come down, arrange to pay off this man, and then we can forget all about it.'

'No. Please. I can stay here. No one will know. Please, Mother. My health… I still need to—'

'And there will be no more of those art classes. Your father said it wouldn't do any harm, and now look what's happened. I knew it was a mistake to let him persuade me.' She placed her hands on her hips and fixed Irene with a steely stare. 'But I need to know who this man is. Tell me who he is, and no more of this nonsense.'

Irene took in a deep breath and exhaled on an exasperated huff. There was no getting around it. Her mother was not going to let up until she answered. 'Joshua Huntingdon, the Duke of Redcliff.'

Her mother stared at her as if she had gone insane. 'The Duke of Redcliff posed naked for you? He stood in this very room without his clothes on?' She pointed to the middle of the room in disbelief.

Irene merely nodded.

Her mother walked over to the easel and stared at the drawing. 'This is the Duke of Redcliff?'

All Irene could do was once again nod.

The furrows creasing her mother's brow smoothed over and a smile twitched at the edges of her lips. She now resembled an art connoisseur observing a particularly intriguing work.

Irene tensed. This was not a good sign. Her mother had no interest in art.

'The unmarried Duke of Redcliff?' she asked, looking up from the drawing to Irene. 'The one who has extensive lands here in Devon and a large estate up in Scotland?'

'I don't know what he owns. I hardly know the man.'

The smile twitching at her lips turned into a full beam. 'I believe you know the Duke very well. Very well, indeed. Better than any respectable young woman should ever know a man, unless of course that man intends to marry her.'

Irene's heart appeared to jump into her throat. 'No, no, Mother,' she said, her voice strangled as she fought for breath. 'It's not like that.' She rushed forward and clasped her mother's arm. 'People pose naked for artists all the time. It means nothing. They are just forms to be painted, like a bowl of fruit. It means absolutely nothing.'

Her mother turned back to the drawing, still smiling. 'Society does not see it that way. The Duke knows the rules. And if need be, we can prove that he has ruined you. This is all the proof we need.' Her smile became self-satisfied. 'He will have to do the right thing. This time I will make sure there is no repeat of what happened with Edwin Fitzgibbon,' she added, as if talking to herself. 'The only exchange of money will be when your father arranges your marriage settlement.'

'No, Mother, please,' she begged. 'The Duke was merely doing me a kind turn. I needed a model and he agreed to pose.' It wasn't entirely the truth but nor was it entirely a lie. And right now, Irene would say and do anything to turn her mother away from the preposterous idea of forcing the Duke to marry her.

'I'll do what you want,' she rushed on, the words tumbling over each other in her desperation. 'We can keep this a secret and tell no one. You're right. We don't want a scandal and neither will the Duke.' Irene doubted that the Duke would care one fig whether he was the subject of a scandal, but there was no need to point that out to her mother.

Her mother turned to her, still smiling. 'No, it won't be a scandal, because the Duke will be marrying you.'

This was insanity. Her mother could not force the Duke to marry her. They barely knew each other. She did not want to marry the Duke, and he quite obviously had no interest in marrying anyone. Including her.

'Please, Mother, I'll come back to London with you,' Irene pleaded. 'We can forget all about this.'

Her mother shrugged off Irene's grip on her arm and continued to smile at the painting.

'I'll never paint again if that is what you want.' Irene's heart seemingly broke as she uttered those desperate words. 'But please, forget all about this, Mother.'

Her mother looked from the drawing to Irene, her expression showing she was oblivious to her pleas. 'My daughter, the next Duchess of Redcliff. Just imagine.' She looked back at the drawing. 'If I'd known your silly artistic aspirations would have such a fortuitous outcome, I would not have put up so many objections.'

'No, Mother, you can't.'

'I really don't know what is wrong with you, Irene.

This is marvellous. I might not approve of the way you've done it, but you've captured the most eligible man on the marriage market, something so many other young ladies have tried to do and failed.' She raised her chin and threw back her shoulders as if she was already the mother of a duchess.

Irene collapsed into the nearest seat, all the fight going out of her. The Duke would not be marrying her—of that she was certain—but this was all so humiliating. She knew he would laugh off her parents' attempt to force him into an unwanted marriage. He had made his feelings on the subject of marriage quite clear and as he already had a notorious reputation, the threat of a scandal was hardly likely to force him to give up his cherished bachelor status. He had also been scathing about those young ladies who chased him. Now he was going to think that she was no different. That having him pose for her was some elaborate ruse to get him to the altar.

She buried her face in her hands, while her mother prattled on about marriage arrangements. Somehow, she was going to have to convince the Duke that none of this was her doing and she was most certainly not out to trap him into this unwanted marriage.

Chapter Six

'It's a shame the Duke has already seen you like that.' Her mother cast a critical eye over Irene. 'But it can't be helped now. I'll have to send for all your gowns. Fortunately the Duke does not attend events during the season so the ones you already have will do and it won't be necessary to have a new wardrobe made.'

With every word the weight on Irene's shoulders grew heavier and she slumped further into the chair.

'Sit up straight, dear,' her mother continued. 'You're almost a duchess, remember. I must send for your lady's maid as well. Once Mabel has worked her magic with your hair and face, and—' she paused, her delighted smile turning to a scowl '—done something with those terrible hands, the Duke will be able to see that you'll make as good a duchess as any other young lady.'

A glint of opportunity opened up for Irene. 'Yes, that's a good idea, Mother. You return to London and arrange everything, and I'll make sure the Duke doesn't see me in this state until you return.'

Her mother sent her a pitying look. 'What century

are you living in, dear? I'll send a telegram to my lady's maid. She will organise everything, and my trunks, along with all that you will require for your courtship, will arrive by the evening train.' She resumed her pacing. 'We'll need to rent a bigger house. This tiny cottage will hardly do. We'll also need more servants so your courtship can take place in a proper, respectable household.'

'Aren't you getting ahead of yourself, just a little, Mother? We're not courting.'

And we never will be.

'I must write to his aunt as well,' she continued as if Irene hadn't spoken. 'I'll remind that good lady that you are the niece of an earl, and that even though you are the child of the second son, you are connected to some of the best families in England, as the future duchess should be. I know that Lady Prudence has been anxious to marry her nephew off to a respectable young lady for quite some time, just as I have been to find a husband for you.'

Panic welled up inside Irene. Hadn't the Duke said his aunt was a formidable woman? Irene did not need two such women as her adversaries.

'But you just said I'm not respectable.' Irene pointed towards the easel as a reminder of all her mother had said about her behaviour, of entertaining men, alone, and naked men at that. 'And there was Edwin,' she added in a quiet voice. 'If the Duke's aunt hears about—

'Nonsense,' her mother cut in, her lips drawing into a tight line before the smile returned. 'We need not mention that man's name ever again. And as for this...' She waved her hand towards the drawing. 'I have met

Lady Prudence on numerous occasions. I know her to be a sensible woman and I am sure will believe, as I do, that it will be in everyone's interest to keep this as our little secret.'

Her mother looked around the parlour that Irene used as her studio. 'So where in this chaos do you keep your writing paper?' She spotted the writing desk in the corner, moved aside the stack of recently stretched canvases with a moue of disapproval and took her seat.

Irene watched in silence as her mother removed a piece of stationery from the drawer, opened the ink bottle and dipped in the fountain pen. Her world was starting to unwind around her and she felt powerless to stop it.

'While you're doing that, I might go for a walk,' she finally said. She was going to have to stop this, and arguing with her mother obviously was not going to work.

Her mother looked up from her writing. 'Didn't you just come in from a walk? And it has started to rain.'

'I love walking in the rain. I won't be long. Hetty will be returning soon so you can ask her to serve you some tea.'

'Good, and I have some tasks for your maid as well.' She looked Irene up and down. 'Make sure no one important sees you dressed like that. After all, a future duchess needs to keep up appearances.'

Stifling a sigh, Irene grabbed her hat and cloak and rushed out of the cottage. She all but ran down the street to where a man was parked outside the local store and was loading his cart with supplies.

She pulled up the hood of her cloak to protect herself from the rain, but also to hide her face from any curious villagers.

'Please, can I trouble you for a ride?' she asked the man, who did not stop in his work. 'I need to visit the Duke of Redcliff's home. I will pay you for your services.'

The man turned to face her, a sack of flour over his shoulder, and a wry smile crossed his face, as if to say he knew exactly why a young lady would be so anxious to see the Duke. It was embarrassing, but nothing compared to the humiliation she would suffer if she didn't speak to the Duke immediately and inform him of the plot being concocted by her mother.

'Right you are, miss,' he said, dumping the flour onto the cart and helping her up onto the front bench. 'I'm going that way myself.'

Irene kept her head lowered, hoping against hope that the man would not recognise her, and she would not become the latest topic of gossip in the village tavern and among the ladies in the tea shop.

She waited with as much patience as she could muster as he continued to load up the wagon, certain that he was taking his time to deliberately prolong her agony. Eventually, he climbed up to the front and joined Irene. With a flick of the reins, they moved off through the village and onto the country roads. Irene willed the plodding horse to move at a faster pace, but it seemed neither horse nor driver were in a hurry.

When they finally arrived outside the impressive gold-and-black wrought iron gates that signalled the entrance to the Duke's estate, he pulled on the reins and brought the cart to a halt. Mumbling her thanks,

Irene reached into her cloak pocket for her small purse, removed all the money she had and pressed it into the man's hand.

With a tip of his hat, and whistling to himself, he drove off, while Irene ran past the gatehouse and up the long, gravel driveway that led to the expansive three-storey home, frantically trying to compose what she would say to the Duke.

Joshua was bored. This morning had been distracting, but now he knew he really should be returning to London. Being stuck inside, staring out the window at the falling rain wondering what to do with himself, was tedious beyond belief. Even the thought of annoying Aunt P wasn't enough to relieve the tedium of his own company. If he returned to London it would be to endless rounds of parties, nights spent in gaming houses and other even less reputable dens of iniquity that catered to bored aristocrats. Even that held no real appeal but it was better than staring mindlessly out the window.

He was sure Miss Fairfax would not be bored. He wondered what she was doing now. She was probably working away intently on another artwork, her pretty face the very picture of intense concentration. How he envied her. She would not be staring blankly out at the rain wondering what to do with herself.

As if he'd conjured her up, the lady herself appeared at the end of the driveway. He wiped the condensation off the window to ensure that his bored mind wasn't imagining things. No, it really was the lady in question, running towards him, her cloak billowing out behind her.

He rushed out the door, down the stairs, through the entranceway and, grabbing an umbrella from the stand, ran down the path.

'Miss Fairfax, you appear to be rather wet,' he said as he opened up the umbrella and held it over the dripping lady. 'Allow me to—'

'I have to talk to you,' she gasped out.

'You need to catch your breath and get out of that wet cloak first.' He took her arm and led her back into the house, where a footman was waiting to take her cloak and his umbrella.

He led the still gasping Miss Fairfax through to the blue drawing room, where a fire had been laid. He had to admit, she looked particularly fetching, with her cheeks a pretty pink and her chest rising and falling rapidly with each gasped breath. He struggled not to focus on her chest, nor on the inappropriate thoughts that were fighting for his attention. Instead, he waited politely until she had taken her seat and caught her breath, then claimed a seat across from her.

The footman entered and asked if he required tea to be served. He looked at Miss Fairfax, who was seated on the edge of the settee as if about to spring up and run away.

'Would you like a cup of tea, or would you prefer something a little stronger to settle your nerves?'

She looked towards the decanter on the sideboard. He signalled to the footman that his services were not required and poured himself and Miss Fairfax a glass of brandy.

She took if from him with shaking hand and downed it like a sailor who had been deprived of his rum ration for far too long. Without comment he poured her another, handed it to her and sat down.

'So what is this all about?'

'My mother,' she said on a gasp, clenching the brandy balloon so tightly he hoped the crystal glass would not break in her hands.

'Your mother?' he prompted.

'My mother has arrived and she saw the drawing I did of you.'

'I see. I assume she is no admirer of my rendition of *David*.'

'No,' she stated emphatically.

'Everyone's a critic these days.'

She glared at him. 'It wasn't my artistic technique she disapproved of. Well, she did, but she always has. Or, at least, the mere fact that I do paint with...' She sighed loudly. 'None of that matters. What matters is the fact that you were...' She waved her hand around in the air.

'I see. Well, she'll be the first woman to criticise my...' He repeated her gesture and waved his hand in the air. 'But there's no accounting for taste.'

She did not laugh at his joke.

'She says we now have to get married.'

Joshua stared at her, then in one gulp, downed his own brandy and rose to pour himself another.

'It's none of my doing,' she rushed on. 'I was not trying to trap you. I don't want to marry you. Honestly, there is no man alive I would less want to marry.'

Joshua smiled to himself. He always suspected she was a sensible young lady, and now she had proved him right. 'I'm pleased you have such a high opinion of me.'

'No, it's just I didn't… When you posed for me I never…'

He laughed. 'You do not need to explain yourself. And you have no need to worry. No one can make us marry if we don't want to.'

She took a sip of her brandy. 'I know that,' she said, her voice a bit calmer. 'I just wanted to make sure that you knew that none of this was my doing.'

'And now I do.'

'I'm so sorry.' She looked up at him, her brow creased, her eyes pleading. 'I never meant this to happen.'

He sat back down on the settee and was tempted to take her hand in a comforting manner, but after their exchange this morning, after experiencing the effect of kissing her hand, physical contact was perhaps best avoided. 'None of this is your fault. You thought you were sketching that other Joshua. Perhaps if you tell your mother, then she will suggest you marry him instead.'

It was another joke that did not amuse her.

'The other Joshua is not a duke.' She sighed loudly. 'I'm sorry, but you're going to have to do something. Deny it was you. Go back to London or hide out in one of your other estates so she can't find you. Something. Anything.'

'While I'm flattered by the strength of your determination not to marry me, you can be assured I will do everything in my power so you do not suffer that fate worse than death.'

Once again she did not laugh.

'Good.' She nodded her head rapidly. 'And you'll

need to do something soon because at this very moment my mother is writing to your Aunt Prudence to tell her you've compromised me and you have to do the honourable thing.'

Joshua finished off his second brandy. The last thing he wanted was to be subjected to an increased level of matchmaking from his Aunt P.

'You do not need to worry,' he said, no longer feeling quite so blasé. 'No one can make us marry against our will, not your mother and not Aunt Prudence.'

'I do hope you're right but my mother is starting to despair. I turned twenty-three this season and we both know what that means.'

Joshua did indeed. She would have had her coming-out at eighteen. Now she would have been through five seasons without securing a husband. Usually that meant both debutante and mother would be desperate, and desperate women would do just about anything to secure a husband before their fate was sealed and they entered the dreaded state of spinsterhood. Although what he couldn't understand was why. Why had some man not snatched up this lovely, clever, talented woman and made her his wife? Sometimes he had as much trouble understanding his fellow man as he did the fairer sex.

'My mother is seeing you as a godsend. Oh why, oh why did I do that damn sketch?'

Guilt seized Joshua. He had thought the entire thing a bit of a lark at the time, but none of this was funny for Miss Fairfax. 'This is not your fault. You made a genuine mistake. The fault lies entirely with me.'

She nodded, then shook her head. 'It matters not

whose fault it is. Not now. But you do believe me, don't you? I wasn't trying to trick you into marrying me.'

'I believe you implicitly. I have never seen a young lady who was more determined not to marry me.'

This time she did smile, a rather lovely smile. If Joshua achieved nothing else this day, and it was likely that he would not, then at least he had made her smile.

She lightly bit her bottom lip. 'I'm not saying there is any reason why some other woman might not want to marry you. It's just… I mean, I don't want to… I'm not saying there's anything wrong with you… It's just—'

'It's quite all right,' he interrupted before she dug herself into an even deeper hole.

She placed her brandy on a side table and stood up. 'Thank you. Now I better return home before my mother causes any more problems.'

'I'll call for my carriage,' he said, heading towards the bell cord to summon a footman.

'No,' she stated firmly, as if he had made an improper suggestion, causing Joshua to raise his eyebrows.

'Sorry, it's just if I return in your carriage Mother will draw all sorts of conclusions. None of them good.'

'You can't walk home in this rain. I insist that you take my carriage.'

She stood up straighter. 'May I remind you, Your Grace, that you are not my husband and never will be? You have no right to insist I do anything.'

'On all those points, Miss Fairfax, we are in complete agreement. But believe it or not I do sometimes like to act like a gentleman, and a gentleman would never allow a woman to walk home alone, and to do so in the rain. Not all my vehicles bear the Duke's crest. I have carriages designed to ensure discretion.'

She sent him a look of condemnation. He was tempted to point out that the carriages had been built during his father's time for that man's illicit liaisons, not his own, but he doubted she would believe him.

'All right, but I will travel alone,' she conceded. 'There is no point giving anyone any more reason to gossip than my journey here will provide.'

'As you wish.' As he pulled on the bell cord she strode out of the room, retrieved her cloak from the servant and waited at the entranceway for the carriage to arrive.'

Joshua joined her and the two waited in silence, as if now that she had established there was to be no wedding, she had no more to say to him. Inside him, there seemed to be so much he wanted to say to her, but he could hardly identify his feelings, let alone turn them into words and arrange them into sentences, so he remained mute.

The carriage arrived and he helped her inside. Before he closed the door she turned to him. 'Goodbye, Your Grace,' she said with a finality that suggested there was no need for the two of them to meet again.

He watched as the carriage drove up the driveway, turned into the country road and took her away from him. She was right in making such a final farewell. It would be better for both of them if their paths never crossed again. At least, it would certainly be better for Miss Fairfax. He had already caused more than enough havoc in her life.

He remained staring at the empty driveway for a moment longer, then retreated into his home to prepare for the inevitable visit of yet another independent, spirited woman. His indomitable Aunt Prudence.

Chapter Seven

Irene should be elated, or at the very least quietly confident. The Duke was on her side. He would be putting a halt to her mother's wedding plans. Once he had informed all concerned that he would not be marrying her, there would be nothing anyone could do about it. Not her mother and not his aunt. Yet neither elated nor confident could describe the unexpected emptiness inside her.

It was all decidedly peculiar. Victory was at hand. So why had this heaviness settled on her? And why did she keep remembering the look on the Duke's face when she told him there were plans afoot to make them marry? He had appeared stricken, like a man standing in the dock and receiving a life sentence.

She should not take offence. Her own expression when her mother had made the same threat had presumably been no different. Although, she had been more concerned about humiliating herself in front of the Duke, rather than horrified by the thought of marrying him. Not that she wanted to marry him. She certainly did not want to marry him. But it would have been somewhat less insulting if he hadn't looked quite so devastated.

She asked the driver to stop on the edge of the village. The carriage might not bear the Duke's crest but she suspected the villagers would recognise it, and everyone would have their theories as to why a young lady was travelling incognito in such a vehicle. And none of those theories would be good for Irene's reputation.

When she arrived back at the cottage, she found it transformed. The parlour was once again a parlour and not doubling as an artist's studio. Her canvases, easels and paints had all gone. The dust cloths that protected the furniture from flecks of paint had been removed, and the furniture had been shifted back into its original position.

'Doesn't this look much better?' her mother said, looking around proudly at the restored parlour.

Irene merely sent her mother a terse smile and reminded herself that this was but a temporary setback. Hopefully, once the Duke made it clear there would be no marriage, her mother would finally realise that her daughter would never marry. Then she would return to London and leave Irene down in Devon, away from the disapproving glare of society. She would then be able to spend her days enjoying her own company and immersed in her artwork. A small ache of loneliness hit her, which she immediately dismissed as a reaction to the turmoil of the day.

'I asked that Hetty girl about larger establishments available for rent,' her mother continued. 'She's quite efficient, I must admit. She went and fetched the little man that handles the properties owned by the Hathaway family. I've arranged for us to move into a much more suitable household as soon as our luggage and the servants arrive.'

Irene moved slowly around the now restored parlour and made no response. Her mother's plans were all for nothing. She would soon learn there was to be no wedding and all would be well. Irene tried to push away her glum mood, caused merely by foolish pride. Why should she care how the Duke reacted to the thought of marrying her? And what did she expect? That he would fall at her feet and say that marriage to her would be no hardship, that he had been waiting all these years for a woman like her to come into his life and save him from his disreputable ways? She scoffed at her own silly vanity. And if he had, which of course he never would, it would have been a disaster. She did not want to marry the Duke.

But she needed to do something to stop her mind from constantly wandering back to that stricken expression on his face. Once again she pictured the way his eyes had grown wide and his mouth had actually fallen open in shock before he drank down his brandy with such desperation. His terror at the thought of having her as his bride couldn't have been more obvious.

All in all, this day had been one humiliation after another.

What she needed was to bury herself in her art. That had always been her refuge and she needed it now more than ever. She looked at her mother, who had returned to the writing desk and was compiling a list with deep concentration, her pen scratching frantically across sheets of paper.

Irene knew returning to her painting would annoy her mother and she would have to endure the full force of her disapproval, but she had to get back to work, to paint away the emotions tumbling around inside her. If she didn't, she was sure she would lose the ability to maintain her polite facade and all her raging emotions would explode out of her, which would be much more harmful to her mother than the sight of her daughter with a paintbrush in her hand.

'Where have you put all my canvases and painting equipment?' she asked with as much nonchalance as possible.

'I told Hetty to burn them,' her mother said without looking up from her writing.

'What? No.' Irene stared at her mother, the room suddenly spinning.

'You're not going to need them now. It would hardly be appropriate for a young lady being courted by a duke to—'

Irene didn't hear what else her mother had to say. She raced out the house, flew down the village street and burst into the cottage where Hetty lived with her family. Her mother and several siblings filled the small kitchen, all busy at a range of activities. Clicking knitting needles came to a halt, stilled knives hovered over piles of cut vegetables and everyone stared at Irene. Even the baby, being bounced on his mother's knee, turned to look curiously at the strange, distraught woman.

'Don't worry, miss,' Hetty said before Irene could choke out her words. 'I know how much you love all your paintings and things, so I've stored them in the shed at the back of the cottage. I doubt if your mother is ever likely to go in there.'

Irene grasped her stomach and sank into a wooden kitchen chair. 'Thank you, Hetty. Thank you so much.'

'Well, I couldn't bear to burn them, especially that one of the Duke.' She sent Irene a quick wink.

'Best you keep away from that one,' Hetty's mother said to her daughter, although Irene suspected she was included in the warning. 'The old duke did enough damage to the young women in this village. I hope the son ain't going the same way—otherwise everyone in this village is soon going to be related to each other.'

'Thank you, Hetty,' Irene said, ignoring the mother's unnecessary words. She did not need any further reminders of what the Duke was like.

Almost as quickly as she had run to Hetty's she returned home, skirted around the side of the cottage and down to the wooden shed at the back of the garden.

Tears welled up in her eyes in gratitude to Hetty. There were all her canvases, paints and easels stored carefully behind the garden implements. No one would be entering the cottage until spring so her equipment would be safe until her mother left, which hopefully would be soon. She retrieved her sketch pad and pencils, sneaked in through the back door and hid them in her bedroom.

The temptation to hide away in her room was all but overwhelming, but if her mother was capable of ordering the burning of her artworks, there was no telling what she would do if she caught Irene with her forbidden sketch pad. And it would just be for a day or two,

Irene reminded herself as she re-entered the parlour. Once the Duke had made it clear there would be no wedding, then her mother would return to London and life could get back to how it had been before she arrived. Irene just had to bide her time.

Her mother was still scribbling her lists, and hardly seemed to have noticed Irene's absence. Sitting in the parlour, she heard the click of the back door opening and closing, signalling that Hetty had returned to prepare the evening meal. Irene waited for her to enter the parlour and make her usual joyful greeting, but she waited in vain.

She released a loud sigh. No doubt, while Irene had been visiting the Duke, poor Hetty had been subjected to a lecture on how she was to conduct herself in the future.

It seemed both young women had been brought to heel by her mother's arrival.

Irene sat and looked out the window. She walked around the room, picked up ornaments, placed them back where she found them and went back to staring out the window.

After such a physically and emotionally exhausting day, the rest of the afternoon and the evening passed as if time had slowed down. For her mother, there was now only one topic of conversation worth discussing. The wedding.

Over dinner the lists of all that was involved regarding the organisation of a wedding were read out to Irene. Fortunately, her mother did not seem to notice that the only contribution Irene made was the occasional 'hmm' of agreement on the choice of flowers, who should design the wedding gown and how it would be best to host the wedding at the estate of her uncle, the Earl of Lanbourne. None of this was actually going to happen, so Irene was determined to just let it all wash over her.

After constant glances towards the clock sitting on the mantelpiece, Irene finally saw the hands move to ten o'clock.

'I think I'll retire early, Mother,' she said, standing up and giving a theatrical yawn, which caused her mother to frown. Before she could be informed that loud yawning was hardly appropriate behaviour for a future duchess, she kissed her mother's cheek and scuttled up the stairs to the sanctuary of her room.

She pulled out her sketchbook and finally had the chance to do some work. Unfortunately, for once, she had not lied to her mother. She *was* tired. Too tired to work, and it seemed also too tired to sleep. Instead, she spent the night, tossing and turning, thinking about all that had happened throughout the day, from meeting the Duke at the cove, to her mother's arrival, to the threat of a forced marriage, to the Duke's look of abhorrence at the thought of marrying her, to his promise that he would thwart her mother's plans. All in all, it had been more eventful than she could possibly have expected when she set off this morning for a gentle stroll along the coast. Finally, she fell asleep, her last conscious thought being to hope the next day would not be so frantic.

Irene's hopes were dashed before the day had hardly begun. Over breakfast her mother's mood went from excited to ecstatic as the first mail delivery of the day brought with it a letter from Lady Prudence.

'Listen to this,' she said, grabbing her daughter's arm as if she was about to run away and almost causing Irene to spill her tea. '"I am delighted to hear that my nephew has expressed such ardent interest in courting your daughter."' She smiled at Irene. 'Isn't that gracious of Her Ladyship to turn something that could be scandalous into something so refined.'

Irene took a sip of her tea and made no response.

'"I shall be arriving by train today and look forward to meeting Miss Fairfax. Please accept my invitation to you and your daughter to afternoon tea tomorrow at Redcliff Estate."'

She looked up, her eyes shining, and beamed the largest smile Irene had seen. Her mother was so happy, Irene experienced momentary guilt that her happiness was soon going to be shattered.

'Afternoon tea with a duke and Her Ladyship, just imagine.' Her mother placed her hand on her heart and sighed. 'Hopefully your trunks will have arrived by then. I think you should wear white, a nice pure colour suitable for a young lady about to be courted by her future husband.

Irene raised her eyebrows but said nothing. There was no point in reminding her mother of what had happened with Edwin. That particular scandal was yet another that was to be conveniently forgotten.

'Or will the yellow tea dress suit you better?' her mother continued. 'Although you did look lovely in that pale blue. Oh, your lady's maid will know what's best.' Her mother went back to rereading the short letter.

The trunks did arrive on the morning train, along with Irene's lady's maid and most of the servants, and they instantly set to work readying the new house.

Once it was set to rights, Irene and her mother made the short journey down the village street to their new residence. Or in her mother's case, it was more a short parade, her imperious posture suggesting she already thought she was the mother-in-law of the local duke and the villagers were little more than her serfs.

'Oh, yes, this is so much more suitable,' her mother decreed when they entered the three-storey house with its large entranceway, elegant dining and drawing rooms and servants' quarters on the top floor. 'This is a house in which you can be courted by a duke.'

Irene merely smiled. At this very moment, the Duke was no doubt informing his aunt that there would be no marriage. He might even have already returned to London. Harsh reality was about to destroy her mother's misguided fantasies. All Irene had to do now was wait and brace herself for her mother's crushing disappointment.

Miss Fairfax had been correct. Her mother had immediately informed Aunt Prudence that Joshua had to do the right thing and marry her daughter. And Aunt Prudence had also wasted no time in writing to Joshua and informing him of how delighted she was that he had finally found a woman he wished to wed. No mention was made in the letter of coercion, nothing was said about the naked painting that had resulted in this threat of marriage, and most certainly nothing had been said about whether or not Joshua wanted to marry.

Instead, he had been told she would be arriving by train the next day and expected Joshua to meet her at the station.

So here he was, pacing up and down the village railway station, waiting for the next train from London and wondering whether now might not be a good time to make a run for it. He could get the first train to Dover and be on the continent by the end of the day. Then perhaps he could flee to the Americas or the Antipodes, anywhere that Aunt P couldn't catch him.

He halted his pacing. But that would not do. He had promised Miss Fairfax he would put an end to all this marriage nonsense, and even if he did flee, he suspected his aunt would follow him to the ends of the earth if she thought she could get him to tie the knot.

No, he was going to have to do the right thing: face his aunt and tell her that he was not about to surrender his bachelor status.

Why his aunt was so set on marriage, he would never understand. Unlike her sister, Joshua's mother, Aunt P had been sensible enough to never marry but did not believe that luxury should be extended to others, particularly not dukes who needed to produce more dukes, for reasons Joshua could never quite understand.

If it had been the formidable Aunt Prudence who had married his father, Joshua suspected she would have kept the old reprobate on a tight leash and curtailed his rakish behaviour. Instead, his father had picked the gentle, sensitive sister, then neglected her and made her miserable. Now his aunt wanted to inflict that fate on yet another innocent young woman. It was unbelievable.

Her letter had also informed him she would be coming to stay for the duration of his courtship, so she could ensure that the entire process was conducted in a satisfactory manner and they could be married as quickly as propriety allowed. She had mentioned that her presence was essential as nothing could be left to chance. In other words, she did not trust him and suspected he would do exactly what he was thinking about now, run off to the Continent or the Americas at the first opportunity.

That showed how little his aunt thought of him, and yet, she still wanted some unfortunate young woman to become his bride.

He resumed his pacing. Not that he had anything to worry about. He had been thwarting his aunt's plans for the last ten years and each season had managed to keep a growing platoon of debutantes at bay. He had avoided marriage many times before and he could easily do it again. And this time he had the added advantage of the latest target being as committed to not marrying as he was.

If he was of a mind, he could feel slightly insulted by the vehemence with which Miss Fairfax had declared she had no interest in marrying him. But he was not insulted. At least that was what he told himself. He was grateful that Miss Fairfax was different from every other debutante he met. She did not want to elevate herself to the highest rank in society and she could see him for exactly what he was, a man who would make a terrible husband.

The train pulled into the station, with much billowing of steam, puffing of smoke and hissing of brakes. The doors of the first-class compartments were thrown open, and his aunt emerged through the smoke, followed by her equally formidable lady's maid.

'Joshua, my dear, this is excellent news,' she said as Joshua kissed her on both cheeks while the lady's maid rushed off to organise the luggage.

Taking his arm, she strode down the platform towards his waiting carriage. 'I've made some inquiries about the Fairfaxes,' she said, getting straight to the point as expected. 'The family is completely respectable. The father is the younger brother of Samuel Fairfax, the Earl of Lanbourne, so they are well connected even if she doesn't have a title.'

The footman opened the door and Joshua took his aunt's hand to help her up the steps.

'I briefly met the young lady at the Cavendish ball a season or so ago,' his aunt continued as she settled herself in the carriage. 'Pretty enough, polite enough. There's a certain, shall we say, backbone there. I don't usually like that in a young lady, preferring a more deferential and self-effacing nature.' She paused for the first time and narrowed her eyes at Joshua. 'But in this case, I believe it might be an advantage. She'll be able to keep you in line.'

Joshua opened his mouth to respond, but his aunt continued. 'I'm not sure why she hasn't married already. Perhaps she is a bit too spirited for most men, but I'm sure you'll manage.'

He smiled. She certainly was spirited, and it was a quality he rather admired. If other men were intimidated by her, then that was their problem.

'I've invited the mother and daughter to afternoon

tea so I'll be able to see for myself what the future duchess is like, but I'm sure she'll be exactly what you need.'

Now would probably be the time to tell his aunt that there was no point in inviting the young lady to tea, and there was no need for Aunt P to acquaint herself with Miss Fairfax as there would be no marriage, so she might as well take the next train back to London.

'Aunt, I'm afraid—'

'After that first informal meeting, we'll need to host a dinner party. I do hope your servants are up to the task,' she continued as if Joshua had not spoken. 'I don't believe you keep a firm enough hand on your servants, my boy. That's something the Duchess will also have to sort out and make sure your home is run as it is supposed to be.'

'My servants do a perfectly adequate job.'

'An adequate job is hardly enough for a duke, especially once you're married. The standards of a married man have to be much higher than a bachelor. I'm afraid your footloose days are about to end, my boy, and you and your servants had better get used to it.'

The carriage pulled up in front of the house. His aunt descended and instantly headed up the stairs, then disappeared down the hallway in the direction of the kitchen, presumably to give orders to Cook and the rest of the staff. Joshua followed along behind, like a schoolboy who had just been given a stern rebuke.

Sometimes, trying to talk to his aunt was like attempting to stop a whirlwind. But he was going to have to interrupt her torrent of words, sooner rather than later, or Joshua suspected she'd have him up the aisle and married off before he'd even caught his breath.

Chapter Eight

There was no time like the present. Wasn't that what people said? His aunt had been operating under a delusion for long enough. It was time to set her straight and put his problems to right, and he needed to do so before Miss Fairfax and her mother arrived for afternoon tea and the opportunity was lost.

Once his aunt had finished giving her orders to his servants and changed out of her travelling clothes, he asked her to join him in the drawing room for morning tea.

The moment she had sat down, and before he was drowned out by another deluge of words, he leaped in. 'My dear aunt, I'm afraid you've had a wasted journey. I will not be marrying Irene Fairfax and have no plans to marry any other young lady any time soon.'

Or any other young lady ever.

He braced himself for the outrage. For her to slam her cup down on the side table and risk destroying the fine porcelain. She did neither, merely sipped her tea, causing Joshua to wonder if she had become hard of hearing.

'I said, I will not be—'

'I heard what you said, Joshua, and there is no need to shout.'

'Good.' He sat down and picked up his tea. That was easier than expected.

'But you will be marrying Miss Fairfax.'

Joshua sighed and placed his tea on the side table. What had he been thinking? It would have been too much to expect an easy conversation about marriage with his aunt. Once again, the Americas and the Antipodes were beckoning. If he caught the late train he could be in London this evening and set sail on the morning tide.

'Unless of course you want to destroy a young lady's fragile reputation,' she said, eyeing him like a bird of prey over the top of her teacup.

'What? No, of course not, but—'

'Before I left London, I told a dozen or so of my closest friends that you were courting Miss Fairfax with the intention of marrying her before the start of the next season.'

'Well, you can un-tell them as soon as you return to London.'

'I'm afraid it will be all around society by now,' she said, not looking the slightest bit afraid of anything. Rather, she looked decidedly triumphant. 'You do know how women like to gossip. It's a frightful vice, but there you are.'

'And when you tell them you made a mistake, they will gossip about that instead.'

His aunt nodded, but that smile still quirking the edges of her lips alerted him that she had another trick

up her sleeve. 'You are right, my dear,' she said, causing Joshua to brace himself once again. His aunt never
said he was right unless she was about to tell him how
wrong he was.

'They will gossip about how a twenty-three-year-old
who is all but on the shelf was courted then abandoned
by the Duke of Redcliff. Her reputation will be in tat-
ters and no man will want to marry a woman who has
been rejected by you. I'm afraid you do have a bit of
a reputation with the ladies, just like your father.' She
sent him a false look of concern. 'People will make as-
sumptions. They will talk. Society will probably shun
her and her mother. It will be a tragedy. But if that is
what you want, you're right, I can't make you marry
against your will.'

Joshua stared at his aunt, unable to believe she could
be so callous. 'That's an appalling thing to threaten,'
he spluttered, barely able to control his outrage. 'You
should have spoken to me first before you announced
our courtship to your cronies. And you couldn't possibly be so merciless as to ruin an innocent young lady's
reputation. She has done nothing wrong.'

His aunt signalled to the footman that she wished for
her teacup to be refilled, then she turned her attention
back to her nephew. 'I'm tired of talking to you about
marriage. I've found countless suitable young ladies for
you and you've rejected every one of them for no good
reason. Now it is time for me to get more assertive. I
will see you married and with an heir and if I have to
blackmail you into doing your duty then that is exactly
what I will do. I owe it to your dear parents.'

This could not be happening. Joshua would not let it happen. 'You're right, Aunt.'

She narrowed her eyes, knowing that he too would not surrender so easily.

'I am exactly like my father. And men like us do not care whose reputation we destroy. If people gossip about Miss Fairfax, then it is hardly likely to affect me.' He adopted his best poker face, hoping his bluff would pay off.

Her smile immediately signalled his failure, proving his suspicion that his aunt would be a demon at the gaming tables.

'Except you are not *exactly* like your father. You, fortunately, are a slightly better man than the old duke ever was. You, my dear, were blessed with a conscience. We both know that, don't we?' With that, she took a victorious sip of her tea.

She was wrong. He was no better than his father. A better man would not have arrived at the Seaton station addled and bedraggled from a night on the tiles. He would not have gone home with a strange woman and taken off his clothes, and would not have seen the whole thing as a bit of a lark.

But damn it all, she was right about one thing. Unfortunately, he *was* cursed with a conscience and he could not see Miss Fairfax's reputation destroyed. But nor would he see her forced into a loveless marriage, all because of his own thoughtless, self-indulgent behaviour.

'But I don't want to marry her and she doesn't want to marry me,' Joshua cried out, feeling as if he was trapped in one of those terrible dreams where you're running as fast as you can but getting nowhere.

'Of course she wants to marry you. You're a duke. She's twenty-three, practically a spinster.'

'Miss Fairfax is not like that. She's like me—she doesn't want to marry.'

'Nonsense. There's no such thing as a woman who doesn't want to marry.'

'Well, she doesn't want to marry *me*, and who can blame her.' He leaned forward in appeal. 'You know what I'm like. I will make her miserable. It will be my parents' marriage all over again and you wouldn't want Miss Fairfax to suffer the way your sister did.'

Aunt Prudence's lips drew tightly together, giving him hope that he had finally made her understand what a bad idea this was.

'Your parents' marriage *was* a success,' she said to Joshua's utter disbelief. 'My sister elevated her family's status and they produced an heir to carry on the Redcliff name.'

'That's hardly my definition of a successful marriage. I cannot imagine two less compatible people. Yes, they produced an heir, but they also made each other completely miserable. Is that the fate you want for me and Miss Fairfax?'

'I want you married, Joshua. I have given you plenty of opportunities to find a woman with whom you are compatible. I am now at the end of my tether. You will be marrying Miss Fairfax, and the two of you will just have to make the best of it. Just as your parents did.'

Joshua glared at his aunt, determined not to be defeated. Vowing to remain unmarried and never subjecting any young lady to a loveless marriage to a man such as him was the *only* way he was better than his father. He would not be letting go of his one and only virtue, not now or ever.

Somehow he was going to have to find a way out of this marriage and he had to do so without risk to Miss Fairfax's reputation. It was obvious that reasoning with his aunt was not going to work. Threats had also failed. For now, Joshua was completely out of ideas, but he had promised Miss Fairfax and he would not let her down. He would have to think of something, and think of something quickly.

Irene's mother meticulously supervised every aspect of her dressing for afternoon tea at the Redcliff Estate, as if she was a general preparing for battle.

She was hurried into her bedchamber several hours before they were expected at the estate, and made to stand in the middle of the room dressed only in her chemise and corset while her lady's maid and mother bustled around her. A series of dresses were removed from the wardrobe and Irene was commanded to try on each in succession, then slowly turn around in front of her mother and Mabel, so the two could observe her appearance from every angle. This was followed by a long, tedious discussion on which dress most flattered her skin tone, which highlighted her slim waist and which accentuated her curves without being too obvious.

Some dresses were immediately abandoned, while others were placed in a separate pile, and Irene was made to try on those for a second inspection. Then the entire discussion was repeated. Eventually, a pale pink dress with white stripes was selected. This, the two women agreed, met all the necessary requirements; the

cinched-in waist flattered her figure, the shade comple-
mented her skin tone, and according to her mother, it
was a colour that presented her as an innocent young
woman eager to be courted for the first time.

Once again, Irene felt it best not to mention Edwin,
nor to allude to the subject matter of the painting that
had got her into this situation, both of which destroyed
any illusions of innocence. It seemed both events had
been entirely forgotten and she was now redeemed as
a young lady untouched by scandal.

The dress finally selected, they moved on to her hair.
Mabel created several styles for Irene's mother's inspection. The two women once again walked around her,
discussing each style as if Irene were merely a collec-
tion of curls, plaits and tendrils. As her hair was repeatedly backcombed, curled, lifted on top of her head or
allowed to flow over her shoulders, she reminded herself to remain calm.

She had nothing to worry about. All this prepara-
tion was for nothing. Her mother had lost the campaign
before the first battle had even commenced. By now
the Duke would have informed his aunt that there was
to be no courtship, that they would not be marrying.
A note would soon arrive informing them the afternoon tea had been unfortunately cancelled. The Duke
might even have left his estate already and was probably now in the arms of some other young woman, if
not in her bed.

Pain gripped Irene's chest, which she told herself
was caused by her lady's maid pulling at her long hair.

When she was finally dressed, Irene received another

order to stand up for further inspection. Her mother frowned and Irene's patience headed towards breaking point.

'I suppose you've done your best with those, Mabel,' her mother said, indicating Irene's hands.

That had to be an understatement. The moment Mabel had arrived she had been instructed to remove every fleck of paint, to rub Irene's hands with lemon juice and oil to try to soften them and to buff her nails in a futile attempt to undo the damage done by paints and turpentine.

'Try and keep these on for as long as possible,' her mother said, still frowning and handing Irene her white lacey gloves.

'Right, I think that's as good as she's going to get,' her mother declared and Mabel nodded her agreement.

No note had yet arrived. Instead, the Duke's carriage was waiting for them in front of the house, to take them to his home. As Irene and her mother drove through the village, her mother adopted that same imperious stance, the one that indicated to anyone who might be looking that she considered herself to be at the very height of society and expected all the little people to look upon her with wonder.

And Irene did, but her look of wonder was in reaction to her mother's delusion that this marriage was actually going to happen.

The carriage drove through the large gates at the entrance to the estate and her mother's look of self-satisfaction seemed to take over her entire body until she was almost quivering with excitement.

'To think, all this will soon be yours,' she said, indicating the grand home at the end of the long driveway. 'It's magnificent, and you will be its duchess.'

Irene had to agree, at least with part of that statement. It was a magnificent home, one that dominated the landscape. Irene couldn't imagine how many rooms were contained in its three stories but there were more than one family could possibly need. If the number of leaded windows in the wing facing the driveway was any indication, they were all but countless.

Personally, Irene would rather have her little cottage, although she had to admit the gardens were sublime. The formal garden in front of the house reflected the artistic talent of the gardeners, with topiary shaped into intricate geometrical patterns, and the greenery of the shrubs contrasting delightfully with white standard roses. This beauty was enhanced by an ornamental lake, adorned with a cascading fountain set against a backdrop of established woodlands, creating a picture-perfect scene. It would be a joy to capture all this beauty in oils.

The carriage pulled up in front of the house, and Lady Prudence and the Duke were waiting for them at the foot of the stone stairs. Lady Prudence greeted Irene as if she were already a member of the family, while the Duke looked on with an expression best described as apologetic.

Irene's heart sank. She wanted to crumple to the ground in a small heap of pink-and-white cotton. His look spoke a thousand words. He hadn't done it. He hadn't told his aunt there would be no marriage. He had let her down.

* * *

Miss Fairfax's look had not been lost on Joshua. He had failed her and was still failing her. Despite racking his insubstantial brain, he had still not come up with a suitable way to fix this unfortunate situation.

While the two older ladies wandered off into the house, chatting together animatedly as if they were already the best of friends, Joshua offered Miss Fairfax his arm. She took it with a resigned sigh and they followed the two women, who were busy plotting their fate, into the house and along the hallway to the drawing room.

'You look lovely today, Miss Fairfax,' he said, admiring her hair, which was a confection of curls and puffiness. She always looked lovely, but it appeared a lot of attention had been paid to this ornate style, which was ballooning out on top of her head, so he felt it his duty to compliment it.

'Don't say that,' she whispered out the side of her mouth. 'They'll think you find me attractive.'

He was about to say he did find her attractive, very attractive indeed, but the stern look she sent him cut off those words before they had left his mouth.

'Mrs Fairfax and I have much to discuss,' his aunt said as the footman opened the door to the drawing room. 'Perhaps you two young people would like to go for a walk before we take tea.'

'What a good idea. Irene loves to walk,' the mother responded. 'She's such a healthy young woman.'

Joshua had heard many similar comments made by mothers about their daughters. He was being informed that the young lady in question was of robust good health, so would be capable of producing the required sons. And the way Miss Fairfax had rolled her eyes suggested the implication of the compliment was not lost on her either.

'Miss Fairfax, would you like a stroll in the garden?' he asked.

'Yes,' she responded and immediately reversed direction and walked back towards the entranceway as if she couldn't get away fast enough, leaving him to follow on behind.

The moment they were down the stone stairs and out of earshot she stopped walking and turned to face him. 'Why didn't you tell your aunt you would not be marrying me?'

'I did.'

'So why is she acting as if we are a courting couple?'

'Perhaps we should sit,' he said, taking her hand and leading her to a wooden bench in front of the garden, all the while trying to think of the best way to impart the unfortunate news.

'Well?' she demanded as soon as they were seated.

'I'm afraid my usually principled aunt has shown a somewhat devious side to her nature. She has told all her friends that we are to wed. She has informed me that if we don't, people will make the assumption that I have had my wicked way with you and abandoned you.'

Her eyes grew enormous as she stared back at him.

'I know,' he responded to her unasked question. 'I didn't think my aunt could behave in such an underhand manner, but she said I have driven her to it. But don't worry, I'll think of something else to stop this marriage without damaging your reputation.'

She looked down at her hands, clasped in her lap, then back up at him. 'Perhaps we can use your aunt's deviousness against her.'

Joshua raised his eyebrows, eager to hear how she was going to succeed in thwarting his formidable aunt when he had failed so dismally.

Chapter Nine

Irene twisted her gloved hands in her lap and drew in a series of slow, calming breaths. She had to get out of this marriage, but what she was planning to do was so desperate she was unsure if it was a move she could take.

'What is it?' he said, reaching over and gently stilling her agitated hands. She pulled them away. She did not need the distraction of his touch, even if it was offered in comfort.

'Your aunt is trying to force you into marriage by threatening to destroy my reputation, and that has given me an idea.'

'Pray, do tell.'

She placed her hand on her agitated stomach and exhaled, long and slow, through pursed lips. She had to do this. If she didn't, she would end up married to a man she didn't want, a man who didn't want her. A man who wanted a string of women in and out of his bed. Women whose names the servants didn't even bother to remember because there were so many. What she was about to do was difficult, even painful, but a moment's pain and embarrassment was better than a lifetime of heartbreak.

'You can tell her that you won't marry a woman with a tarnished reputation,' she burst out before she could change her mind.

He raised his eyebrows in questioning confusion.

She drew in another deep breath to try to still her jittering stomach and looked out at the garden.

'You know Edwin Fitzgibbon, I presume?'

He gave a snort of disapproval. 'That cad. I have, unfortunately, met him on one or two occasions. And that was more than enough.'

'I too have unfortunately met Edwin on many occasions and I know him rather too well. He courted me in my first season. He even proposed, although he never officially asked for my hand.'

The Duke's shoulders tensed beside her. If he knew Edwin Fitzgibbon's reputation, then he probably knew exactly what she was going to say, but it still needed to be said.

'Then he called it off,' she said quietly, looking down at her clasped hands. 'My father paid him handsomely so he would not brag about his…conquest. That is the only reason why society never heard what had happened.'

'The bastard.' He jumped to his feet, his raised hands tightly clenched. 'I'm sorry for my language but there is no other word to describe that man. Your father should have beaten him within an inch of his life. That was what he deserved, not being paid for…for what he did to you.'

She shook her head. 'Please. Sit down. It does not matter now.'

Slowly his fists unclenched. He sat down beside her, his breath still coming in loud bursts through flared nostrils.

'But don't you see? We can use this to our advantage. You can inform your aunt of my…association with Edwin. Then I'm sure she will understand why you do not wish to marry me.'

Once again he jumped to his feet. 'I'll do no such thing,' he all but shouted.

She reached out and took his hand, needing to make him see that it was their only option.

'Please, sit down,' she pleaded.

He looked down at her, his lips tight, his nostrils flared, then drew in a long, slow breath, exhaled and took his seat.

'I cannot do that,' he said through clenched teeth. 'I abhor the way young women are held to a different standard than men and I will not be party to it. And I abhor men like Fitzgibbon who think it a great lark to seduce debutantes, never thinking for a moment what harm they do.'

She stared at him, trying to take in the intent of his words. *Men like Fitzgibbon?* Wasn't he like Edwin? A man who seduced women without thought of the damage he caused? But there was no time to think of that right now. There were more important things at stake.

'But it would work,' she said, turning towards him on the bench. 'Your aunt will understand. No man will want to marry a woman who is not chaste.' She cringed at the use of such a word but knew that was the way the world would see her. 'Everyone knows that men, particularly ones of your status, want a virgin for a wife.'

'Not this man. I couldn't care less about such things and despise men who do.' He turned to face her. His expression softened and he took hold of her hands. 'What happened with Fitzgibbon is unforgivable, but only because Fitzgibbon's behaviour is unforgivable, not because of you. And even if I discovered that you'd had a thousand lovers I would still not see it as a reason for ending an engagement.'

Confused thoughts whirled through her mind: memories of her parents' crushing shame at having to pay off her seducer; the accusations she had endured from her mother, as if the entire episode had been her fault; and the blame she had placed on herself for being so stupid and falling for Edwin's charm so easily and so completely.

It had been so hard to tell him about Edwin, and she had expected him to show his true colours, just as Edwin had once he got what he wanted. To shun her and see her as tarnished, just as the rest of society would if Edwin had not been paid to keep silent. Instead, he was looking at her with such affection, such concern, as if she had been wronged.

She could not but admire him for holding such views, although under the present circumstances, it might suit them better if he was as hypocritical as the rest of society. 'But you don't have to tell your aunt that,' she said quietly. 'You could say that you are outraged by this revelation.'

He snorted and shook his head. 'My aunt would not believe me. She knows me only too well. She would see it for exactly what it was, a ruse to get out of this marriage. She's already tried to blackmail me by using your reputation, so telling her about Fitzgibbon will only give her further ammunition.'

She sighed, her shoulders slumping in defeat.

'I am so sorry. Sorry that you are in this predicament, and sorry that you ever had the misfortune of meeting that…' He released her hand and stared out at the garden. 'That cad Fitzgibbon. I'll happily horsewhip him for you, if you wish. It's certainly no less than he deserves and would give me a great deal of pleasure.'

'No, please do not do that.' Even though it was something she had often wished she had done herself.

He gave a small, mirthless laugh. 'Although, he's now suffering from a much worse fate than that. He was forced to marry Lady Beatrice Dankworth and I hear she makes his life a living hell.'

They sat in silence for a few minutes, Irene feeling surprisingly relieved that she had unburdened herself, even though that had not been the intention of her revelation.

She had expected him to blame her, the way her parents had, and for him to be governed by the same double standards as the rest of society. Even men who had countless mistresses before they married expected the woman they took as their wife to be pure and chaste.

If he had judged her, it would have provided her with more reason to despise him, to see it as yet more proof that he was just like Edwin.

But the Duke was not like that.

On that point at least, she had to reassess her opinion of him. And unlike Edwin, he did not approve of the seduction of debutantes. While Hetty and Hetty's mother had said the old duke was notorious for seducing village girls and servants, neither had any evidence that the present duke did the same. And Hetty had said his servants had only good things to say about him. Although Irene could not forget Hetty had also said the servants never bothered to remember the name of the new woman in his life because she would soon be replaced.

Irene was perhaps giving the Duke too much credit. He was still a rake, albeit one with some redeeming traits, but a rake nonetheless. And while he did have the admirable trait of not holding double standards for men and women, in this instance it would be better if he was not quite so admirable.

He turned on the seat to face her. 'Since this is the time for confessions, I too have a confession to make.'

Whatever it was, she was sure it would not matter—after all, he meant nothing to her—but she braced herself anyway.

'I am also not a virgin.'

She stared at him, at his look of wide-eyed innocence, then despite their dire situation, she burst out laughing.

'It's true,' he said, joining in on her laughter. 'Please don't hold it against me.'

Irene continued laughing like a giddy schoolgirl, causing the tension to leave her body. She would never have imagined that this difficult conversation could possibly end in laughter, and she found herself leaning towards the Duke, sharing in this joke.

When their laughter finally settled she looked at him

and smiled. 'We still haven't found a solution to our problem. What are we going to do about our marriage?'

He shrugged and patted her hand. 'Don't worry. You're intelligent and I have a certain animal cunning. Between us I'm sure we'll come up with something.'

Irene could only hope that he was right.

Joshua was pleased he had made Miss Fairfax laugh. He had seen the anguish on her face and had wanted to take her in his arms while at the same time beating Fitzgibbon to a bloody pulp for causing her such despair. He could do neither, so making her laugh was the next best option.

And laughter had gone some way towards calming his own raging emotions. And, to his shame, anger at Miss Fairfax was among them. He was angry that she would think him such a lowlife that he would use her history with the cad Fitzgibbon against her. He knew he was a bounder, but even he would not sink that low. Although he did know that many men who lived an equally dissolute lifestyle as himself still expected the woman they married to be a virgin. Even Fitzgibbon himself had said he would only marry a woman who came to his marriage bed intact and not spoiled by another man.

Joshua continued to seethe as they returned to the house, once again wishing he could vent his anger on Fitzgibbon. He had heard the man bragging of his conquests for the entertainment of his friends and at the time had despised him for it. The thought that Miss Fairfax was among the debutantes he had seduced made his blood boil. She deserved a man much better than

Fitzgibbon and much better than himself. Whether she wished to marry or not was her choice, but she still deserved to be loved, and to have a lover who appreciated what a remarkable young woman she was.

As they entered the house he continued to fume, wishing he could give Fitzgibbon the beating he deserved. But she did not want that. So he would honour her wishes as much as they pained him.

And she was right. They needed to focus their energies on finding a way out of this difficulty. Then Miss Fairfax would be free to find a man worthy of her.

He opened the door to the drawing room. They halted in the doorway and exchanged defeated looks. Their two adversaries were on the settee, their heads close together in deep conversation, and Joshua knew exactly what the topic of conversation would be. Both women looked up and beamed identical smiles of delight.

'You two look the picture of romantic bliss,' his aunt said, causing Mrs Fairfax to smile all the brighter.

He cast another glance sideways and found Miss Fairfax was doing the same. They gave matching ironic laughs, then she frowned, no doubt worried her mother would interpret their exchange as collusion, when the only collusion was their agreement to stop this marriage.

'I just knew you would enjoy your walk,' his aunt continued as they took their seats on the matching settee and the footman served them tea. 'It's spectacular in autumn with the bright foliage, but you are going to love seeing it in spring with the blossoms. Even in winter it's simply marvellous.'

His aunt smiled at Mrs Fairfax. 'Your mother tells me you like to dabble in art.'

'She does more than dabble,' he said, leaping to her defence. 'She is a talented artist. One who deserves to be encouraged.'

Miss Fairfax sent him a wide-eyed look of warning, and Joshua inwardly cursed himself. It would not do to praise her in front of their adversaries. They might get the wrong impression.

'You'll find plenty of subjects for your watercolours on the Redcliff Estate,' his aunt continued.

'She paints in oils,' he said, forgetting himself immediately. 'And she's already found plenty of subjects to her liking.'

Miss Fairfax blushed and moved uncomfortably beside him, causing Joshua to suppress a smile. He had not meant to allude to the incident of him standing in front of her, stark naked. Nor had he intended to cause her embarrassment, although she did look decidedly pretty with pink tinging her cheeks.

'She did a magnificent sketch of one of the coves the other day,' he said, trying to redeem the situation.

She blushed a darker shade of red and Joshua admonished himself again. How had he managed to forget he had been naked on that occasion as well?

Aunt Prudence raised her eyebrows, reminding him that nothing much was lost on that wily old woman. Perhaps he should stop talking. He did not want his aunt to interpret Miss Fairfax's blushes as an attraction between them, especially as her discomfort was caused by his own miscreant behaviour. A quality which she clearly did not find attractive.

'I believe you have an estate in Scotland as well as this magnificent estate in Devon,' Mrs Fairfax said. That was a much safer topic, even though he knew exactly why it was asked. Mrs Fairfax was interested in his wealth and was trying to ascertain just how affluent he was about to make her daughter.

'Yes, but I don't get up there as often as perhaps I should. Nor do I spend that much time at this estate.'

'Although I believe you've found a good reason to spend a lot of time in Devon in recent days,' Aunt Prudence added, smiling at Miss Fairfax and causing Mrs Fairfax to beam the largest smile he had ever seen.

Joshua had nothing to add to that statement, so he sipped his tea, as did Miss Fairfax. Her reason for adding nothing to the conversation, he could not say, but his own purpose was clear. He did not want to risk saying anything else that suggested he was attracted to Miss Fairfax. That was an aim that would be easier to achieve if he wasn't so damn captivated by her. So remaining mute and revealing nothing was the best option.

While the two older ladies chatted on, discussing the wedding as if it were a foregone conclusion, he looked at Miss Fairfax. She was slowly turning her cup around in her saucer, no doubt occupied in the same way as himself, thinking of how to get out of their predicament. He sent her a sympathetic smile, but her frown suggested it was no consolation.

The interminable afternoon tea finally over, they said their goodbyes.

At the carriage door, he took her hand and held it perhaps for a tad longer than necessary while gazing into her eyes. He knew the older women would interpret this as a gesture of affection, but it was a silent conversation intended to tell her not to despair. Somehow, he would make sure she was not forced to become his bride.

Chapter Ten

'I believe that went rather well,' Irene's mother said as the carriage took them back to their new residence. 'Lady Prudence was quite taken with you and said she could tell immediately that you would make the ideal duchess.'

Irene scowled, enjoying the fact that it was a very un-duchess-like thing to do.

'Lady Prudence also said she is so very pleased that the Duke has finally found someone to settle down with. She said she even suspected this was going to be a love match.'

'Hmph,' was the only response Irene was prepared to make on that.

'She said that you make such a lovely couple.' Her mother's smile could almost be called a simper. 'And I must say I do agree with her. The Duke is handsome, you must admit, and so charming.'

Irene refused to comment. Yes, there was no denying he was handsome. He was a womaniser; being handsome and charming were surely two of the main requirements. He was also surprisingly compassionate, with enlightened views on women, but she would not be informing her mother of those qualities.

'And Lady Prudence didn't miss the way you looked at each other. As she said, she had never seen a man and woman look at each other with more affection.'

'Oh, for goodness' sake,' Irene said as the carriage came to a halt. 'We are not a love match. There is no affection. This is a marriage that has been forced on us and you know that very well, as you are the one doing the forcing.'

Irene had had enough. This needed to come to an end. If the Duke wasn't going to do it, then it seemed it was all going to be left to Irene.

As they entered the house, her mother continued to prattle on about the graciousness of Lady Prudence and the beauty of the estate, as if oblivious to Irene's outburst.

'Redcliffe Estate is so grand,' she said, as she handed her hat and coat to a servant. 'It makes your uncle's home in Shropshire seem quite shabby in comparison.' She lifted her chin and adopted that now familiar imperious posture. 'Oh, how he and his wife are going to be envious that it is the minor member of the family who is elevated to such an exalted position. His wife has always looked down on us for just being addressed as Honourable, rather than Lord and Lady. Now my daughter will be addressed as Your Grace and live in one of the most magnificent homes in all of England.'

Irene continued to grit her teeth and waited until they were inside the drawing room and all the servants were out of earshot. She did not want this particular conversation with her mother to be discussed in the servants' hall.

She had made the difficult decision to tell the Duke about her relationship with Edwin Fitzgibbon and it had not worked, but that was not to say it would not work on her mother.

'Mother, I will not be marrying the Duke for the simple reason that I do not want to deceive him,' she announced, interrupting her mother as she continued to bathe in the expected glory of being the mother of a duchess.

'Deceive him? What on earth are you talking about?' her mother said, still with that self-satisfied smile.

'He thinks he will be marrying a young lady who is chaste and we both know that is not true.' Irene cringed, not just because she was lying to her mother, but because she had never before openly talked about what had happened with Edwin.

Her mother's hands shot to her neck. The smile died, and she looked quickly at the closed door, fearing that her words might have been overheard. 'Never mention that again,' she said, through clenched teeth. 'You do not want the servants talking.'

'But it's the truth, Mother, and if it comes out after the marriage the Duke and Lady Prudence will know that we tricked them.'

Her mother lowered her hands and gave a tentative smile. 'By then it will be too late. You will be the Duchess and there will be nothing anyone could do about it.'

Irene stared at her mother, aghast. 'You are willing to deceive them?'

'Yes. Certainly.' She lifted her chin. 'When you have

a daughter of your own you will understand the lengths a mother will go to to find her a suitable husband, but thanks to me you will be much better placed as your daughters will have a duke for a father, not the second son of an earl. My dear, you are twenty-three and this might be your last chance to find a suitable husband. Desperate times call for desperate measures. So, let's speak no more of this matter.'

Her mother picked up her embroidery as if that was the end of the conversation. Irene stared at her. She could not leave it there, not if it provided her only escape.

'Mother, if you make me continue with this courtship, I will reveal to the Duke everything that happened between Edwin and myself.'

Irene's conscience pricked a little harder, but she was desperate, and as her mother said, desperate times call for desperate measures. And surely her behaviour was no worse than anyone else's in this entire sordid affair. Her mother was prepared to lie to the Duke and Lady Prudence by omission and both women were determined to make two people marry against their will. And the esteemed Lady Prudence was blackmailing the Duke, threatening him with the destruction of Irene's reputation if he didn't marry her. If it was good enough for a woman of her standing to use underhand methods, then surely it was good enough for Irene. Ironically, the only person behaving with any decorum was the Duke.

She waited for her mother's outrage, for shouting, tears, remonstrations, something. But her mother merely looked up from her embroidery.

'I would advise against such actions, my dear. Sometimes it is wisest for a wife to keep things from her husband which will have a detrimental effect on marital harmony. And if you think it will cause Lady Prudence to halt this marriage, I believe you will discover you are very much mistaken. Lady Prudence informed me that she is determined that this time her nephew will be marrying, no matter what. I suspect she will have the same view as myself. As long as no one else in society officially knows about it, a scandal is not a scandal, and it is best ignored.'

'Then I shall make sure that all of society does know.' Irene was unsure how she would do that. It wasn't something you could introduced into a polite conversation and she was hardly likely to take out an advertisement in *The Times*.

But it had the desired effect. Her mother's lips had tightened into a thin line and she had dropped her embroidery onto her lap. 'And kill your father in the process. Is that what you want?'

'What?'

'Your poor father never truly recovered from the shock of discovering what you had done. Do you know how degrading it was for him to have to pay off Fitzgibbon? Now, when he is growing older and his health is starting to fail, are you saying you would be such a selfish girl as to humiliate him and expose him to ridicule? He has suffered so much. Now all he wants is to see his daughter respectably married and her scandalous past buried.'

'Father is unwell? Why didn't you tell me? And why are you down here and not in London tending to him?'

'I came down here to make sure you were behaving

yourself, and I'm staying to make sure you get married. If you were more capable of finding a husband for yourself then I would be able to stay in London and tend to my ailing husband.'

'I must go to him.' Irene rushed towards the door.

'Sit down,' her mother called out. 'You will do no such thing. You will stay here and court the Duke. If you want your father to get well again you will give him what he most wants in the world, to see his daughter married.'

Ignoring her mother, Irene rushed up the stairs to her bedchamber and grabbed her clothes out of the wardrobe and drawers. This was appalling. How could her mother just leave her father behind when he was unwell? She pulled open a portmanteau and stuffed it full of clothing for her journey.

Her mother entered her bedroom. 'Stop this immediately.' She pulled clothing out of the portmanteau and shoved them back in the drawers. 'If you want to help your father, the best thing you can do is marry the Duke.'

Irene returned to the drawers and once again pulled out the stockings and undergarments. Her mother tried to pull them out of her hands and stop her frantic movements. 'If you go rushing up there full of all these threats and objections to this marriage, you will only make him sicker. Stop behaving like an impetuous, impudent child and start behaving like a responsible daughter.'

Irene dropped the pile of clothes onto the bed and sank into the chair. Damn it all, her mother had won. She was right. The scandal with Edwin had wounded her father deeply and she could not cause him further pain, especially now that he was unwell.

'I'll call for Mabel to unpack, shall I?' her mother said as she departed, once again looking decidedly pleased with herself.

Joshua was out of ideas. As his valet helped him dress for dinner he went through his options, as limited as they were. Running away to the Antipodes or Americas was out of the question. If his aunt made good on her threat, he would leave behind a ruined young lady. Miss Fairfax appeared not to care about her reputation, but surely all that showed was how this situation had clouded her thinking.

He had seen how ladies were treated by society when their reputation was compromised. He sighed loudly, causing his valet to pause momentarily as he brushed down Joshua's dinner jacket.

It was barely credible, but Miss Fairfax would rather be shunned and be the topic of vile gossip than become his bride.

While he was somewhat insulted by the strength of her objection to him, he was also impressed by her good sense. She was right, and her low opinion of him was well deserved. Although he would not have thought marriage to him would cause a young lady so much despair that she would gladly sacrifice her good name rather than suffer such a fate.

But she *was* in despair and he owed it to her to free her from this situation. He just wished he could think of how he was going to do that.

He joined his aunt in the dining room. She smiled

at him, and he was reminded of a satisfied cat looking at a cornered mouse.

'That all went rather splendidly, did it not?' she proclaimed as the footman served the first course. 'Miss Fairfax is a delightful young lady, is she not?'

Joshua flicked open his napkin. 'She is.' There was no point denying it. Miss Fairfax was indeed a delightful young lady.

'And so pretty.'

'Yes.' That too was something Joshua could not deny, although he would go further and say that Miss Fairfax was beautiful, with big soulful blue eyes that changed with every emotion, from icy blue when she was angry, as she often was with him, to warm and inviting when she smiled. And her brown hair, woven with threads of gold and copper, was certainly lustrous. It made a man wonder what it looked like when released and flowing around her shoulders, or what it felt like when you ran your fingers through the thick locks. Like silk or satin, he imagined. And he had rarely seen such luminous skin. Yes, Aunt P was right—she was pretty. But that did not mean he wanted to marry her.

'And so elegant,' his aunt continued.

'Yes, she's certainly elegant,' he agreed and resumed eating his soup. He could not possibly dispute that her movements were elegant, and as for her figure, it was as if it had been designed to tempt a man. Her hands could not exactly be described as elegant. He smiled to himself, although it was possibly her hands that he admired the most as they reflected her passion and love of art. Or was it her figure he admired the most? Those soft, feminine curves, that small waist he could imagine encircling, those rounded hips he could imagine running his hands over, those full… He coughed and moved uncomfortably on his seat. 'Yes, very elegant.'

'All in all, she will make an excellent duchess.'

Joshua merely hmphed an agreement. Yes, she *would* make an excellent duchess, just not for this particular duke. She deserved much better than him. She deserved a man she could respect, admire and love and that certainly wasn't him. And she deserved a man capable of love and fidelity, and that just wasn't in him.

'I believe you should announce the engagement immediately and the two of you should marry as soon as propriety allows,' his aunt continued as the footmen removed the soup bowls and served the fish course. 'We wouldn't want to rush things. With your reputation a sudden marriage would get tongues wagging and that simply would not do.'

Joshua huffed out his exasperation, causing his aunt to send him a stern look.

'You can write to the newspapers this evening and send it off by tomorrow's post,' his aunt said as if that was the final word on the matter.

Joshua slumped down in his chair. His fate and that of Miss Fairfax was about to be sealed and there was nothing either of them could do about it. He had failed her. That lovely, talented young lady was about to become his fiancée.

Slowly he sat up straighter as a kernel of an idea started to form in the recesses of his mind.

'I shall write to the papers immediately after dinner and ask Charles to get them in the post first thing tomorrow,' he informed his aunt, causing her to raise one eyebrow.

He continued smiling as he ate his salmon, his hearty appetite suddenly returning. He had found his answer. The solution was so obvious. He would put up no further objections, concede complete defeat and do exactly what his aunt wanted.

Chapter Eleven

'We will get engaged.'

Irene stared at the Duke, suspecting being an imbecile was yet another of his faults. That was his clever plan? That was why he had rushed over to her home so early in the morning, when they had barely finished breakfast?

'And we'll have a nice long engagement.'

Irene raised her hands, palms upwards to signal that what he was suggesting was no plan at all, not unless one considered complete capitulation to be a plan.

'A really, really long engagement,' he said, dragging out the words *really*. 'An engagement that goes on and on and on and never actually results in a marriage.'

'Oh.' That actually wasn't a bad plan.

'Your mother will be happy. Aunt Prudence will be happy.'

'And we will be happy,' she added.

'Very happy indeed.' They smiled at each other, a conspiratorial smile that made Irene's heart soar. He took hold of her hands and Irene's smile faltered slightly.

She fought to ignore the way his touch sent little quivers running up her arm and how her heart appeared to have skipped a beat. She should not be having such reactions. For so many reasons she most definitely should not be having such reactions.

'We'll just have to come up with a series of excuses as to why the wedding has to be put off, again and again,' he said.

Think, Irene, think, she admonished herself, determined to focus on this very good plan and not on her very bad reactions.

'Well, I suppose I could make a bit of a fuss about the wedding gown. I believe that's almost expected from the bride. I could insist that it be designed in Paris by the House of Worth, then claim that they're so booked up it will take simply ages before they can design a gown fit for a duchess.'

'Excellent.'

Irene thought it best not to mention that she suspected the famous couturier would give priority to the wedding gown of a duchess.

'And I could say I have business dealings in America that simply have to be sorted out before we can marry.'

'Good. What else?'

He looked up at the ceiling. 'I could tell Aunt Prudence that it's essential that the bedchamber be refurnished before the wedding so it is more modern and acceptable for my new bride.'

Irene's cheeks grew warmer. It simply could not be because he had mentioned the bedchamber, their marital bedchamber. It had to be something else. Anything else. The excitement of working together on this plan, perhaps.

'And I could be really fussy,' she forced herself to continue. 'Demanding that it be remodelled again and again.'

'Excellent. And by then we will have had time to come up with more delaying tactics. This could go on for years and years. In the meantime, nothing in our lives will have to change. You can continue to live as you like, with the added freedom being the future wife of a duke will bring.'

Freedom. That wonderful, elusive concept. And he was right. As the fiancée of a duke, a supposedly future duchess, no one would question the way she led her life. She could spend her days painting. Her mother would not be able to criticise anything she did and would hopefully return to London, knowing, or at least thinking, that her job was done.

Her father would be pleased that all scandal was well and truly behind her, and that would be just the tonic he needed to improve his health.

Her smile grew brighter. It *was* the perfect plan.

'I too will be free,' he continued. 'Free from Aunt P's constant matchmaking and as an engaged man I'll no longer be pursued by legions of debutantes. I can go back to doing whatever it is I do with my days. I don't know why I didn't think to do this years ago.'

She dropped his hand as if it had seared into hers. She did not want to think what the Duke would be free to do.

He raised a quizzical eyebrow at her changed demeanour and she made herself smile, as if unaffected by this discussion. It mattered not what he did. Nor did it matter how many women he had in and out of his bed. She cared not one jot. At least, she did not want to care one jot. But her heart, hammering inside her chest, and the twisting sensation in her stomach suggested otherwise. She breathed in deeply and slowly, not a particularly easy thing to do when one is holding a forced smile, but it was essential she get that inappropriate reaction under control. He was to be her fiancé in name only. She would have no rights over him, and that included not having the right to be jealous. If that was what this strange reaction was.

She placed her hand on her stomach. She was not the sort of woman to forget what type of man she was dealing with. She was a woman who had been burned once and would never be burned again, even by a man who was charming and good-looking. *Especially* by a man who was charming and good-looking.

'You don't need to worry,' he said, his face suddenly serious, and once again taking her hand. 'I will do nothing that will cause you any distress.'

Irene cringed. Had he read her mind, or seen her befuddled reactions? She hoped not, and in future she had to remember to be more rigorous about keeping her guard up.

'It goes without saying that you will also be free. Should you,' he explained, shrugging, 'become enamoured with another man I will put no obstacles in your way.'

'What? Oh, yes.' Irene knew that was most unlikely to happen. No man had caught her attention since Edwin. That was, until now, and she was surely only drawn towards the Duke because circumstances had thrown them together. There was no other possible explanation as to why she was having these peculiar reactions to a man who could not be more unsuitable.

'If that happened you can merely call it off,' he continued. 'Aunt P will have to accept that situation. Her threat to ruin you won't work if you're already promised to another man, and your mother is unlikely to put up any objections, provided you are to wed someone suitable, and I'm sure any man who captures your heart will be eminently suitable.'

Irene composed herself. As much as it pained her, she had to agree to the same condition. 'And if *you* become enamoured with another, then we will call off the engagement.' There it was again, that terrible sensation that felt horribly like jealousy.

He laughed. 'Believe me, there is no danger of that. I will not become enamoured with any other woman.'

But there will *be other women*, that little green-eyed monster whispered in Irene's ear. *Lots and lots of other women.* Irene wanted to swat the monster away, to tell it she didn't care. He could have as many women as he wanted; all it would do was prove that she was right about him. That he was a rake, a lothario, a cad, a bounder, a… Well, whatever he was, he was a man Irene could never be attracted to.

'Will you be returning to London soon?' She kept her voice as indifferent as possible, as if merely making polite conversation, and not waiting for him to confirm her suspicions that he was just itching to get back to the decadent life he lived in London.

'No, I think for appearances' sake it might be best if

I remained in Devon for a while at least. After all, we still have to convince Aunt P and your mother that this engagement is genuine. You know what they're like. If either of them gets a hint of a suspicion that we're fooling them and we have no intention of actually marrying, they'll have us up the aisle before we can catch our breaths.'

Once again, Irene had a reaction she knew she should not be having. She was actually pleased that she would continue to see the Duke, even if it was only for a while. That too was inappropriate. Surely, she did not want to see the Duke, did not want him in her life. And even if he did stay, for a while at least, it would not be long before he returned to his real life in London, a life full of parties, music halls and a revolving door of women. If she was to avoid a repeat of the heartbreak she had felt when she discovered Edwin's deception, it would be wisest if she kept her heart in check. Although, with her hands still in his, it was becoming increasingly difficult to remember how she was to do that.

Remember Edwin. Remember what heartbreak felt like. Remember what humiliation was like. You never, ever want to experience that again.

And at least this time she knew exactly what the Duke was like. Unlike Edwin, he was not trying to deceive her and he was certainly not trying to seduce her.

Heat shot through her body, sizzling deep into her core, at the thought of the Duke actually trying to seduce her. An image of him nuzzling her neck, of his hands moving over her body entered her mind, more as a feeling than as an image. She swallowed quickly and took a step backwards. Where on earth had that come from? Wherever it was, it needed to go back there and not rear its head again.

'Yes, I suppose you're right,' she said in what she hoped was a composed voice. She was unsure whether the Duke remaining in Devon was a good or a bad thing. Yes, she wanted to see more of him—there was no point denying it—but not if it caused these sudden, inappropriate, even dangerous upsurges of emotions.

He gave her an apologetic smile. 'Until my aunt and your mother leave Devon, I'm afraid, we're going to have to pretend to be a courting couple.'

'Oh. I see,' she said uncertainly. 'Going for walks, taking tea together, that sort of thing?'

'Yes, and you could do things, like, I don't know, flutter your eyelashes at me.'

They looked at each other, then both burst out laughing, Irene's coming more from embarrassment than amusement.

'I'm afraid I'm not much of an eyelash flutterer.'

'No, I suppose not. But how do women usually act when they're in love?'

They feel like they're melting inside every time they look at you. Their skin feels alive, as if desiring to be stroked. Their lips tingle, aching to be kissed. It's as if they're being thrown around in an emotional tempest and don't know what to think or how to act. That was what Irene could have said, but instead she frowned in thought.

'I don't know. I've never been in love.' Edwin hardly counted. She had thought herself in love, but it had been a sham. She had not been in love with the real man, only the image he presented to her. A carefully crafted image designed to make her lower her guard and trust him. That had not been love, merely a cruel, deceitful illusion, but it didn't make the pain of his rejection any less real.

'No, me neither,' the Duke said, and Irene didn't know whether to be relieved or annoyed. He'd had all those women, so many that his servants did not bother remembering their names, and yet he loved none of them.

'This might present a bit of a problem for us,' he added.

'Well, when my friend Amelia looks at the man she is in love with, her face seems to soften. Her eyes appear to sparkle. She often leans towards him and seems incapable of not touching him.'

'Like this?' The Duke once again took her hand. He stared deep into her eyes with an intensity that literally took away Irene's breath. Just as she had described to him, she was incapable of looking away; his eyes held her prisoner, drawing her in. Pulled by an invisible thread, she moved closer towards him. Her heartbeat increased its tempo, the pounding spreading through her body, throbbing and pulsating until it all but consumed her.

'Yes,' she whispered. It was not just an answer to his question but a wish, one that came from the bottom of her heart. Whatever he was thinking, whatever he wanted to do, her answer would be yes, oh, yes.

The door opened. 'Your Grace, how delightful,' her mother said. Irene turned towards her, as if in a daze, then quickly stepped back, embarrassment gripping her.

She could just imagine what this scene must look like to her mother. They were standing so close together they were almost touching. The Duke was holding her hand against his chest, and they were staring deeply into each other's eyes. Everything about their behaviour suggested they were a courting couple, a young couple in love who were anticipating a happy marriage. Irene fought to think of an explanation for their behaviour, then remembered that they *were* engaged. They were supposed to look like a young couple in love.

'I've just come to inform Miss Fairfax I will be sending off notices of our engagement to the newspapers this morning,' the Duke said.

Her mother clapped her hands together, rushed over to Irene and kissed her on the cheek. 'Oh, that is wonderful, simply wonderful. And I believe that now you are officially an engaged couple you can drop the formality and call each other by your given names,' she said, smiling at them both.

'Will that be acceptable to you, Irene?' he asked, with a cheeky smile.

'I believe it will be, Joshua,' she responded, and damn it all, she heard her voice soften when she mentioned his name. She hoped he would think that was merely part of her performance, just as the way he was looking at her with such ardour was all an act.

Her mother indicated that they should sit, and with her hand still in his, he led her to the settee. When they sat down, he was so close his thigh was almost touching hers. Irene was unsure what she wanted to do, move closer or move further away. But what she did know was being so close to him was making her light-headed. The warmth of his body was burning into hers. The crisp citrus scent of his cologne and his own musky masculinity was surrounding her, all of which was making it difficult to think straight.

'I'm so pleased you have made it all official,' her mother continued, and Irene fought to focus on what was being said and not the way she was feeling.

'And I must say, this announcement has certainly brought colour to your cheeks, my dear,' her mother continued. 'I've never seen you look so radiant. Doesn't she look beautiful, Your Grace?'

'Indeed she does,' he replied, and smiled at her in a manner that looked disconcertingly like a man who meant it.

It's not genuine, she reminded herself as she stared back into those deep brown eyes. *It's all designed to fool your mother*, the rational part of Irene's mind said, but the susceptible part of her mind wished it was true, and he did indeed think she was beautiful and that he was in love with her.

Irene dragged in a steadying breath, forced her gaze away from the Duke, and smiled at her mother. The Duke's plan was a good one, and she knew it was essential she do nothing to ruin it. But right now, seated beside him, her hand in his, she was starting to have her doubts. How was she going to survive having to spend time with this man, to pretend they had an affection? He was a man she knew she did not want, but unfortunately one towards whom she now had to admit that despite her better judgement, she was hopelessly, undeniably attracted.

Joshua could do this. He had to do this. It was his clever plan after all, so there was no backing out now.

He'd saved her reputation while at the same time avoiding breaking his own vow of staying single. And instead of subjecting her to marriage to him, all he was subjecting her to was an engagement. It was perfect. Well, almost perfect.

This scheme would be a lot easier if Miss Irene Fairfax wasn't so damn attractive. How was he going to pretend to be in love with her, when he was so deeply, so undeniably, so hopelessly in lust with her? Why did she have to have those big blue eyes, those tempting, full pink lips, that body that he was longing to hold and caress?

But it was a lust he most definitely would not be acting on. She had been hurt once before, by that blackguard Fitzgibbon. He would not hurt her again. In this way he knew he was the better man.

As Mrs Fairfax prattled on about something, wedding flowers or veils or whatever, he sat up straight like a good, attentive fiancé and repeated to himself that he could do this. He would merely have to exercise some self-restraint and discipline. When it came to women, that was something he had never before had to do. But then, he had never before become involved with a woman like Miss Fairfax. And quite deliberately so, for the very reason that he did not like to exercise self-restraint and discipline.

And to make matters worse, he was going to have to do that while pretending to be in love.

He was wrong. This was not even remotely a clever plan at all. It was possibly the most foolhardy plan he had ever come up with in a lifetime of devising foolhardy plans. It had seemed like such a good idea when it had popped into his head last night. It had continued to seem like a good plan when he had explained it to Miss Fairfax this morning. It wasn't until he was staring into her eyes, trying to imitate the look of a man in love, that the major flaw in his plan became painfully obvious. He wanted her. Wanted her so much it hurt. Even now, at this inappropriate time, he wanted to take her by the hand, lead her somewhere private, strip her naked so he could kiss every inch of her lovely body and make love to her in every way he could possibly think of. And when it came to making love to a woman, he prided himself on being highly inventive.

He supressed a groan. This was going to be torture, but perhaps it was his punishment, his penance for living a life where he had only ever thought of his own pleasure. He wasn't a religious man, but if a vengeful God wanted to punish a man such as him, putting him in the company of Irene Fairfax and telling him to keep his hands, and other body parts, to himself would be a particularly inventive and cruel way of exacting divine retribution.

'Don't you agree, Your Grace?' Mrs Fairfax smiled at him.

'Indeed I do,' he replied, having no idea what he had just agreed to.

'No,' Miss Fairfax shot back, her pretty face pinched in annoyance. 'I thought we'd agreed that we wouldn't marry for some time, perhaps next June, when the weather is at its loveliest.'

'Yes, right, June, when the weather is at its loveliest.' He smiled at Mrs Fairfax.

'Oh, but a winter wedding can be so glorious,' her mother said with a pout.

'I agree, a winter wedding would be best,' he said, causing Miss Fairfax's eyes to grow wide.

'But I believe it would be best to wait until next winter,' he said, frowning in concentration. This statement elicited a smile from his non-fiancée and a frown from his not-to-be mother-in-law. 'As my aunt has pointed out, a sudden wedding might get the tongues wagging.'

'Yes, perhaps,' the mother reluctantly conceded.

All they had to do now was find a reason why a winter wedding would not suit, but they had more than a year to come up with suitable excuses to delay the wedding further. Between the two of them, Joshua was confident they would be able to do so.

He smiled in reassurance at Miss Fairfax. She returned his smile and without thinking, he placed his other hand over the one he held. She really did have an enchanting smile, like a beautiful bloom opening in the sunshine. He continued to smile back at her, unsure why he was doing so, just knowing that looking at her caused warmth and lightness to flood through him.

'That's if the two of you can wait until next winter,' the mother said. He forced himself to turn away and back to Mrs Fairfax, who was also smiling, that same victorious smile that his aunt had constantly worn since informing him he was to wed.

'We're actually looking forward to a long courtship, aren't we, my dear,' he said, giving Miss Fairfax a quick wink.

'Yes, we are,' she responded. 'After all, we hardly

know each other and it will give us plenty of time to ensure that we are suited.'

'I think it is already obvious that you are ideally suited,' Mrs Fairfax said, placing her hands over her heart. 'My daughter married to a duke is wonderful in itself, but for it to be a love match is more than I could ever have hoped for.'

Miss Fairfax tensed beside him. He squeezed her hand in reassurance and to stop her from blurting out that she was not in love with him, that she hardly knew him and what she did know of him she did not like. That would ruin the plan, and if he was being honest, although he knew it to be true, it was not something he needed to hear.

'Your daughter deserves nothing less than to marry a man who loves her,' he said, causing the mother to smile even brighter and the daughter to look at him in confusion.

Joshua could add that she not only deserved a man who loved her, but also one who was capable of being loyal and faithful. In other words, a man who would make a good husband, and that was not him.

Instead of saying any of that, he stood up to take his leave.

'If you ladies will excuse me, I need to give my aunt the good news that we have decided on a winter wedding.' Joshua could only hope that shrewd old lady would be as easy to convince regarding the reason for the delay as Miss Fairfax's mother had been.

As he left the Fairfaxes' home, he could not help but wonder about his change of mood. He had arrived full of enthusiasm for his foolproof plan but he was leaving full of doubts and confused emotions. He still thought it a good plan, at least, the best plan he could come up with. He just wondered whether he was up to the demands it presented. He had to pretend to be in love with a woman who caused him to think decidedly improper thoughts every time he looked at her. He had to make sure that under no circumstances he acted on those improper thoughts. And he had to hope that at some time, preferably sooner rather than later for the sake of his sanity, she met someone else she really did want to marry. Then he had to be man enough to accept that although Miss Fairfax was a woman he wanted, she was a woman he would never have. Then he would have to happily look on as she became another man's.

Chapter Twelve

News of her engagement brought Irene's three closest
friends rushing down to Devon. When they arrived on
her doorstep, straight from London, she realised that she
had erred terribly. They had always shared everything
since they first met at Halliwell's finishing school, and
she had failed to share with them something so monumental as getting engaged. They had to read about it
in the newspapers. Her only excuse could be she had
been befuddled by what had happened, and the speed
with which it had occurred, that she hadn't had time
to inform them first before they announced it to all of
society.

'Why didn't you tell us you were to marry?' Emily
said as they entered the ~~cottage~~ house

'And to the Duke of Redcliff,' Georgina added, taking off her hat and coat and handing them to the footman.

'I'm so happy for you,' Amelia said, causing Irene
to frown. Amelia had recently married Mr Devenish
and had not long returned from her honeymoon. Love

had made her radiantly happy, and she quite obviously thought, or at least hoped, that her friend was also now in love.

This was all going to take some explaining. They continued chattering and firing questions in her direction as she ushered them into the drawing room. She waited until the footman had closed the door before starting.

'I'm so sorry for not writing to you,' she said. 'This all happened so quickly that I didn't really have a chance.'

'That's the best way,' Amelia said, her hand on her heart. 'Once you know you're in love you might as well marry as quickly as possible. Waiting is far too hard.'

'I'm not in love.' Irene said quietly so no servants would overhear. She knew how fast gossip could spread in a small village and it was essential that nothing untoward got back to her mother or Lady Prudence. Discretion was essential.

'This is not a real engagement. It's just a ruse to put off my mother and the Duke's aunt, who are determined to marry us off.'

All three friends frowned as one.

'Why?'

'How?'

'What happened?'

Irene was unsure who had asked which question but it hardly mattered. 'I painted a…a portrait of the Duke. Mother saw it and insisted we marry.'

The three sets of eyebrows raised in question.

'But we're not going to actually marry,' she rushed on before those questions could be asked. 'We tried to discourage my mother and his aunt but they are determined. It was the Duke's idea that we pretend to give in, get engaged but never actually marry.'

She looked from one friend to the other, hoping they would understand.

'A painting?' Amelia asked. 'What sort of painting?'

'Why would a painting mean you have to marry?' Emily said.

'Can we see it?' Georgina added.

The three friends nodded, causing Irene to blush slightly. 'Well, yes, I suppose so.' She could hardly refuse to let her friends see the painting. She had originally intended to submit it as part of her portfolio so she could gain entrance to another art academy, so it wasn't exactly taboo. 'Mother objected to my painting and wanted all my artwork burned.'

Her friends gasped in unison.

'But it's all right. My maid of all works stored them in a shed at the bottom of the cottage I was staying in when I first arrived.'

'Then let's go and have a look,' Amelia said, standing up.

With surprising reluctance Irene led her friends out the house, down the street to her little cottage.

Why she should be reluctant she was unsure. After all, it was just a painting. Hadn't she said that repeatedly to herself and her mother? Just light and form, no different to a bowl of fruit? Normally she was proud to show off her work to her friends, who were always so supportive. It must be because of all the trouble that the painting had caused that she was feeling hesitant.

They entered the garden shed, where her artwork, paints and easels remained stacked and abandoned.

The three women turned over canvas after canvas and admired the work. Then Georgina gave a loud gasp. 'I think this might be the painting in question,' she said turning the canvas towards her friends. The other two rushed forward, and Irene watched their eyes grow wide, and give each other a series of sideways glances.

'Excellent brushwork, isn't it?' Emily said, causing the other two to nod in a robotic fashion, their eyes still fixed on the painting.

'And she really has captured the Duke of Redcliff,' Georgina added. 'I've met him on a few occasions, although he's always had his clothes on.' She giggled and looked over at Irene, then covered her mouth with her gloved hand.

'I had heard he has a bit of a reputation with the ladies,' Amelia said. 'I think we can all see why.'

This comment caused all three to cover their mouths to stifle a giggle.

'So your mother saw that painting and decided you had to marry him?' Amelia continued, finally looking up at Irene.

'Yes.'

'I suppose she wondered what had happened before he got into this state,' Emma said, waving her hand in front of the painting. 'She was possibly curious as to how you had managed to get the Duke to take off his clothes.'

All three looked at her in expectation.

'It was a mix-up,' Irene said in a rush, taking the painting out of Georgina's hands and placing it against the wall so the back of the canvas was facing out. 'I thought he was an art student who I had arranged to come and pose for me. He didn't enlighten me until it was too late.'

Georgina giggled again. 'That sounds like the Duke. He's rumoured to be quite the rascal by all accounts.'

'Hmm,' was all Irene could respond to that. 'Mother saw the painting, and once she discovered it was of a duke she saw her opportunity to force him to marry me. She wrote to his Aunt Prudence, who is equally determined to get her nephew married off, so our fates were sealed. All because of that stupid painting.'

They all looked at the canvas, which was now hiding its secret.

'Lady Prudence and my mother managed to back us into a corner and give us no choice but to marry,' she continued. 'So the Duke came up with the plan to get engaged but to never marry. Now we have to act like we are a courting couple, even though we don't even like each other.' She shrugged as if that was a simple statement of fact and not a cover for a range of complex emotions that Irene couldn't even begin to explain. 'Anyway, now that you've seen what caused this catastrophe, shall we return to the house and take tea?'

With a final look in the direction of the accursed painting, they left the garden shed. As they walked back along the village streets they made polite conversation, but Irene could just tell they were still bursting with questions.

Once they were settled back in the drawing room and tea had been served, Irene tried to divert them with questions about their own lives. The friends laughed along with Georgina as she regaled them with her latest method of putting off yet another suitor determined to marry her for her substantial marriage settlement.

They expressed their support and admiration as Emily told them of her work in the slums of London.

And they listened with rapt attention as Amelia talked of her new life with Mr Devenish. Every time she said her husband's name she became candescent. Irene had been pleased for her friend when she had fallen in love, but until today she had never envied her. If envy was what she was now feeling. It was all so confusing. She had no reason to feel envy. She was happy for her friend, but she did not want a life like that. She did not want to be married, and if she did it would certainly not be to the Duke of Redcliff.

'It really is wonderful to be in love,' Amelia finished with a sigh, and looked towards Irene.

'I'm sure it is and I'm very happy for you,' Irene said, shocked at how prim her voice sounded. 'I *am* very happy for you,' she repeated, meaning it. *But I am not in love*, she wanted to add, *so there is no need to look at me like that.*

Anything further Amelia was about to say on the subject of love was cut off when Irene's mother entered the room. In fact, almost all conversation between the friends came to an end for the rest of the afternoon as her mother used every opportunity to remind them that Irene would soon be a duchess. And the same topic dominated conversation through dinner and into the evening, much to Irene's chagrin.

She was, however, pleased her friends went along with the charade, although in Amelia's case it did not appear to be an act. It seemed now that her friend had found love she thought that everyone else should also be in love. Throughout the evening she kept giving Irene knowing looks, as if she knew more about what Irene was feeling than Irene did herself. If her mother hadn't been present she would have made it clear to Amelia, in no uncertain terms, that she was not in love. And if she ever did find herself in that elusive state it would most emphatically not be with the Duke of Redcliff.

The following day, her friends returned to London, back to their busy lives, but the afternoon train brought another visitor. Her father arrived, anxious to meet his future son-in-law.

Just like her friends, he turned up unexpectedly on the doorstep, full of excitement. But there was one fundamental difference in the manner with which Irene greeted her father; she pretended that she too was excited about the coming nuptials.

The moment he was inside, with the servants still present, he enfolded her in a series of exuberant hugs and the usually taciturn man couldn't use enough words to express how pleased he was that his daughter was soon to wed.

'I thought you were poorly,' Irene asked him once her mother had finished greeting her husband. 'So poorly you were confined to your bed.'

'What? No, I'm in the peak of physical condition,' he said, rubbing his round stomach as if his healthy appetite proved his case.

Irene raised her eyebrows and looked at her mother, who was the very picture of contented innocence.

'Mother said—'

'I believe I may have exaggerated somewhat due to my concern over your father's well-being,' she cut in. 'Before I left for Devon you did mention you were feeling under the weather,' she added, turning to her husband.

'Did I?' her father asked. 'Well, whatever it was, hearing that my daughter is to marry must have been just the remedy I needed.'

'Exactly,' her mother said, once again smiling contentedly, as if that were enough of an explanation for her outrageous lie, one that had led Irene to think if she didn't marry the Duke she would be responsible for making her father sicker, and perhaps even worse.

'Yes, you've recovered in much the same way as Irene did,' her mother added, sending Irene an arched look. 'I believe you said you had to come down to Devon for the sake of *your health*.'

Irene gave her mother a tight smile. Yes, she too was guilty of stretching the truth, but it *was* for the sake of her health. If she had been stuck in London and unable to paint she was sure she would have gone completely mad.

'It seems the Duke is responsible for improving the health of both my husband and my daughter,' her mother added, staring at Irene as if daring her to contradict this statement.

Irene decided it was best not to rise to the challenge. After all, wasn't she supposed to be happy to be engaged to the Duke, so why should she object to how it came about? Whether her mother realised this or not, Irene could not ascertain, but her mother sent her a jubilant smile, took her husband's arm and led him into the drawing room.

'So when am I going to meet my future son-in-law?' her father asked as he waited for the ladies to take their seats. 'When am I going to meet the man who has put a bloom on my daughter's cheek and a sparkle in her eye?'

'We're dining with him and Lady Prudence tomorrow night, so you'll be able to make all the necessary arrangements,' her mother said, referring tactfully to the marriage settlement.

'Good. Hopefully he'll pass muster and I can officially give him my blessing for this union.'

Everyone in the room knew that her father's blessing was a mere formality. Irene's mother had made the decision, and her father would acquiesce. Plus, the engagement had been announced so there was no going back now.

As her parents continued to discuss arrangements for the wedding, Irene fought to squash down her guilt about deceiving her father. She knew that the scandal with Edwin had broken his heart, and she had seen how much it pained him to have to pay off such a man to save his daughter's reputation. Now he thought all that was behind them. His daughter was in love and she was to wed a man at the pinnacle of society.

She looked at her mother, who was sitting up tall in her seat, her chin lifted, that imperious expression appearing every time she mentioned the Duke or Lady Prudence. If anyone should be feeling guilty, it was her mother, not Irene. She had forced her into this fake engagement, had even lied about her husband's health to trick her into a marriage to an inappropriate man. No,

Irene had no need to feel guilty. But that awareness did nothing to stop shame from washing through her every time she looked at her happy father.

Chapter Thirteen

The dinner should have meant nothing to Irene. And yet, that evening she found herself dressing with more care and attention than ever before. Even in her first season, when she was a naive young lady anxious to make a good impression, she had not spent such a long time fussing over her appearance.

Being courted by Edwin had not resulted in her trying on each gown several times, nor caused her to sigh because she was sure that no gown would be good enough.

She stared at the mounting pile of silk, satin and chiffon on her bed. She had to make a choice. So, after examining each gown carefully and repeatedly, she finally selected the pale lemon one with the sheer lace sleeves and silver embroidery.

She had made her decision, but that didn't stop her from looking at the mountain of discarded gowns and wondering.

'An excellent choice, miss,' Mabel declared once she had finished doing up the row of buttons down the back.

'The sash at the waist accentuates your curves. That colour brings out the gold highlights in your hair and the neckline is so feminine.'

Irene looked down and wondered if it was, perhaps, a bit too feminine. Was the neckline a tad too low? Did the fine lace ruffled along the edge draw the eye, rather than conceal her décolletage? And was that what she wanted? For the Duke to look at her with genuine desire, rather than feigned admiration, designed to fool his aunt and her mother?

She gave herself a small shake. No, she did not want that, and even if she did, which she didn't, the Duke did not see her in that way. She was a means to an end for him. Her purpose was merely to protect him from the hordes of debutantes who *did* want to marry him, and from his matchmaking Aunt Prudence. She was just a ruse so he could return to the women he really wanted, and it would be foolish to think otherwise.

Mabel picked up her ivory-handled comb and brush and hovered expectantly over Irene as she sat at her dressing table. 'Shall I style your hair in the French manner?' Her eager face suggested she would be crushed if Irene said no.

Irene nodded, even though she really did not want the Duke to think she had gone to too much trouble for his sake. She would hate him to get the wrong impression and think she actually cared about his opinion. But surely, it would be cruel to disappoint Mabel.

Her lady's maid set to work with gusto, until Irene's hair was elegantly backcombed, plaited and piled on top of her head. Only a few strategically placed curls were allowed to escape, and were precisely draped over

Irene's shoulder, as if the artifice was entirely unintentional.

Once she was ready, she entered the drawing room, surprised that she had kept her parents waiting. Usually Irene was ready long before her mother, and anxious to get whatever social occasion she was being dragged to over and done with as quickly as possible.

'You look lovely, my dear,' her father said, kissing her lightly on each cheek.

'Do a slow turn,' her mother ordered. Irene did so as her mother made a scrupulous examination from every angle. 'Yes, you will do,' she finally declared.

'She'll more than just do,' her father added. 'She is perfect. The perfect duchess.'

Irene smiled, trying to control the conflicting thoughts and emotions battling for dominance. She would not feel guilt for deceiving her father, she told herself. She would not feel anxious at seeing the Duke again. She would not wonder what he thought of her appearance. She would go to the dinner, pretend to be a happily engaged young woman. She would remind herself that none of this was her fault. And most importantly, she would remember, at all times, that this was a pretence for the benefit of her parents and Lady Prudence.

The Duke's coach arrived and as they drove through the early-evening light, the fluttering in Irene's stomach informed her that despite her determination, one emotion had won the battle. The closer they got to the Duke's home the greater her sense of jittery anticipation.

Stop this immediately, she told herself repeatedly. Even the dratted Edwin had not caused her to feel so nervous. And this was all just for show. She was not going to dinner with her betrothed. She was not about to meet the man she had fallen in love with. And yet her nerves were obviously finding it impossible to separate play-acting from reality.

They arrived at the house and the Duke was waiting outside. He opened the carriage door and reached out his hand to help Irene down the small steps. She looked into his eyes to offer her thanks and paused. Why had she never noticed before how his eyes weren't just brown, but held a golden light, like the flickering of warm flames, or those first rays of sunlight in the morning?

They really were stunning eyes, ones that drew you in and held you captive.

She smiled at him. He slowly smiled back, causing warmth to radiate through every inch of her body.

If Irene had ever seen a more handsome man she couldn't possibly remember when. She had seen countless men dressed as he was tonight, in a black evening suit with white shirt and tie and a brocade waistcoat, but when had she ever seen one wear it so well? Never. That was the only answer to that question.

'Come on, my dear,' her father said with a light laugh. 'We can't stay in the carriage all evening.'

Irene blushed. What a fool she must look, standing at the top of the stairs staring at him as if bewitched, but as an artist she was merely admiring the colours of his eyes, nothing more. She placed her hand in his, and even through her silk gloves she could feel his skin burning gently into hers, causing warmth to tingle up her arms, across her chest and into her heart.

'You look beautiful,' he murmured as she stepped down. She looked up at him and under his gaze that was exactly how she felt. Beautiful. Even desirable.

Her mother alighted from the carriage and greeted the Duke, then introduced him to her husband, who gave the Duke a hearty handshake and patted him on the back, as if he was already giving the courtship his blessing.

They entered the house and as if from a distance, Irene could hear her parents chattering away happily as they moved through the entranceway, down the hallway to the drawing room. Suddenly feeling shy, she followed on behind, the Duke at her side.

Lady Prudence greeted Irene and her parents and once they were seated conversation flowed easily, although Irene seemed to have been struck dumb, something that had never happened before. The Duke sat next to her on the divan, and like herself, he too seemed to have lost the ability to talk, something that she had hitherto not seen in the usually loquacious duke.

While conversation whirled around them, all she could think of was the way he had looked at her as she stepped down from the carriage. It was as if she was the only woman in the world, as if he was gazing upon a woman of such exquisite beauty that she had enchanted him. And that was how she had felt. As if she was an adored enchantress.

She looked towards him and smiled. He smiled back and that peculiar tingling sensation once again erupted inside her, making her even more conscious of her body. She had never before been more aware of how her breasts moved as she breathed, nor how the silk fabric of her gown caressed her skin.

She moved slightly closer to the Duke. Despite all her previous reservations, she wanted to be near him, but not just sitting next to him in this drawing room, but alone, so he could look at her in that manner again, so she could gaze back into those deep brown eyes.

When the gong announced dinner was served, the Duke stood and once again held out his hand. She looked up at him, and holding his gaze placed her hand in his, as if it were more than her hand she was offering.

In silence they paraded down the hallway to the dining room. The Duke pulled out Irene's chair, and as she took her seat she breathed in deeply, filling her senses with the fresh citrus of his cologne and the underlying masculine scent that was uniquely his. She closed her eyes briefly, savouring its spicy quality. As he pushed in her chair, his jacket briefly rubbed against the naked skin of her arm like a gentle caress, sending tingles fizzing through her.

Chatter once again whirled around her as the others took their seats, and Irene tried to bring herself out of the dreamlike state she had descended into. Although she had no appetite, she attempted to take at least a few morsels of the lobster bisque that had been placed in front of her.

'Miss Fairfax tells me that you are also a fine artist,' she heard the Duke ask her father.

Her father smiled at her. 'I used to dabble in my youth, but business took me away from it.'

'But you must be proud to have a daughter who is such a highly talented artist,' the Duke said. 'One whose work is worthy of being hung in the best galleries any-where in the world.'

'Oh, I wouldn't go that far, Your Grace,' her mother said before her father could answer.

'I would,' the Duke replied, causing her mother's patronising smile to die. 'Her ability to capture light is unsurpassed and even her sketches evoke so much emo-tion in the viewer that you completely lose yourself in the scene. It's almost a transformative experience, as all great art should be.'

Everyone stopped eating and stared at him in sur-prise, including Irene. No one talked with such pride and passion about Irene's art. At least, no one had be-fore.

'What are you working on at present?' the Duke asked her enthusiastically, breaking the startled silence. 'I'm sure we'd all love to hear.'

Irene looked over at her mother, who bore a pinched-lip expression.

'My daughter is too busy with the wedding prep-arations at the moment. And really, her painting can make such a mess. There is nowhere suitable for her to paint, not if she is to use oils. Watercolours, on the other hand—' she smiled at Lady Prudence '—they are so much more respectable and so much tidier. Much more appropriate for a young lady.' Her simpering smile was bestowed on Irene. 'And a future duchess.'

'If you're worried about the mess and there's nowhere suitable in your present residence, then the gatehouse at this estate would be perfect,' the Duke announced, ig-noring the underlying meaning beneath her words. 'It's not being used at the moment. One of the rooms could be cleared out and turned into a studio.'

'That would be marvellous,' Irene gasped out, suddenly finding her voice. 'Thank you.' Pleasure bubbled up inside, almost making her dizzy. Her mother couldn't possibly object to such an arrangement. After all, he was a duke, and, as far as her mother was concerned, her future husband. Whatever he said was the final word on the matter. And he had just given her the freedom to paint and her own place to do so.

She smiled at him, a smile that contained a wealth of emotion, gratitude being paramount amongst them. He had been right. This engagement would give her greater freedom. She would soon have her very own studio, something she had never had before. She wanted to hug him in thanks. Well, she wanted to hug him full stop, but instead she merely repeated her thanks.

'Excellent,' the Duke continued. 'You can visit the gatehouse tomorrow, choose the room that has the best light for your studio and I'll send my carriage and driver to pick up all your painting equipment.'

Irene looked at her mother, who had the decency to blush slightly, but not so much decency that she was prepared to inform the Duke she had ordered the burning of all Irene's paintings and equipment.'

'Thank you, that would be ideal,' Irene said, this new freedom of being the fiancée of a duke making her bold. 'Everything is stored in the garden shed at the back of the cottage I used to live in. If your driver can pick it up and deliver it to the gatehouse I can resume painting immediately.'

'Excellent,' the Duke said. 'That's all sorted.'

For once it was Irene's turn to send her mother a jubilant smile.

And for the rest of the dinner, that was all she seemed
capable of doing. Smiling. The Duke had promised her
freedom, and that was what he had delivered. Despite
being trapped in an engagement she did not want, for
the first time in her life she was free. Free to do what
she loved more than anything else in the world, to paint
whenever she wanted, and no one could object. It was
the most exhilarating feeling and it had all come from
the unlikeliest of sources, Joshua Huntingdon, the Duke
of Redcliff.

After dinner, the ladies retired to the drawing room,
leaving the Duke and her father alone to talk. Such
a conversation would usually fill a young lady with
trepidation, and strangely, it *was* making Irene anxious. She had complete faith in the Duke and knew he
would make a good impression on her father. And if
he didn't, it shouldn't worry her. In the unlikely event
that her father found him wanting, believed he was not
good enough for his daughter, the engagement would
be called off. And that was what she wanted. Wasn't it?
Wasn't that what she told her friends? Wasn't that what
she had told herself, repeatedly?

And yet, those annoying butterflies had resumed
fluttering their wings inside her stomach. Why they
should come back to life now she had no idea. If the
Duke made a good impression, they would continue
with their false engagement and never marry. If the
Duke made a bad impression, the engagement would
be called off, and they would never marry. Either outcome was acceptable so nothing about the conversation

between her father and the Duke should cause her any concern. That was what she reminded herself as she placed a comforting hand on her stomach.

The door opened. The three women turned to face the two men and released a collective sigh of relief. Both men were smiling and in the middle of an animated conversation. They turned to face the ladies, and both smiled at Irene, then her father smiled at her mother, while the Duke sent her a quick wink.

That unspoken conversation said it all. The Duke had passed muster. A marriage settlement agreeable to all had been reached. The marriage was going to happen. Except it wasn't. For a moment, Irene's smile inexplicably quivered.

Conversation resumed, and the rest of the evening passed in a convivial manner, with Irene and the Duke adding little, just sitting together and playing the role of a courting couple in the company of their elders. A role Irene was finding came surprisingly naturally.

On the journey home her parents continued to be in high spirits. As Irene seated herself in the carriage, her father patted her on the knee, while her mother smiled on.

'I know I've already given my blessing for this union,' he said, then smiled at his wife. 'Well, your mother told me to, which is the same thing.' He gave a jovial laugh, which her mother joined in on. 'But I just had to tell you, my dear, you do indeed have my blessing. He's a capital fellow.' Her father leaned in closer. 'I never did take to that Fitzgibbon, found him a bit shifty and I was proved right. I didn't like to say anything at the time as you seemed enamoured with the chap.'

'Let's talk of that no more,' her mother interjected, the smile gone.

Irene agreed. Although she was tempted to point out that Lord Fitzgibbon was another man whom her mother insisted would make an ideal husband, and a man she had all but told Irene to encourage in his amorous advances, a man she had often left her alone with, thinking that a marriage was imminent.

'But the Duke, well, he's cut from a different cloth,' her father continued, then frowned slightly. 'The father wasn't much, I'll admit. There were quite a few rumours about him, but the son, no, the son will make you a fine husband.' He sat back and continued to smile as if all was right with the world.

Irene stared at her parents in disbelief. Hadn't they sung Edwin's praises as well when they thought he would marry Irene, despite his man's reputation. Now they were saying that the Duke would make her a fine husband. They must have heard the rumours about him. Did her parents walk around with blinkers on? When it came to marrying their daughter off to a man with a title, it seemed they did. Had they ignored all that they had heard about Edwin because he was an earl? Were they prepared to ignore everything they had heard about the Duke just because they wanted their daughter to become a duchess?

Unbelievable. They were smiling like the proverbial cats who had got the cream, happy that they were marrying their daughter off to a womaniser, a man no better than Edwin.

Well, that wasn't quite right. Unlike Edwin, the Duke made no secret of his dissolute ways. And unlike Edwin he didn't hold double standards for women, believing they should remain chaste while men were free to do as they wished. And unlike Edwin he didn't seduce debutantes.

He didn't *need* to seduce any woman.

He just needed to look at them the way he had been looking at her all night and they would fall into his arms, and into his bed.

A shudder of realisation ripped through Irene. How could she criticise her parents for falling under the Duke's spell when she had done the exact same? She had been like a woman entranced from the moment she had seen the Duke standing at the bottom of the carriage steps.

Like so many other women she had done what she told herself she would never do, become bedazzled by his charm and good looks. She stared out at the dark night and her own startled reflection looking back at her from the carriage window.

The awareness that she had fallen under his spell was bad enough, but it was worse than that. Despite everything she knew about him, she still wanted to be with him. Wanted him to look at her the way he had looked at her tonight. Wanted to feel those intense emotions that erupted within her when she was near him.

It was a shocking revelation. One she was ill prepared to deal with. She could hardly ask her mother for advice. What do you do when you have strong feelings for a man you are engaged to, a man you're not going to marry and a man for whom you know it would be wisest to have little to no regard?

It was a conundrum, and while she was solving it,

she was going to have to keep this bewildered state to herself. Heaven knows what would happen if her mother ever got wind that she was actually starting to have feelings for the Duke. There would be no way she could delay the marriage, not until next winter, and certainly not indefinitely.

'Now that is all settled, I shall return to London tomorrow,' her father said as the carriage pulled up in front of their house. 'I've got a marriage settlement to arrange,' he said, smiling indulgently at Irene.

'And I shall accompany you,' Irene's mother added. It seemed this night was full of surprises.

'Now that my daughter is officially engaged, and to a duke no less, there's no more for me to do down here in Devon.'

Irene suspected she wanted to return to London society to bask in the glory of being the future mother of a duchess. But as it further freed Irene she would happily allow her mother to bask to her heart's content, especially as it meant she could now drop all pretence. Although what she was now pretending she was starting to forget. Was she pretending to care for the Duke? Or was she pretending to care for the Duke while pretending not to care so he wouldn't know she was starting to care for him? It was all too confusing and giving Irene the beginnings of a headache.

'That's what a young woman in love looks like,' her father said as he helped her down from the carriage. Irene could inform him that this was what a thoroughly confused young lady looked like. One who was being thrown about by her emotions so she didn't know what to think or what to feel. If that was what love was, it was a very disconcerting state indeed.

But she merely smiled and said nothing.

Joshua couldn't stop smiling. Tonight he had experienced something that was completely new and unexpected. Something he would like to experience again and often. He had achieved something and it felt good. He had made a difference to someone's life, especially her life, and he could even claim to have contributed to the world of fine art. Yes, he felt decidedly pleased with himself.

He doubted he would ever forget the sight of Miss Fairfax smiling at him, of her eyes shining as if she was about to cry with pleasure. It had been such a small thing to do, to offer her the gatehouse, but the smile of gratitude on her face made him feel like he was the most benevolent man in the world.

It was something he definitely should do more often if it made him feel like this.

He poured glasses of brandy for himself and his aunt, took his seat, swirled the amber liquid around the bottom of the brandy balloon and continued smiling.

And he didn't just feel pleased with himself because it was Miss Fairfax whom he had helped. There definitely was a sense of satisfaction in knowing he had helped a struggling artist. He had meant every word he said about her talent, and such talent should never be stifled. It should be allowed to grow and flourish, and he had helped in a small way to make that happen.

He took a sip of his brandy, as if giving himself a reward.

Yes, tonight he had shown himself to be a better man than he had hitherto thought, and not just because he had helped Miss Fairfax and the art world in general. Tonight he had proved conclusively that he was not entirely like his father.

Over the years the old duke had offered the gatehouse to many a beautiful young woman. But his thoughts had never been about helping the young woman, and he certainly had not been concerned with furthering the arts. That old lecher had only one reason for allowing a young lady to live in the gatehouse: to satisfy his own rapacious needs.

Joshua's poor mother was forced to ignore her husband's constant trips down the gravel driveway. She must have known that one of the local lasses had been secreted away there. He had mistresses in London, but that was never enough for the old satyr. He also liked to have one close at hand during his infrequent visits to his estate.

Now the son had offered the gatehouse to a beautiful woman as well, but he had done so for a higher purpose.

Hadn't he?

Joshua looked down at his brandy balloon, his self-satisfaction wavering slightly. Was it a mere coincidence that the first woman to whom he made that offer also happened to be the most attractive woman he had ever met? A woman who was not only beautiful in appearance but who held a certain fascination for him and had such a passion for art that it gave her an incandescent glow?

No, that had nothing to do with it. It *was* a mere

coincidence that she just happened to be a woman he found attractive.

He was still aware that despite their engagement Miss Fairfax was off limits. He was not the sort of man to make such an offer and have an ulterior motive. That would make him even worse than his father. At least the succession of young ladies who had lived in the gatehouse knew exactly what the old duke wanted. No, it was not like that. Joshua had no ulterior motive.

'Do you think you'll be able to wait until next winter?' his aunt asked, interrupting his thoughts.

'What? Yes, of course I can.'

Answering the question despite having any knowledge of what it was in regard to.

His aunt raised her eyebrows. 'From the way the two of you were looking at each other tonight, I thought perhaps you might like to bring the wedding forward.'

He stared at his aunt. She was talking about the wedding. He should have realised. That was all she ever talked about.

'No, we have to wait until next winter. Miss Fairfax wants her gown designed by someone special.' He shrugged, trying to remember what she had said. 'Apparently there's someone worthless in Paris who she insists has to design the wedding gown.'

His aunt gave an indulgent laugh. 'The House of Worth in Paris, I believe you mean.'

'Yes, something like that.'

'And it is kind of you to offer her the gatehouse.'

'It was nothing,' Joshua said. 'It has stood empty for so long it will be good to see it being used again.'

His aunt once more raised her eyebrows, a gesture

that spoke a thousand words. He wanted to tell her she was wrong. He was not like his father. He had offered the gatehouse to Miss Fairfax for one reason and one reason only.

'She needs somewhere to paint,' he blurted out as if defending himself from her unspoken accusation. 'And you heard what her mother said—she objects to the mess she thinks oil paints make.'

'I think it is an excellent idea to turn the gatehouse into an art studio,' his aunt continued.

It was Joshua's turn to raise his eyebrows. When had his aunt ever had any interest in art? And she had never before approved of a young lady who did anything other than devote all her efforts to securing a husband.

'You do?' Joshua asked cautiously.

'Yes. After watching you two lovebirds tonight, I believe the more you see of Miss Fairfax the less you are going to be capable of waiting until next winter. I suspect we are going to be hearing wedding bells much sooner than you think.'

Joshua chose not to reply. It was good that they had fooled his aunt—after all, that was their intention—but she was wrong. There was only one love in Miss Fairfax's life, and that was art. It would never be him, and for that he was eternally grateful.

Chapter Fourteen

Freedom. That was what Irene would focus on. She would put aside all other confusing emotions and focus on the wonder and joy of freedom. She could spend every day and evening with a paintbrush in her hand and no one, not even her formidable mother, could object.

As she stood on the platform waving at the train carrying her mother and father back to London, she wanted to dance up and down the platform, such was her sense of exhilaration.

Her mother had agreed that as Irene was now engaged, her lady's maid could act as adequate chaperone during her courtship with the Duke. Irene had tried to argue that Hetty, her maid of all works, would be more than capable of doing the job, but quickly saw that she was pushing her mother a tad too far on that one. Particularly when her mother mentioned that Hetty had defied her instructions and not burned Irene's paintings and equipment. But it mattered not. Irene had no need of a chaperone, and Mabel was about to find she had plenty of spare time on her hands.

With her parents gone she would have peace. She would no longer have to pretend to be enamoured with the Duke in front of her mother; she was free to be herself. Or was it pretend to not be enamoured with the Duke? Whatever it was, she would not think of that now. Instead she would think only of the joy of freedom. Glorious, wonderful freedom.

This engagement had solved two problems. She now had a painting studio and never again would her mother drag her to a society event. Never again would she have to stand with the leftover young ladies. Never again would she have to listen to her mother lecturing that she should make more of an effort to be delightful and witty, that men did not want to marry women who were obsessed with art. She was free. And it was all thanks to the Duke and this fake engagement.

Several servants had also stayed behind to care for her and the house, although Irene suspected they too would be struggling to find enough to occupy themselves as she intended to spend all her time doing what she loved, painting.

All in all, it was more than she could ever have hoped for.

She remained standing on the platform as the train disappeared around the corner, leaving only a puff of smoke drifting in the air as a reminder of its departure.

And to that end, instead of returning home she went straight to the garden shed at the back of the cottage to retrieve her paints, easels, canvases and other equipment. As promised, the Duke's carriage arrived, and the driver loaded her equipment inside, packing it carefully against the leather benches. Irene couldn't wait to get started, so she squeezed herself inside with the piles of equipment and, still smiling, drove to the Duke's estate.

As requested, the carriage driver came to a halt at the gatehouse and, despite his protestations, she helped him unload the equipment.

During her trips to Redcliff Estate she had hardly noticed the building before. The red-brick facade, Gothic arched windows and crenelated roof had presumably been designed to deter intruders, but to Irene it could not present a more welcoming sight.

Once everything was stacked beside the front door she dismissed the driver and walked up to the house, still enveloped in that delicious lightness of spirit.

Before she had mounted the stone steps to the front entrance the Duke emerged and raced down the steps towards her. Dressed in a cream linen suit he looked just as wonderful as he did last night, and Irene wondered whether she should ask to paint him again.

She swallowed and struggled to regain her composure as liquid heat rushed through her veins.

Never think of that again. Never ever, she admonished herself as she tried to forget the sight of his naked chest, of his hard flat stomach, his...

Stop, stop, stop.

Using a level of self-control she had hitherto not known herself capable of, she smiled at him, willing her burning cheeks to settle down and praying he did not inquire as to the source of her embarrassment.

'To the gatehouse,' he said, extending his arm towards her.

Not trusting herself to speak, Irene nodded in response, took his arm and accompanied him back down the gravel driveway towards the building that was soon to be her studio.

Focus on painting. Focus on your freedom. Focus on anything except the man beside you and the memory of him standing naked in the pose of David.

The Duke unlocked the door then ceremoniously handed the keys to Irene. He stood back and with a flourish of his arm, indicated for her to enter.

The interior was just as she had hoped. Large windows and high wooden beamed ceilings meant every room was flooded with light, making it the perfect studio. Downstairs was furnished as a living area, so she was obviously not the gatehouse's first occupant.

'I believe the rooms upstairs have the best light,' the Duke said, as she continued to look around in awe.

Without responding, she rushed up the stairway, anxious to find her new studio, and she knew exactly where it would be. The corner room she had seen outside, the one with large sash windows on the north and east sides that ensured the room got plenty of natural light.

'It's wonderful,' she announced, entering the room and doing a small twirl. Not only was it light and airy, but also the room overlooked the estate's gardens and the woodlands.

'Would you like any of the furniture removed?' the Duke asked from the doorway.

She looked around at the chaise longue, and the armchairs arranged around a low table. 'No, there's still plenty of space for me to paint.' She turned to face the Duke. 'Who used to live here?'

'Oh, various people,' he said, entering the room,

moving to the window and staring out at the scenery. 'My father used the gatehouse for entertaining.'

'I see.' Irene was determined not to react or sound ungracious. She knew exactly what sort of entertaining his father would use it for, and who had stayed here in the past, but the gatehouse's history mattered not. She had her own studio, something she had wanted for as long as she could remember.

'There's also a bedchamber,' the Duke said, still staring out the window. 'If you paint late into the evening you are most welcome to stay over, and you can always either take your meals at the house or we can arrange for a meal to be sent down to you.'

'Oh, yes, that would be wonderful. Once I start painting I often lose track of time so it will be wonderful if I don't have to return home.'

'Right,' he said, turning from the window. 'While you're getting acquainted with the house, I'll bring up your painting bits and pieces.'

While the Duke carried her equipment up the stairs, Irene wandered around the house. Her suspicions as to what the old duke used the gatehouse for were confirmed when she saw the bedchamber. The room was dominated by an enormous four-poster bed, draped in red velvet. Curtains in the same heavy fabric blocked out the light, or perhaps ensured that no one could see what was taking place inside.

Irene should be outraged at such a sight, but she wasn't. Instead, she entered the room and lightly stroked the velvet fabric, then moved it to her cheek, loving the feel of the sensuous fabric against her skin. She looked at the soft, inviting feather mattress, imagining what it would be like to luxuriate in such a bed.

'That's the last of it,' she heard the Duke call out. She quickly dropped the fabric and left the bedchamber.

Her easels had been set up, her paints and other equipment placed on a shelf and her canvases were all lined up against the wall, including the one of David. Irene was tempted to pick it up, to run her finger along the sculptured muscles of his arms, down the line of his chest, to those slim hips and those long, muscular legs. He really was everything David should be. Strong, resourceful, impressive, although she doubted the original David had a cheeky smile and an irreverent sense of fun.

She smiled. He returned her smile and for a moment neither spoke.

'Thank you so much for this. You don't know how much this means to me,' she finally said, her voice quiet.

'I am pleased that I can help an artist of your quality.'

It was so wonderful to hear those words. All her life she'd had to either fight to be allowed to paint or had to do so in secret. Even when her father reluctantly allowed her to go to art school, she was never given anywhere adequate in the house to paint, and the other students and the tutors never took her seriously, always assuming she was merely a wealthy woman who wanted to indulge in a little hobby. But unlike anyone else the Duke took her seriously.

'Thank you,' she repeated.

'No need. But I should stop disturbing you and let you get on with your work.'

'You're not disturbing me,' Irene said, although she

knew that to be a lie. He *was* disturbing her. She looked towards the painting of David, then back to the Duke. How could he not disturb her? A better answer was, *You are disturbing me, in a way that is both exciting and unnerving, and I don't want you to stop disturbing me.*

They continued gazing at each other. Irene's skin tingled, just as it had when she had stroked the velvet fabric against her cheek. The pounding of her heart, the throbbing deep within her, which had started when she saw that large four-poster bed, intensified. Irene knew what she was feeling: desire. She knew she shouldn't be feeling it, but also knew she didn't care.

'And do you have any ideas of what you will be working on?'

It was a simple question, but Irene had to concentrate before she answered. 'I suppose I had better focus on landscapes. After my mother's reaction to my—' she looked towards the painting leaning against the wall '—to my *David* it seems the world is not ready for a woman painting nudes.' She gave a little dismissive laugh that sounded false to her ears.

'Your mother is not here,' he reminded her. 'No one is here. At least no one who will criticise you. If you want to paint nudes there is no one to stop you.'

'Hmm, perhaps.'

'If your fiancé doesn't object then no one else will have the right to,' he said and sent her another of those heart-stopping smiles. 'Not your mother and not those stuffy old art tutors who banned women from life classes'

She smiled at him, not entirely convinced.

'You will be making a breakthrough for women artists everywhere, showing the world that women are not only capable of creating works as good as any male, but better.'

Warmth engulfed her. She loved his enthusiasm and the way he was so encouraging of her art.

'Well, I suppose it would be a waste not to finish my *David*.' She walked over the canvas, picked it up and placed it on the easel. 'Especially as it caused us so much trouble.'

'I think you may have flattered me somewhat,' he said, looking over her shoulder at the painting.

'I did not,' she laughed. 'I painted exactly what I saw.'

'I'm not criticising. I'm happy to be flattered.'

She laughed again. He did not need to be flattered. In Irene's eyes he was perfect. The perfect embodiment of the male physique. And that perfect male was standing behind her. So close all she had to do was lean back and she would be touching him, touching the hard planes of his chest. He was so close his arms could easily encase her. So close, all he had to do was bend down slightly and he could nuzzle the sensitive skin on the side of her neck.

Her temperature soaring, she turned slightly and looked at him over her shoulder. He was no longer looking at the painting, but at her. His gaze moved from her eyes to her lips, and as if under some control that was not her own, she parted them.

As if he was following her unspoken wish, his hand lightly stroked her cheek, his touch as soft as velvet. She tilted her head and, willing him to do more, turned further towards him, looked deep into his eyes, her lips parted, her breath coming in soft, insistent gasps.

He took hold of her chin and leaned in closer. But not close enough. She moved towards him, lifting up onto her toes, her lips so close to his she could feel his soft, caressing breath.

Then he kissed her. His lips touching hers so lightly she could barely feel them. This was what she wanted, but she wanted more. Had to have more. Desire making her reckless, she slid her hands around the back of his neck and kissed him back, harder, with more insistence.

His kiss immediately turned from soft and tentative to urgent and hungry. Heat surged through her as the pounding tempo of her heart accelerated. He wanted this too, as much as she did. His arms wrapped around her waist, pulling her in firmly against his body. Her soft curves melted into hard muscles, her breasts against his chest, her hips pressing into him, their thighs touching.

Reacting, not thinking, she rubbed herself against him, needing to relieve the mounting tension building up inside. A delicious tension she knew only he could free her from.

Just as she had fantasised, his kisses moved from her lips to her neck and he nuzzled the sensitive skin beneath her ears. A sigh of pure pleasure escaped her lips.

'Oh, Irene,' he murmured, the sound of her name increasing her aching need for him.

'Joshua,' she said on a soft breath, loving the feel of his name on her tingling lips. 'Oh, Joshua.'

His lips returned to hers, hot and demanding, as if he wanted to devour her. And that was what she wanted, needed, with every sensitised part of her body. Not thinking, just feeling and wanting, she kissed him back with a fervour that would have once surprised her, but nothing surprised her now.

His lips withdrew from hers. He closed his eyes, dragged in a deep, slow breath, took hold of her hands and removed them from where they had wound themselves around the back of his neck. Irene continued to gaze up at him, unsure what he was doing, but waiting for those lips to return to hers.

'We shouldn't have done that,' he said, his voice husky, his hands still holding hers.

Irene tried to make sense of his words. Of course they should have. The only thing they shouldn't have done was stop.

'That should not have happened,' he said, his voice stronger.

'Why not? After all, we are engaged.' Irene knew there was no logic to what she was saying. It was a false engagement, designed to keep others happy. It meant nothing and they would never marry. That reality pushed through the fog of her brain. She too stepped back, her confused mind trying to make sense of what was happening.

'Perhaps it should not have happened, but it did, and I have no objections,' she stated.

He smiled, that smile that never failed to do perplexing things to her insides.

'I too have no objections. But believe me, it is something I should not do, not if I am to continue to act like a gentleman.'

Then don't act like a gentleman.

She took a step towards him, her hands outstretched.

'I think I should go before I completely forget myself,' he said, turning from her.

Then forget yourself, if that is what you want. I've certainly forgotten myself.

That was what she wanted to call out, but something stopped her. Pride? Confusion? So instead, she watched him walk out the room and down the stairs.

The front door clicked shut. He was gone.

Chapter Fifteen

Joshua should not have done that. He most definitely should not have done that. What on earth had he been thinking? As he raced back down the gravel path towards his house, he knew the answer to that question. He had not been thinking. He had reacted, and any sensible thoughts that *had* tried to force themselves into his addled brain had been drowned out by something louder, more insistent than logic and reason. Lust. A lust he most certainly, most categorically should not have been feeling, and even more certainly, more categorically, should not have acted upon.

When he'd offered her the gatehouse he had intended it to be an act of generosity, nothing more. Yes, just like his father, he had made the offer to a beautiful woman, but it most categorically was not for the same reasons his father would set up a young lady in the gatehouse. It was so Irene would have the freedom to paint, not because of any devious reasons of his own.

At least that had been what he had told himself. It hadn't taken long for his true nature to come to the fore, to show him that he was not like his father after all. He was worse. At least his father never tried to deceive himself.

It had taken only a matter of minutes before he had acted upon his urges, and now he was scuttling away like the coward he knew himself to be. But at least he wasn't a complete cad. He *had* stopped. That was something, wasn't it? Not much, but something. Every aroused part of his body, every lustful desire, every raging impulse, had been urging him to lift her up, carry her through to the bedroom, strip her naked and satisfy himself deep within her. Like a starving man presented with a banquet, he had been insensible with hunger for her. A hunger stronger than he had ever felt before, and yet he had stopped.

But if he was a better man, he would not be regretting that decision with every rampaging inch of his body. A better man wouldn't have anything to regret.

He forced his legs to keep propelling him forward, away from Irene.

Irene.

It had been wonderful to say her name, and even more wonderful to hear his name being whispered by those lovely lips.

His walking slowed down. He stopped. Turned. He could go back. He could once again hear her whisper his name to him. He took in a deep breath, then forced himself to turn back towards his house and keep walking.

Joshua groaned loudly, not caring who heard. All his life he had worried that he was as bad as his father, but he wasn't. He was much worse. His father was never a hypocrite. His father would never have offered the gatehouse to a young lady, telling himself he was doing it for the young lady's benefit, then immediately set about seducing her. Even his father would not lie to himself in that manner.

He really was deplorable. And despite knowing that, he still wanted to return to her. He still wanted to go back to those waiting lips, back to that luscious body, back to that sensual, passionate woman. He had known she was passionate about her art and now he knew that under that no-nonsense exterior was a woman who smouldered. Her kisses were unlike any he had experienced, as if a wildness was just waiting to be unleashed. And by God he wanted to be the man to unleash it and discover where it would take them.

He clenched his hands into tight fists, digging nails into flesh. He would not become his father. He had few rules in his life, but one he had always tried to live by was that he never seduced naive women. Every woman he took to his bed lived outside of society's conventions and would not be harmed by a dalliance with him. And damn it all, that simply was not Irene.

She was forbidden fruit; she had to be for both of their sakes and he would not give in to temptation. But by God he was tempted by the forbidden Miss Fairfax.

His walking slowed yet again, his feet dragging. Was that all this was? Did he want her so much *because* he knew he couldn't have her? His father could never resist a conquest. Was he just as bad? Even as he tried to tell himself that he was the better man. Was he?

He forced himself to resume his rapid pace, as if trying to run away from himself and his unforgivable desires. Then ran up the steps to his home, through the entranceway, and as if finally safe behind the thick oak doors, he stopped.

How on earth was he going to cope, knowing that she was just a short walk away? Every time he looked out a window at the front of his house he would be able to see the gatehouse, and know that she was there. This was going to be torture.

He paced up and down the entranceway. Perhaps he should return to London. Yes, that was what he should do. He should put as much distance as he could from the source of his lustful desire. In London he would hopefully not think of the touch of her soft lips, the feel of her full breasts pressed into his chest, of her hips and thighs rubbing against him, tempting him to ignore what was right and give in to his baser instincts.

'Oh, there you are, Joshua,' his aunt said.

He stared at her as if unsure who she was and why she was in his house. Then it came crashing back. She was the reason for all this. She was the reason why he could not make a cowardly retreat back to London. He was an engaged man and he needed to act like one. Or, at least, the way he thought an engaged man should act, and he suspected they did not behave like a randy schoolboy who had forgotten all sense of propriety.

'Have you been to visit Miss Fairfax?'

'Yes,' he shot back as if confessing to an accusation. He breathed in deeply to compose himself. 'Yes, I've just come from the gatehouse. I wanted to ensure she had settled in and had everything she needed.'

And I wanted to kiss her senseless and unforgivably do so much more.

'And has she?'

'Has she what?'

'Settled in and got everything she needs.'

'Oh, yes, I believe so.'

His aunt raised her eyebrows and smiled in a somewhat peculiar manner. 'Good. It will be so convenient having her just at the end of the driveway. You'll be able to spend so much time together and really get to know each other intimately.'

Joshua suppressed a groan. He did not want to think about spending time with Irene, and he most certainly did not want to think about getting to know her intimately. Well, he wanted to get to know her intimately, more than he'd ever wanted to do anything before, but he would not be. He most categorically, most emphatically would not be.

Irene had no regrets. She had just kissed a notorious rake, a man who had so many women in his life that his servants didn't bother remembering their names, but she didn't regret anything she had done.

She placed her fingers on her still tingling lips. No, that was wrong. She did have one regret. She should have done more to encourage him to stay, to continue kissing her, caressing her, until he relieved the fierce desire building up inside her, a desire for him.

She must be one of the few women alive who had found herself in the arms of a rake who had then acted like a gentleman. Edwin Fitzgibbon would not have done so.

Irene shuddered, wishing she had not remembered that man. His kisses had been nothing like Joshua's. Edwin's kisses had been more like an unwanted but necessary prelude before he had taken what he really wanted. And take it he had, quickly and coarsely. And once it was over his arrogant smile had revealed his true character. She shuddered again and forced that memory out of her mind.

Joshua's kisses were not like that, and if his kisses were any indication, then making love to him would not be like that other, passionless, hurried act. She touched her neck, running a line along where his lips had caressed her. Until today, her only knowledge of what happened between a man and a woman had been what occurred between her and Edwin.

She had never wanted that repeated. Had never wanted any man to ever touch her again, and certainly had not wanted a man to kiss her. But she wanted Joshua to kiss her, wanted him to show her what it was really like to be in the arms of a man who knew women, who knew how to please them, a man who wasn't just interested in taking what he wanted.

Her hand gently caressed her neck. He had awakened something within her, something she liked, something she wanted to explore. And despite his hasty departure, the way he had kissed her showed that he *did* want her, wanted her with an equal fervour.

She had watched him racing up the path away from her and seen his struggle. Several times he had stopped, as if about to return to her. Her pounding heart had accelerated, her breath had caught in her throat and with her longing thoughts she had tried to draw him back to her. But he turned away from her, and each time it was like another pierce to her heart.

How could he be so cruel? He had kissed her, given

her a taste of what was possible, then he had taken it away, leaving her desperate for more.

And why would he be so cruel to himself? She knew enough about men to sense when they wanted a woman. And yet he had walked away from her. Why?

This was madness. She wanted him. He wanted her. Why had he not just taken her? Wasn't that supposedly what men like him did? She was his for the taking, they were even engaged and yet he had not accepted what was on offer. Once she might have resisted him, but those days were now gone.

After that kiss all vestiges of resistance had been stripped away. How could she possibly resist being taken in his arms again? How could she not want to feel those lips on her burning skin and the touch of his strong, muscular body against hers?

She was past caring about his reputation. She just wanted him. Wanted to feel that glorious, aching torture that consumed her body when she was in his arms, for him to satisfy the craving he ignited within her.

And to get what she wanted, what she had to have, all she needed to do was somehow convince a rake to stop acting like a gentleman, to stop treating her like she was some sort of saint and do what he did best, what he had a reputation for.

Chapter Sixteen

Once again Joshua found himself standing at the drawing room window staring out towards the gatehouse.
It did make a change from staring out the window of
his bedchamber, but the effect on his mood was no different.

'I've made a decision,' his aunt said from behind
him. He hadn't heard her come into the drawing room
and didn't turn towards her as he asked, 'Have you?
And what decision is that?'

'I believe it is time to return to London. I've done
my job and you hardly need my presence any more. I
believe Miss Fairfax has a lady's maid to perform the
function of chaperone, so I will leave you two young
people to get on with your courtship.'

A groan welled up inside Joshua. Aunt Prudence's
presence was providing a much-needed barricade
against him throwing aside all sense of right and wrong,
storming the gatehouse and like a marauding invader
claiming what was not his to take.

He turned towards her and sent her what he hoped

was a sincere, cajoling smile. 'But Aunt, I will miss you terribly. Surely you can stay a little longer. Don't you want to oversee the courtship? Wasn't that what you said when you first arrived, that your presence was essential to ensure that everything went smoothly and resulted in a marriage?'

Her eyes grew wide and her eyebrows nearly reached her hairline. She was evidently as surprised as he was by this plea. Usually he was going to extreme lengths to get his aunt to leave him alone. Hadn't that been the reason why he had fled down to Devon in the first place? As for needing her to ensure he actually got married, well, that just showed how worried he was at the thought of being left alone. He was not concerned about whether they did or did not get married. He was concerned about how he would act if he didn't have his aunt's eagle eye keeping him from straying down the path to places he should not go.

'I'm pleased to see you are now in total agreement with me,' she said, those quizzical eyebrows still raised. 'But I believe my presence is now a hindrance rather than a help. I have noticed you are spending too much time with me and not enough time with your fiancée. Once I am gone then you can dedicate all your time to what you are supposed to be doing. Courting that young lady.'

'But Aunt—'

She held up her hand. 'My mind is made up. I have booked a ticket on the afternoon train so you will soon be free of my interference.'

And free of your restraining influence.

How was Joshua going to cope? Perhaps he should

join her and return to London on the afternoon train. Back to his life. Away from temptation.

This engagement was supposed to give him freedom. It had certainly freed him from Aunt Prudence's matchmaking, and he would never again be chased by a young lady who fancied herself as a duchess, but he had never felt more trapped. Trapped by his own lustful thoughts, his own desires, his own obsession with a woman who could never be his.

'Now do the right thing,' his aunt continued. 'Spend time with Miss Fairfax. Pay attention to her and let her know how much you admire her. Young ladies like to be flattered. They like men to make a fuss of them. I've seen how you've been moping about. Stop doing that. Go to her and show her how you feel.'

With every word Joshua winced. If his aunt knew how he really felt, she would not be encouraging him to see Miss Fairfax but would be locking him up in a dungeon so he could cause no further harm.

She waited for his answer. When none came, she strode out of the drawing room and he heard her calling to her lady's maid to organise their departure. Joshua once again turned back to stare out the window and remained standing there until he was summoned to luncheon.

He made one last attempt to convince his aunt to stay as she ate a hearty meal and he moved his food around on his plate.

'While I'm flattered that you are so desirous of my company, my mind is made up,' she said as she dabbed her lips with her napkin. 'And I won't need you to accompany me to the station.'

With that she bustled off to ready herself for her departure. Joshua returned to his observation post, and was still there when he watched her carriage roll away, up the driveway, then halt outside the gatehouse.

His aunt disappeared inside. After a brief period while Joshua watched on anxiously, she reappeared, sent a wave in his direction and climbed back into the carriage. Then she was gone.

This was ridiculous. He could not spend the rest of his life standing here and doing exactly what Aunt Prudence had said he was doing: moping.

What he should do was return to London, back to his life, back to all those women who were not forbidden fruits. He turned from the window and took a few paces towards the door, then returned to the window.

The problem was, he didn't want to go back to London. But nor could he stay here. And he particularly did not want to become a permanent fixture standing at the drawing room window staring out at his estate.

He moved from the window, walked a circuit of the drawing room, and returned to stare back out the window.

Irene would not be moping around, wondering what to do with herself. After his own sleepless night, he often saw her arrive bright and early in the morning. And that would be the last he saw of her until she took a carriage back home late in the evening. She did not spend her days pointlessly staring out of windows. She was productively engaged in her art, no doubt absorbed in something that gave her immense pleasure. She had an all-engrossing passion, whereas he, he had nothing.

He was just an aimless aristocrat with nothing to do except gallivant about town.

That was what he needed. Something to divert his attention. Something that absorbed him fully. Something about which he could get passionate. Unfortunately, the only thing that he was passionate about, the only thing that absorbed him fully, was a certain young lady who was not for him and never could be.

He left the window and collapsed into a chair. It really was hopeless. Women did not do this to him. Yes, he loved women, the more the merrier. Like his father, he was a moth to a flame when it came to a pretty face and a pleasing figure. And like his father he never looked back when he moved from one woman to another, and never had any regrets about the way he lived his life.

Until now. Now he was racked with regrets. Regretted not filling his life enraptured by a passion like her. And he both regretted kissing Irene and stopping. He most certainly should not have kissed her, yet walking away was one of the most admirable things he had done in his pointless life.

But how he wished he had stayed. If he hadn't walked away, would he still be obsessing over her? Would those lips be tormenting his dreams, both when asleep and awake? Would he be behaving like some love-struck adolescent, wondering what she was doing now, wondering if she was thinking of him? Would he have been reduced to this idiotic state? Those were questions he simply could not answer.

And the longer he remained here the more elusive the answers were going to become.

Leave Devon. That was what he had to do. He stood up with more determination than he felt, crossed the room and pulled the cord to summon his valet.

'Charles, pack my bags,' he instructed when the man appeared. 'I'm returning to London on the next available train.'

'Very good, Your Grace,' Charles said, and departed.

Good. Decision made. Now he could stop moping. Next he would tell the housekeeper he would not be in residence for the foreseeable future. Then he would inform Irene of his imminent departure.

He collapsed back into his chair. That would mean seeing her again. But he had no choice. He had to. To leave without saying goodbye would be unforgivably bad manners. He placed his head in his hands.

What on earth was wrong with him? All he had to do was drop in on his way to the station, in much the same way his aunt had. Surely he wasn't such a lech that he wasn't capable of saying a quick farewell without succumbing to his dissolute nature.

Joshua was also unsure of the answer to that question but did not feel up to testing himself quite yet. He once again summoned his valet to tell him he would not be returning to London today.

He would wait until he had the strength to make that final goodbye.

He wasn't coming back. That was becoming increasingly obvious. Each day Irene arrived at the gatehouse full of expectations. Each day, before she departed from her home, she told her lady's maid that it was unnecessary for her to accompany her. Each day she started off thinking, today would be the day when Joshua returned. Each day she went home disappointed. She knew he was still at the house. Occasionally she would catch sight off him when she left and arrived, and each time she did, it sent her pulses racing.

She knew what the sensible thing to do would be. Put that kiss in the past and forget all about him. Remember that she was here to concentrate on her art. And she did, but as if under some compulsion to inflict further agony on herself, she spent her days finishing off the painting of David. It was pure torture to work on his naked body, on his divine face, on the contours of his muscles, and yet it was also oddly cathartic as it provided a focus for her constant internal agitation.

Once she had finished she stood back and admired her work. It was the most intense painting she had ever completed, and she wondered if other people would be able to see the strength of the artist's emotions when they looked at the work.

Now that she was finished, she should move on to another work. She placed a fresh canvas on the easel to work on her sketch of the cove. That too featured Joshua, but merely as a small figure, swimming into the scene. As she painted, memories of that day flooded back. Of how he looked emerging from the sea, of him gazing at her sketches as if entranced by what he saw, of how she had begun to see a different man under that devil-may-care surface he presented to the world.

When she had finished, she sat the two paintings together. She had changed so much since she'd first made those sketches, and it was all because of him. But now he had gone and he had left her with all these emotions that she didn't know how to manage.

But there was one thing she did know how to do. Paint. And that was what she would do. She would create an artwork that expressed her feelings. Memories of Velázquez's *Venus* entered her mind, of that sensuous woman lying naked on a silk-draped chaise longue.

When she had seen the painting on a visit to Rokeby Park she had always been impressed by the use of light to highlight the subject. She had admired the flowing lines of the woman's body and the genius of the artist. Now she knew how that woman felt as she lay in that languorous pose waiting for her lover.

Like Irene, her body must have ached for his touch. She too would have been sensually conscious of her body, of her skin, of her breasts. She too must have throbbed for him, deep within her core.

That was what Irene wanted to capture.

To that end she draped the chaise longue in red velvet from the bedchamber, moved a full-length mirror so she would be able to see her reflection and found a smaller mirror in the bedroom. No Cupid would be holding her mirror, depicting the presence of the god of physical love, so she had to be content with propping it up against the wall.

Then she stripped off her clothes, lay on the chaise longue in the sensual pose that Velázquez's model had adopted, placed the hand mirror so she could see her reflection in the full-length mirror. It was the exact same pose, except Velázquez's Venus did not have a sketch pad in front of her.

She moved on the velvet fabric, loving the feeling of

it against her naked skin and released a gentle sigh. It was easy to imagine what was going through the model's mind when she posed for the famous artist. Just like Irene, she would have been completely aware of her body, of her sensitive skin aching to be caressed, of her breasts yearning for her lover's touch, of her mounting desire that only he could quench.

She picked up her pencil and reminded herself of why she was lying in this pose. She was supposed to be capturing that sensual feeling on paper. She would create a modern version of the old master and prove to herself and the world that no subject should be taboo for a woman artist.

Remaining as still as possible, she drew the lines of her body. Soon she became caught up in her art and forgot about everything else. It was one of the many reasons she loved the act of drawing. It completely took her over and made her forget everything else, even if just for a moment.

As if from a far distance the sound of gravel crunching under feet entered her mind, but she chose to ignore it. That was followed by the more distinct sound of someone knocking on the door and entering the gatehouse. She reached for her chemise. Joshua called out her name, his boots resounding on the stairs.

Something stilled her hand. The chemise dropped to the floor. She resumed her pose. As if intoxicated by what she was doing, she waited and watched the door reflected in the mirror.

He entered the room. Came to a sudden halt in the doorway. Irene knew what he was seeing. She could see herself reflected in the tall mirror. Her naked body was laid out before him like a tempting offering.

'Irene, I'm sorry… I—' he croaked out, pointing towards the hallway, his eyes never leaving her body. 'I—' He took a step towards her, his words evaporating before they were fully formed.

She rolled over, looked into his eyes and stretched out her arms towards him.

Chapter Seventeen

Leave. Now, an internal voice called out to Joshua as he took a step towards a sight more beautiful than even his wildest imagination could have conjured up. And *beautiful* seemed inadequate to describe her creamy skin, those full breasts, the nipples already tight in expectation, those long legs and that enticing dark mound.

'Irene, are you sure?' Joshua's body hoped she would say yes, while a small, fading part of his brain still hoped she would say no.

When she nodded, that small part was completely drowned by his surging desire. Hardly aware that he had moved he was across the room and had taken her in his arms, desperate to lose himself in her erotic beauty. He had never seen a woman look more sensual, more arousing, and he had never been more aroused. He wanted to take her now, fast and hard, and relieve his surging need that had been building and building since that first kiss.

But he also wanted to worship her beautiful body. So he forced himself to slow down, to fully experience every pleasure.

Be gentle, he told himself as he kissed her, but the fierce hunger inside him meant he kissed her like a man possessed. And he was possessed. He wanted her more than he had wanted any woman before, as if his life depended on it.

Her arms were immediately around him as she returned his kisses with matching fervour. Lifting herself off the couch towards him, her soft body melding into his, those full, luscious breasts rubbing against his chest, tempting him, tormenting him.

His kisses left her lips. He kissed her neck, urging himself to go slowly, to savour the feel and taste of her silky skin, her gasps of pleasure further swelling his hard arousal.

His hand moved to her breast. Cupping the full mound, he gently ran his thumb over the hard bud. She lay back on the bed, her eyes hooded, gasps coming faster from her parted lips. He watched her beautiful face as he cupped both breasts, teasing the tight nubs with his thumbs. A flush consumed her breasts, throat and chest, letting him know more loudly than words ever could that this was what she wanted. She moved languidly under his touch, her back arching, those beautiful round buttocks moving sensually, invitingly. If there was anything more beautiful than an aroused woman, Joshua was yet to see it. And Irene in this heightened state was the most beautiful sight he had ever seen.

Taking one nipple in his mouth, he heard her cry out his name, and her hands slid through his hair, holding him in place. Her sighs growing louder, faster, he moved to the other breast, taking the nipple in his mouth, loving the feel of her full breast and the taste of the tight nub.

As he continued to torment each hard bud, his hand slid slowly down her back, over the round of her buttocks and around to her mound of soft hair. He paused. Waiting for any objection. None came. He moved his hand between her legs. They parted, allowing him easy access.

Watching her beautiful face, slowly, gently he stroked.

Her back arching, she moved to his rhythm, her cries coming louder and faster. When she placed her hand on top of his, forcing it harder onto her nub, he knew she was completely lost in the experience. His fingers slid along her cleft, parting her feminine folds, and his finger stroked her opening.

'Yes,' she murmured in encouragement. He pushed inside her, loving the way her tight sheath encased him.

'Yes, yes,' she cried again as he increased the pressure, his palm rubbing her harder, his finger entering her deeper.

Almost immediately, her body gave a small shudder. It had happened so quickly she had obviously been ready for him, waiting for him. She wanted him as much as he wanted her. Had she been thinking of him, fantasising about them making love, just as he had?

And he did want to take her fully, to lose himself inside her, but that part of his brain that still knew right from wrong held him back. He would be content with pleasuring her. He would take his own pleasure in worshipping her beautiful body as she deserved to be worshipped.

To that end, he kissed a line down her lovely round

stomach, his kisses moving down to her mound. She parted her legs, either knowing what he wanted to do or reacting under impulse. Whichever it was, Joshua had no time to consider as he moved between her parted legs.

Her first cry of 'Oh' was one of surprise, then the sound came again and again, each time louder and louder.

His tongue stroked along her cleft, savouring her beautiful feminine taste. Finding her bud, he licked, suckled and nuzzled, encouraged by her increasing groans, which grew louder, faster, urging him on.

Satisfaction consumed him as a ripple shuddered through her, a final sigh of contentment escaped her lips and her body, which had been tense with excitement, relaxed back onto the couch completely sated.

Joshua's own arousal was now throbbing hard within his trousers, demanding release. Once again he kissed her lips, both wanting and not wanting her to encourage him further.

She opened her hooded eyes and gazed into his eyes. 'I love…' She swallowed. 'I loved that, but I want you to make love to me,' she said, her voice barely a gasp.

He drew back but she wrapped one naked thigh around his waist.

'Are you sure, Irene?' he asked, his voice like an unrecognisable groan.

She nodded. 'I'm not a virgin,' she whispered. 'My reputation is already ruined.'

Joshua cringed. He did not want to be like Fitzgibbon, a man who used trickery to take what he wanted, who saw women as merely conquests to be tallied up. Nor did he want to be like his father, a man who took what he wanted, caring nothing of the consequences.

He gently stroked the soft skin on the inside of her thigh, then moved her leg away. She grabbed his hand and placed it on her breast and wrapped her other naked thigh around his waist.

'Please, Joshua. I'm not a virgin but no man has made love to me. I want you to be the first man to make love to me.'

Joshua knew he was lost. Completely lost. It was still wrong, but it was a wrong he wanted so badly he no longer cared.

Unable to hold back any longer, he pulled open his trousers and placed himself between her legs. Rubbing himself against her feminine folds, he could feel how ready she was for him, but when he reached her opening, he paused.

'Are you sure?' he asked one more time, knowing from her expression, from those gasping lips, that flush that had consumed her body, what the answer would be.

'Yes. I'm sure. Make love to me, Joshua.' Her hands encircled him, running down his body and cupping his buttocks, pushing him towards her.

Using a level of self-control that tested him almost beyond his endurance, he slowly entered her, watching her expression for any sign of pain or objection. Her arched back, the rhythmic movement of her buttocks taking away any remaining doubts, he pushed into her deeper and deeper until he was fully encased in her sheath.

Joshua released a deep, loud groan of pleasure. This was what he had been thinking of, fantasising about, wanting so badly it was all but killing him. But he had not thought being deep within her would feel so good, had not thought anything could feel this good, this right, as if they were now joined, body and soul.

He pulled out of her, and slowly pushed himself back in, loving the sound of her sighs, coming in time with his movements and the feel of her thighs holding him tighter. He let the rhythm of her moans guide him, their increasing intensity telling him she did not want him to hold back.

Her thighs moved upwards to grip his waist, and she tilted her pelvis, allowing him to enter her even deeper. As he thrust into her harder and faster, he watched her beautiful face. Her head was tilted back, her eyes closed, her mouth open as her moans grew louder and her ecstasy climbed to a higher and higher peak. When she grabbed hold of his shoulders, her fingernails digging into his flesh, he knew she was close. He increased the tempo, thrusting faster and faster, until she let out a final loud cry and collapsed back onto the bed.

He wanted to throw all caution to the wind, but he forced himself to withdraw just in time, before his own satisfaction came, and collapsed onto her soft body, his heart beating so hard within his chest it seemed to be trying to escape and take flight.

As his panting breath and beating heart slowly resumed their normal rhythm, Joshua knew that everything had now changed between them, and an unanswerable question crashed into his head. *What happens now?*

Irene lay back on the chaise longue, loving the weight of his body on hers. She had imagined what it would be like to have him kiss her again, caress her, make love to her, but had never imagined it could be so earth-shatteringly wonderful.

With Edwin it had been quick and painful, both physically and emotionally. There had been no pleasure for her, but the look of smug satisfaction on Edwin's face made it clear that not only had it given him immense pleasure, but also that he had seen the entire act as one in which he was the winner and she the loser.

She lightly kissed Joshua's shoulder in thanks. He had shown her what it was like to be made love to. He had taken her to a level of pleasure that she had not known existed. With him she had felt loved, cherished, even worshipped. It had been so sensual and had given her the confidence to abandon herself to the pleasure.

But she couldn't help but wonder, *What happens now?* They had been thrown together by a misunderstanding. They had been forced into an engagement neither wanted. They were both committed to never actually marrying. Now they had made love. And it was all Irene's doing. She had literally presented herself to him, had lain naked in front of him. It was no surprise that he had accepted what she was offering. What man wouldn't?

She could not solely hold him responsible in any way for what had happened. She had wanted him, wanted him so desperately she had been prepared to do anything to get what she wanted. Now she had to let him know that he was still free. She did not expect this encounter to mean they now had to marry.

He lifted himself off her and smiled down at her. She smiled back, her heart once again starting to race. He was so handsome, so wonderful, so loving. But he was not for her. They had made a pact and just because she had wanted him so fiercely that she had all but thrown herself at him, nothing had changed. And she had to tell him. Tell him now. She could see that look in his eye, that deep, penetrating look as if he wanted to possess her. That was how he had looked before he had entered her. It was wonderful to see him look at her like that, and she so wanted him to make love to her again, but she had to let him know that she expected nothing from him.

'That meant nothing,' she blurted out before she could change her mind.

He winced as if she had slapped him and she realised how cruel her words must have sounded. 'I mean, it did mean something...to me, anyway. It was wonderful. It was... Well, really, *really* wonderful...' She knew she was burbling and for some reason she felt unaccountably shy. After what they had just exchanged, after how she had behaved, the way she had exposed the depth of her need to him, it was absurd that she should now feel coy. But she did.

She bit her bottom lip lightly as she tried to compose her words. 'I just mean, as wonderful as it was, it changes nothing between us.'

'I believe it changes everything,' he said.

'No, no, I mean, well, yes it changes things, and you know, if you want to do that again, then yes, good.'

He laughed lightly and kissed her burbling lips. 'I am pleased to hear that,' he said, his lips still tantalisingly close to hers. 'And believe me, I want to do it again, soon and often. But I do need a bit of time to catch my breath.'

She moved slightly closer towards his lips, aching for his kiss, but she had to ignore her desires and try to get her words in order. 'I just mean, it doesn't change our arrangement. I didn't…you know, do, well, you-know-what because I expected you to marry me as a result.'

He smiled down at her once more. 'Whatever your *reasons*, I'm very pleased that we did.' He gave her that cheeky smile that never failed to cause her to melt inside. 'You know what.'

She returned his smile, whatever it was she wanted to say to him disappearing from her mind. Something about freedom, something about nothing changing. Whatever it was, it was impossible to remember words when your body was remembering the touch of his hands, the feel of him inside you, bringing you surging up to the pinnacle of ecstasy.

She lightly kissed his shoulders, her lips then moving down his chest.

'I seem to be getting a second wind, so would you like to do you-know-what again?'

'Oh, yes, please,' Irene responded, the increasing throbbing between her legs drowning out any thoughts of what their future might hold. All she wanted was to immerse herself in the present and the immediate pleasure to come.

With that, he picked her up and carried her through to the bedchamber and placed her in the middle of the bed. He stood at the foot of the bed, staring down at her as he removed his clothing. As each garment was discarded, Irene's anticipation grew more fervent, until by the time he joined her on the bed she was so frantic for him that she wrapped herself around him, needing to feel him inside her, immediately.

As he made love to her again, she knew that thinking of the future could be left for another time. Right now, this was where she wanted to be; this was where she wanted to stay.

And they did, throughout the rest of the day, into the evening and through to the following morning.

Chapter Eighteen

Joshua opened his eyes to the sight of an empty bed. The sheets were tossed into knots and the pillow still bore an imprint of Irene's head, but she was gone. He closed his eyes, gripped by an unfamiliar sensation. What on earth was wrong with him? Waking up to find the young lady he had spent the night with gone should not affect him like this. A forlorn emptiness should not be taking hold of him.

If anything, he should be pleased he did not have to go through the ordeal of making small talk in the cold, sober light of day. To awake to an empty bed would usually make him feel like a man who had been given a lucky reprieve.

Last night he had told Irene that everything had changed now that they had made love, but it wasn't just their circumstances that had changed; something in him appeared to have altered as well. What it was he was unsure, and while it was peculiar and somewhat unsettling it was far from unpleasant, unlike this sense of loss at her absence.

But he had no time for introspection. He needed to find her.

'Don't move,' he heard her command from across the room.

He smiled as relief washed through him, and unable to obey he sat up. She was seated on a divan by the window, sketchbook in hand.

'Oh, I told you not to move,' she said, putting down her sketchbook. 'I was trying to catch your sleeping form.'

He rose from the bed and crossed the room to look at what she had created.

'Is that how you see me?' he asked, looking down at the sketch of his body, lying on the bed, the sheets barely protecting his modesty. He was sure she had flattered him; no man actually looked like some sort of Greek god when they were sleeping.

'You are the ideal subject, especially when you're asleep.'

He laughed. 'Is that how you like me, asleep?' He leaned down and kissed the side of her neck, and she all but purred with pleasure.

'Only when I'm sketching,' she said, the pencil dropping from her hand.

'I'm not asleep now, and I can think of much better things to do with my body than pose for you.'

She angled her head so he could kiss her waiting lips. As he did so, he picked her up and carried her back to the bed, laid her down in the middle and removed her chemise, then stood at the foot of the bed so he could revel in her beauty.

He so wished he too was an artist so he could capture this moment and be able to treasure it for ever. She was simply the most beautiful woman he had ever seen, with her lovely, inviting body laid out before him, her long brown hair curled around her shoulders, those full breasts pointing towards him as if in invitation, those long legs lying sensually on the bed as she waited for him.

He looked into those blue eyes, hooded with desire, and at those full, parted red lips, her breath already coming in quick gasps of anticipation. They had made love repeatedly last night but Joshua doubted he would ever be able to sate himself of her.

He joined her on the bed and took her in his arms. Making love. That was what this was. With Irene it wasn't just an enjoyable physical act; it was something different, something more intense. He was expressing how he felt about her, and what he felt was something he couldn't name as he had never experienced it before.

It was exhilarating, intoxicating yet left him strangely vulnerable, as if for the first time in his life he was not fully in control of his emotions. No woman had made him feel like that, but then he had never before met a woman like Irene. Yet now was not the time to think of that. Now was the time to just enjoy the profound pleasure of the moment.

Now was the time to kiss every inch of her beautiful body, before losing himself in the rapture of making love.

Once they had both shuddered to another climax he held her close, never wanting this moment to end, never wanting her to leave. But she would leave one day, wouldn't she? Or, as impossible as it was now to imagine, he would one day leave her.

He wasn't the type to commit, remember. He wasn't the marrying type. Her head rested on his shoulder. His arm still around her, he kissed the top of her head. Or *was* he the marrying type? No, he was not, and as painful as such a conversation would be, he needed to let her know that. When this ended, as it inevitably would, it would all be his fault, not hers. He simply was not designed for fidelity.

'Irene, you know that I will never deliberately hurt you.'

'Mmm,' was all she replied as she ran her fingers lightly over his chest. But he refused to be distracted. This had to be said.

'I never want to hurt any woman, especially you.'

She rolled over onto her stomach, lifted herself up on her elbows and looked down at him. 'I'm glad to hear that, but what's this all about?'

He drew in a long breath. 'I suppose you know about my reputation.'

She bit her bottom lip, nodded and he could feel her tense slightly.

'Well, it is nothing compared to my father's.' He closed his eyes briefly as images of his crying mother entered his mind, and of him as a young boy fruitlessly trying to comfort her while his father once again left the house, either back to London or down to this very gatehouse.

'He hurt my mother, again and again, with his philandering. I never want to be like that. I never want to cause anyone any pain. That is why I vowed at a young age never to marry.'

She nodded slowly.

'I know we should not have made love,' he continued. 'But I wanted you so much. I still want you so much.' He lightly stroked her cheek. 'And that frightens me,' he added quietly, his words inadequate to express how deep that fear ran.

She lay back down on her back and was silent for a moment. 'You don't have to feel that way,' she finally said as if talking to the ceiling. 'I wanted you to make love to me. I don't expect anything else from you. Nothing between us has to change. We can still pretend to be engaged and never marry.'

She had already made such a declaration, but at the time he had been so intoxicated with lust he had barely heard what she said, and certainly had not registered its implications.

'No, nothing has changed between us,' he said. He should be feeling pleased that they were in agreement, but the tightness in his chest did not feel like pleasure.

He took hold of her hand, lifted it to his lips and gently kissed each finger, wishing he was a different man, wishing he could offer her more, wishing he was the man she deserved.

She rolled over onto her stomach and kissed his lips, lightly and sweetly, then smiled at him. 'Nothing has changed between us, but you have changed me. And for that I thank you.'

He gently stroked her cheek. 'What has changed?' he asked, wondering if she too was feeling as if the earth had somehow tilted off its axis. Like him, was she no longer sure of anything any more, only aware that she was now somehow profoundly different?

She drew in a deep breath. 'After what happened with Edwin I never wanted a man to touch me ever again.'

Joshua's muscles tensed at the mention of that man's name, his hands clenching into fists. He went to sit up, feeling the need to take action, to do something, but she put her hands gently on his shoulders to ease him back onto the bed.

'But I wanted *you* to touch me, wanted *you* to kiss me.' She smiled at him. 'And do so much more.' She gave him a saucy smile, then her face became serious. 'You have given me back part of myself, something that I had shut down, and—' she lightly kissed his shoulder '—you've opened up new parts of me I never knew existed.'

He wrapped his arm around her waist and flipped her onto her back, causing her to giggle. 'In that case, let me open those parts once again.'

'Oh, yes, please do,' she said, still giggling as she wrapped those long, luscious legs around his waist, until he stifled her giggles with his kisses.

Despite being exhausted by their love-making, sleep did not come easily for Irene. Their pledge to each other kept circling in her mind, tormenting her.

Nothing had changed.

But for Irene, everything had changed.

His first kiss had caused her to throw all caution to the wind. It had made her want him with a desperation akin to a madness. She had to have him, had to know what it was like to be made love to by such a magnificent man. She had got what she wanted, but she had deluded herself, lied to him and lied to herself.

Was still lying to him. But that was something he could never know. When she had offered her naked body to him she had been desperate for him to make love to her. She got what she wanted. She had no right to expect any more.

Nothing had changed.

She had made that promise. Now she would have to abide by it.

Finally, she slipped into a fitful sleep. When she awoke she saw Joshua across the room, looking through her sketchbook. She wished she had paper and a pencil in her hand, so she could draw his strong naked form, silhouetted against the light streaming in from the large windows.

He looked over at her and smiled. 'You really are superbly talented. You should have an exhibition. Although perhaps don't display this particular sketch.'

He turned the sketchbook towards her, with the drawing she had done while he was asleep. That was one done just for her own memories, and such an explicit work by a female artist would be sure to shock society.

'No, I'd never do that. That is just for me, so I can remember last night.'

He flicked the sketchbook closed. 'But you really should have an exhibition. And I could arrange it.' He returned to the bed, but instead of lying down as she'd hoped, he sat on the edge and looked at her, his face earnest. 'I have many connections in the art world, men I went to school with. I even have a friend, George West-wood, who owns a gallery in Grosvenor Square. I can contact him and tell him about your work. I'm certain he will want to display your work.'

'No,' she said firmly, not liking the direction the conversation was going. She did not want him think-ing he owed her. He couldn't give her love or commit-ment so he would help her in her career. What was that? Payment?

He looked taken aback by her abrupt reply. 'No? Why not? Your work deserves to be shown to the world. Well, perhaps not that sketch of me,' he said, pointing to the sketchbook. 'But your other paintings. Rather than trying to get into another one of those art schools that make it clear they don't really want women artists, you could get established on the art scene without them.'

'I said no.'

'But I'm sure if I showed George your work, he'd be delighted to display it.

'I said no,' she repeated, louder.

He placed the sketchbook on the bed and turned fully to face her. 'Why not? Isn't this what you want? To be an established artist?'

'You know it is, but I don't want to have my work displayed because you have friends with art galleries. I don't want my work to be hung in those galleries be-cause I am engaged to a duke.' She grabbed her che-mise, pulled it on and covered herself up. He had ruined everything. His offer seemed like nothing more than payment for what they had just exchanged.

'No one needs to know.'

She gave a dismissive laugh, climbed off the bed and

looked around for the rest of her clothing. 'I think your friend already knows you are a duke.'

'But he doesn't need to know the paintings were done by my fiancée. He doesn't need to know there is any connection between us at all. If I take a selection of your paintings up to London and show them to him, just to get his opinion, he can make up his own mind.'

He stood up and pulled on his trousers as if about to rush off to London immediately.

'Believe me, no gallery owner will mount an exhibition just because a duke shows him the works,' he said as he pulled on his shirt. 'They're businessmen. They also have to maintain credibility in the industry. No one would display your work just because I'm a duke and you're my fiancée, but if it makes you uncomfortable I can keep that to myself. I can just say they are works by a talented artist I've discovered, one whose work I want him to have a look at so he can give his opinion. I can even leave the suggestion that they mount an exhibition up to them.'

She shrugged. 'No one mounts exhibitions of women artists.'

'Ah, and that's where we can have some fun,' he said, sitting back down on the bed. 'I won't tell them you're a woman. We won't tell anyone until after the critics have raved about this new, original and highly talented artist. Then we'll tell them that they've just fallen over themselves to praise a female artist.

He smiled at her, obviously delighted with his plan. She didn't smile back.

'I'll just tell them they're the work of a recluse. Which is really the truth. Once they discover that this reclusive artist is actually a woman they'll have to eat their words and throw away all their prejudices.'

She could see some merit in his argument but remained unconvinced. 'You have a lot of faith in my work. You don't know that the gallery owner will be interested. You don't know what the critics will say and you certainly don't know that we are going to revolutionise the art world.'

'I have no more faith in you than your talent deserves.'

Irene smiled at him, not just because his words were so flattering but because he looked like a different man. Gone was the louche rake she had first met. All she could see now was a man fired up with determination.

'Right,' he said, taking her by the hand. 'Let's go and look at your paintings so we can decide which ones I should take up to London.'

He led her through to the studio and they stood in the middle of the room, surrounded by all the works she had completed since arriving in Devon.

'Not that one,' Irene said, pointing towards the painting of David.

'No, perhaps not,' he said, looking at it with a critical eye.

Irene's heart seemingly sank to her stomach. He didn't like it. She had put her heart and soul into that work. It reflected how she felt about him, how she had longed for him, how she had been yearning for him to return to her.

He turned towards her, his face serious. 'It is a masterpiece, Irene, but you are right. If I show that to the gallery owner he will know that the artist is not just someone I have a passing acquaintance with, and not just because I'm naked.' He approached the painting. 'You've captured so much emotion, so much intensity. No one could ignore that this is a painting of the artist's lover.'

'You weren't my lover when I painted it,' she said quietly.

He turned to her and smiled. 'That makes it even more personal. While I was thinking of you, imagining taking you as my lover, you were painting this.' He looked back at her *David* and smiled. 'But this painting should remain something just for us, a memory of the time when we were too foolish to realise that we needed to be together.'

Irene's heartbeat fluttered within her chest. Was that a declaration of love? It almost sounded like one, although he had not actually said the words. Was he also saying they had a future together? Again, it sounded like it, but he had not actually said it. Was Irene reading too much into his words?

No, nothing had changed.

'Right, this is going to take some time,' he said, changing the mood to one of brisk efficiency. 'I had better call for some food to be delivered to the gatehouse.'

He did up the buttons of his shirt and checked to make sure he looked respectable, although everyone at the house would not have failed to notice he had spent the night at the gatehouse.

Remembering her own situation, she quickly grabbed a piece of paper, scribbled a note and handed it to Joshua. 'Please have this delivered to my lady's maid so she does not worry about my absence.' Or even worse, suddenly appear at the gatehouse, curious to know what had happened to her mistress.

Irene did not want Mabel reporting back to her mother what she saw, although what she would see would be two people who were engaged to be married looking at artwork and having a discussion about art. That would hardly cause a scandal, but Irene still wanted everything that happened between herself and Joshua kept private, even innocent acts such as this.

With a kiss goodbye, he departed, and with surprising efficiency he returned, back in her studio and back scrutinising her paintings, his face serious as he moved from one to the other.

'Choosing just a sample is so difficult,' he said as he held up her painting of several village children playing marbles on the footpath, while village life swirled around them. 'They're all so good and each one displays a different aspect of your talent.' He looked up at her and smiled. 'But I do love this one. You've captured the children's serious faces, as if what they were doing was of monumental importance.'

'It was, to them.'

'I think that's why this one is such a delight. It's not sentimental but shows that childhood intensity so beautifully.'

He picked up another, and once again frowned in concentration, causing Irene to swell with pride. He was looking at each painting as an objective critic and he was impressed with what he saw. It was so different from most people's reaction. Her tutors at the art school barely looked at her work, assuming that she would never amount to anything. After all, no one was ever going to take a woman artist seriously, whereas the male students had a chance of achieving fame, of maybe one day even being accepted into the Royal Academy. No such future lay in store for Irene, so they did not waste their time on her.

Her friends were always supportive, and for that she was always grateful, and now Joshua was also encouraging her and gave every appearance of being genuinely proud of her achievement.

He placed the painting on the floor, picked up another and a smile crept slowly over his lips. 'This one I have to take up to London.' He turned the painting to face her. It was of the cove, the one she started sketching on the day she saw him swimming. 'Not just because I'm in it,' he said, still smiling. 'But because it is masterful.' He turned the painting back to look at it. 'Your talent really is sublime,' he said quietly, as if to himself.

'At least no one can tell you're naked in that one,' she said with laughter in her voice.

'Perhaps one day you could actually paint me with my clothes on.'

'Now why would I want to do that when you look so good naked?'

He nodded towards the sketch of her, still lying on the couch. 'I could say the same about you, my darling.' He turned and smiled at her. 'But let's not think of that right now or I'll become distracted.'

Irene was tempted to tell him she had no objection if he did get distracted but he had already turned back to her art and was looking carefully at another painting of the cove, this time depicting the aftermath of a storm, with debris strewn along the beach.

The afternoon passed in the companionable activity of examining each painting in turn, discussing it objectively, until by the end of the day, they had six paintings that represented the breadth of Irene's style.

Once again, he departed, this time carrying her paintings to the carpenter so he could crate them up and Joshua could take them up to London.

While he was occupied Irene took the opportunity to return home. She sneaked into the house, like a thief in the night, and was pleased to see the servants had taken advantage of her absence and were absent themselves, doing heaven knows what. Only Hetty was present.

'Good afternoon, miss,' she said, greeting Irene in her usual cheerful manner. 'I've packed your portmanteau. I'm assuming you'll be staying at the gatehouse for a while.'

Irene sent her an embarrassed smile. Of course Hetty would know. Gossip spread faster than the wind in a village, but it was too late to care about that now. She had done what she vowed she would never do, fallen completely under Joshua's spell, and there was no point denying it.

'Thank you, Hetty,' she said. 'Would you be so kind as to take it out to the coach driver.'

Even if the village did not already know of her involvement with Joshua, seeing her travelling in his carriage would have alerted the ever-vigilant gossips, but so be it. If being gossiped about was the price she had to pay for being in his arms, then it was a price she was prepared to pay.

When she returned to the gatehouse, Joshua was

waiting for her. 'I've booked to travel up to London on the next train,' he said, causing her heart to sink.

'Don't worry. I'll only be gone a few days, and when I return I'm sure we'll have some good news to celebrate.' He wrapped his arms around her and kissed her, long and hard. 'And that's just a sample of how we will be celebrating,' he said when they finally broke apart.

With that he departed. Irene had no idea whether he would be successful, but her heart swelled every time she thought about the faith he had in her talents.

Once his carriage had departed, she turned from the window and picked up the sketch of herself, lying in the position of Velázquez's Venus. While he was away in London, she would make a start on the painting so she could present it to him as a gift, a memory of what they had shared.

It would be a painting that would depict everything she felt about him, that would say what she couldn't express in words. She wanted to capture the passion, the yearning desire she had felt for him before they became lovers, and once again felt for him now he was gone, even if it was only for two days.

She would miss him while he was gone, but he would soon return and she would be waiting for him.

Chapter Nineteen

Joshua had a purpose. For the first time in his life he was doing something that felt important and it filled him with an unfamiliar sensation. Pride? That was probably it. It was not an emotion he was familiar with but he rather liked it. He was about to launch a new artist, about to grant someone an opportunity they might otherwise not have; that was surely something to be proud of.

The fact that the artist was Irene made it even more worthwhile. But he had not lied to her, had not been trying to flatter her. He could see that she possessed real talent and that was the main reason why he was doing this. Even if she wasn't his lover, he would want to help her achieve the success that was denied to her because she was a woman.

He arrived in London in the early evening, so had a night to kill before the gallery opened in the morning. Under such circumstances, he would normally visit one or more of his clubs, then go on to a party or some other form of entertainment. Instead, he spent a quiet evening at his town house contemplating the day to come.

This too was a novelty. Joshua never stayed at home when he was in London. And after spending time down in Devon he would usually be even more keen to be among his fellow revellers, but not this evening. Tonight he was content with his own company. Another novel experience. Usually being alone was to be avoided at all costs, much preferring to be with people whose lives were just as futile as his than to spend time with his own thoughts. And he most decidedly had never spent any time thinking about the latest woman in his life, but thoughts of Irene never left his mind. Memories of her smile were his constant companion. It was all so peculiar to feel like this, but also extremely pleasant.

The next morning he awoke still with that strange sense of purpose, and arrived at the Westwood Gallery in Grosvenor Square, just as his friend was opening up.

'Joshua, how good to see you,' George said, clapping him on the back. 'What brings you here so early?'

Joshua signalled to his carriage driver and footman to bring in the unpacked paintings. 'I want your opinion on this artist who I discovered down in Devon.'

As each painting was presented to him, George looked at it carefully, not just with an art lover's gaze, but with the eye of a businessman. Joshua knew what he was thinking. Would these sell?

When he nodded, Joshua released his held breath.

'They're exquisite,' George said, confirming what Joshua already knew. 'Are there any more? I'd love to host an exhibition.'

'Yes. The artist has quite a catalogue. I've just brought a sample of the different styles.'

'Then let's do it. Tell me more about him. Where

did he study? Where else has he exhibited? When can I meet him?'

Joshua gave his prepared speech about the reclusive artist who wanted to remain anonymous and how the exhibition could only be mounted if that anonymity was guaranteed.

George nodded slowly, considering what Joshua had said. 'Intriguing. An anonymous artist, a recluse, an undiscovered genius. Yes. That should fire up the public and the critics' imaginations. They'll all be anxious to know who this unique talent is.' George leaned forward and squinted at the signature in the corner of the painting, the initials revealing nothing. 'But surely you can tell me.'

''Fraid not. I promised the artist.'

'Hmm, well, if he insists, I suppose I too will have to stay in the dark.' George stood up from peering at the signature and shook Joshua's hand. 'I'll schedule an exhibition for next month. That won't be too soon to get more paintings up to London, will it?'

'Not at all. Not at all.'

Joshua left the gallery further swelling with that feeling he now knew for certain was pride and a sense of achievement. He could hardly wait to get back to Devon and tell Irene the good news, but the new Joshua seemed to have not only found a sense of purpose, but good manners as well.

He knew he should dine with Aunt Prudence before returning. She would be disappointed if he didn't, although the old Joshua did not usually worry about disappointing anyone, especially his matchmaking aunt. But his new-found warmth towards the world encompassed even that indomitable woman. And after all, she was partially responsible for this euphoria that had possessed him.

If she hadn't been so annoyingly determined to marry him off, she would never have brought Irene into his life. His aunt had unintentionally made him happier than he would once have thought possible. The least he could do was show her he was now an improved, responsible nephew.

'My darling aunt,' he greeted her as he arrived at her Mayfair town house. He kissed her on the cheek and took a seat across from her in her parlour.

'You look different,' she said, staring at him through narrowed eyes. 'More…' She twirled her hand in the air as she tried to capture the right word. 'Less…' She repeated the gesture.

'More or less what?'

'I don't know, but something has changed since I last saw you in Devon.' She continued staring at him then slowly smiled. 'It's all due to Miss Fairfax, isn't it?' His aunt clapped her hands together. 'Didn't I say she was exactly what you needed and would make an ideal duchess?'

In his good mood, Joshua chose not to point out that Irene was the last in a long line of so-called ideal young ladies his aunt had selected for him to marry. As a gambler, or at least, a former gambler, he knew what the odds were. She'd have to get it right eventually. And get it right she had. Perfectly right.

'Although even I couldn't predict it would be such an immediate success and you would fall in love with her. You are in love with her, aren't you?'

He stared at his aunt. Was that what he was feeling? Was that why the world suddenly seemed a brighter place? Was that why he felt such benevolence towards the world and everyone in it, including his aunt? Was that why he couldn't stop thinking about Irene? Was he in love? It was another emotion Joshua couldn't readily identify. But if this was love it was rather wonderful.

'So, have you decided to bring the wedding forward?' his aunt continued before Joshua could confirm or deny her claim. 'Why wait until next winter? Why not marry sooner?'

He continued to stare at his aunt as if dumbstruck. These were all good questions and worthy of consideration. He and Irene had agreed not to marry, but if his aunt was right that he had fallen in love with her, wasn't marrying the most logical thing to do? He wanted her in his life, could not imagine his life without her, did not want to imagine his life without her. He wanted her, and only her, for the rest of his life. He had been making things so complicated when really, it was all so simple, so obvious.

He rose from his chair, crossed the floor and kissed his aunt once again on the cheek. 'Perhaps. I'll ask Irene when I return and let you know.'

He would have to do more than just ask her when she wanted to marry—he would have to ask her *if* she wanted to marry, and he could only hope the answer would be yes.

Irene stood back and admired her work. She had made good use of their time apart and was pleased with the progress she had made.

When she had started the painting, she had been trying to express how she felt at the time, how she had been aching for Joshua. Now it had captured a sated woman, a woman who was still waiting for her lover, not with unfulfilled yearning but with anticipation.

She stared at the painting of herself and wondered what sort of present it would make. Would it be a memento of the beginning of their relationship that they would treasure in the years to come? Irene knew that was what she hoped.

She didn't know what their future held, didn't know where their futures would take them, but one thing she did know for certain: her feelings for Joshua had grown even stronger now that they were lovers. They had promised each other freedom, but the only freedom she wanted was the freedom to be in his bed, the freedom to be in his life, for ever.

Her thoughts were interrupted by the sound of carriage wheels on gravel. He was back. She quickly pulled off her painting smock, ran to the mirror to check her appearance, brushed down her skirt and took a quick breath to compose herself.

Then she heard female voices calling out loudly, several male voices responding and the sound of another carriage travelling up the driveway. Had he brought guests with him? That was unexpected, and somewhat disappointing. Perhaps it was the gallery owner. But they had agreed she was to remain anonymous. He wouldn't go back on his word, would he?

She moved to the window and saw the two carriages drive around the fountain in front of the house, people leaning out the windows and calling to each other. The carriages halted, the doors flew open and more people than they were designed to carry tumbled out, including several women, all in a state of disarray and, she suspected, a state of intoxication.

Did they not know that Joshua was away? Irene continued watching, expecting the footman to inform them they had made a wasted journey and they would soon be departing. With much hilarity they entered the house. That was peculiar. She waited, assuming the footman had made a mistake and soon the butler would intervene and the raucous party would be on their way. That didn't happen.

Whatever was happening at the house, it was none of her business. She pulled her smock back on, returned to her easel and tried to focus on her work. Her gaze kept straying to the window. Who were these people and what were they doing in Joshua's home when he was absent?

Eventually her curiosity got the better of her. Once again, she discarded her smock, draped it over a chair and walked up the driveway to the house.

The same footman greeted her with a polite bow and the butler raced down the hallway towards her. 'Good afternoon, Miss Fairfax,' he said, looking uncharacteristically flustered.

'I saw a carriage draw up. Has Josh— Has the Duke returned?' Irene asked, knowing the answer.

'No, miss. But he has guests, and they have made themselves at home in the green drawing room,' he said with a hint of disapproval.

'Is this a common occurrence? Do guests often turn up when the Duke is away.'

'Yes, miss. Such things have been common in the past.' His manner suggested he hoped, in the future, when Irene was mistress of the house, it was an occurrence that would cease.

Irene walked through to the green drawing room, curious yet hesitant to meet these presumably uninvited guests.

She opened the door and came to a halt in the door frame. The noise of their arrival had alerted her that they were a raucous group but that had still not prepared her for what she saw. Irene was used to people either sitting politely and chatting or standing in small groups sipping their drinks. Even the crowd from her art school, who were considered bohemians by some, only breached etiquette by being rather boisterous and high-spirited.

What Irene saw reminded her of Rubens's paintings of nymphs and satyrs. They had not long been in the drawing room and yet empty bottles were already strewn around the room and the red faces and dishevelled appearances of the men suggested they had already consumed a large amount of alcohol. But it was the young ladies that shocked her the most. One was draped over a settee and two men were taking turns to kiss her, while another couple of young ladies by the window were engaged in what could only politely be described as an amorous embrace, much to the enjoyment of the men watching.

The nearest man turned towards her. 'And who do we have here?' he said, rising unsteadily to his feet and stumbling in her direction. 'Has good old Joshua arranged some local entertainment for us?' He crossed the room with surprising speed for a man in his condition and took her arm before she had a chance to turn and run. She could smell alcohol and it wasn't coming from the glass in his hand. It seemed to emanate from his very skin.

'You really are a beauty, aren't you?' He increased the grip on her arm. 'Come and sit on my lap and I'll put a smile on those pretty lips.' He turned to the others and shouted above the noise of raised voices and loud laughter. 'Doesn't this one look like she needs cheering up and I'm just the man to do it, if I do say so myself.'

He turned back to her and gave her a lecherous smile that turned her stomach.

'Who are you and what are you doing here?' She demanded.

'The Earl of Musgrove at your service, ma'am,' he said, releasing her arm and making an unsteady bow. 'Now, talking of servicing...'

Irene swatted away his hand, which had picked up a tendril of her hair.

'Now, don't be like that. You'll upset me,' he said with a laugh and took a swig from his brandy balloon. 'I don't mind a feisty woman as long as she lets me win in the end.' He looked over his shoulder at the other men, so they could share in this joke.

'Joshua is in London. Does he know you? Did he expect you?'

'Oh, Joshua, is it? Well, well, well. It seems good old Josh has got rather friendly with this beauty already.' He slowly raked his eyes up and down her. 'Better not let the fiancée know that he's still up to his old tricks.

That won't go down too well, especially as they haven't even tied the knot yet.'

'I am his fiancée,' Irene said, louder than she had intended.

This brought the activities in the room to a halt and they all turned to stare at her.

'Are you indeed?' the lecherous man said, his expression not changing. 'So you're the one who finally managed to bag the title of Duchess of Redcliff. I hope you know what you're letting yourself in for.' He laughed and looked towards his friends, who were watching the exchange with gleeful, almost cruel expressions. 'If the Duke hasn't already shown her, perhaps it's up to us to let her know what life is going to be like when she weds the Duke.'

A loud hurrah went up from the group. The amorous couple, who had momentarily stopped what they were doing, resumed their passionate embrace, and one of the men caressing the young lady on the settee began unbuttoning the front of her gown, which caused her to squeal with laughter.

Irene's hands shot to cover her mouth.

'Don't worry about them,' the lech continued. He wrapped an arm around Irene's shoulder in a clumsy attempt at comfort. 'As far as I see it, you've got two choices. Try and change the Duke, something that is bound to end in failure, or just accept him as he is and join in the fun. And if you join in, I can assure you, you will find lots of ways to enjoy yourself.'

Irene pushed his arm away and took a step backwards.

'It's going to be like that, is it?' He shrugged. 'Looks

like you're going to be just like the old Duchess of Redcliff. She made the mistake of trying to change the former duke and quickly learned that was a waste of time. Try that and you too will end up a miserable old crone who stays at home while the Duke is out carousing. If that's what you want, well, it's your loss, but if you change your mind…' He sent her another of those stomach-turning smiles.

Irene backed out of the room, needing to get away from these appalling people. She slammed shut the door, which resulted in much laughter and jeering. Unable to move, she leaned against the door frame, her legs weak beneath her.

She should not have been so shocked. Hadn't she been warned what the Duke was like? Hadn't she heard about his reputation, about the countless women who moved in and out of his bed, of the carousing? And yet she had chosen to forget it, just because he had made her writhe in ecstasy. What a damnable fool she had been.

Joshua himself had even told her that his father treated his mother badly, that he'd had countless mistresses, and even kept them in the gatehouse. Just as Joshua was doing with her. He had said he didn't want to hurt any woman, including her, and that was why he had vowed never to marry.

He had told her all this. He had actually warned her. He had not lied to her. She had lied to herself.

She had tried to convince herself that nothing else mattered as long as he was in her life, had even wanted to believe it was different between them, that she was different to every other woman who had passed through his life.

How could she be such a fool? Hadn't her time with Edwin taught her anything? She had wanted to believe it was different with him as well. She had been flattered by his attention. Had chosen to ignore the warning signals. And now she had done it all over again.

And this time it was so much worse. She had become so besotted with Joshua she had not only forgotten who he really was, but had also dropped every barrier she had built to protect her. Now she could no longer deny it. She was a woman who had fallen completely, hopelessly in love with the wrong man. A woman who had been desperately trying to convince herself she expected no more than the delirious happiness of being in his arms, in his bed.

She forced herself to start walking back to the gatehouse. As much as she wanted to, she could not blame Joshua. He had made no promises, had never given her any indication that she was anything more than just another woman in his life. The only person she could blame was herself. She should have known it would end like this, sooner or later, and perhaps she should be grateful that it was to end so soon.

That lecherous man, that Earl of Musgrove, was right. If she remained with Joshua, she would end up just like the previous Duchess. Miserable and wanting to change the Duke, to turn him into a man he simply would never be.

Well, that would not be her fate. She would not stand back while he took other women as his mistresses. She could not bear it.

They had promised each other complete freedom when they became engaged, and now it was time for

Irene to honour that promise. But she could not stay around and be witness to his dissolute lifestyle and she most certainly would not be part of it.

If she was to save herself from being completely crushed, there was only one thing she could do. She had to ensure she never saw the Duke of Redcliff again. That was the only way she could stop herself from once again falling for his seductive appeal and deceiving herself as to the man he really was.

Chapter Twenty

Being away from Irene had been hard but it had been well worth it. Joshua couldn't wait to see the expression on her face when he told her about the gallery owner's enthusiastic reaction to her work.

As he sat in the train carriage taking him back to Devon, Joshua could barely contain his frustration at how such a modern, rapid form of transport could travel so slowly. He wanted to gift Irene this news as soon as possible, and he wanted to be back with her. Immediately and for ever.

He couldn't help but smile at how much his life had changed since he last took this train from London to Devon. On that trip he had been hiding from his aunt and her constant matchmaking. Now he was grateful for the very thing from which he had fled. His aunt had achieved her goal. She had matched him with his future duchess and he couldn't be more grateful to her.

Not only had his aunt achieved what he would once have thought impossible. She had convinced him he did want to settle down and marry. It was hard to believe but it was true. And there was only one reason why his world had been turned on its head. His aunt had matched him up with Irene Fairfax. The woman he loved. The woman he wanted as his wife. It was unbelievable and yet extremely believable. Knowing Irene as he did, how could he feel otherwise?

How could he not want to spend the rest of his days with someone who made his life worthwhile? How could he not want to wake up next to her every day, go to sleep with her in his arms every night?

When he had last been on this train, he had been fleeing from the thought of marriage. Now he was returning to Devon with the intention of proposing. Something that a short time ago would have been unimaginable.

They stopped at another station and Joshua frowned out the window, willing the passengers to move faster and the train to recommence its journey.

Finally, the train pulled into the Seaton station. This time he had telegrammed ahead and his carriage was waiting for him, and he told the driver to drop him off at the gatehouse.

Before the carriage had come to a halt, he jumped out and rushed up the stairs to her studio. She wasn't there. His smile grew even wider at the memory of how he had entered her studio and found her lying on the chaise longue, her beautiful naked buttocks towards him, looking at him over her shoulder, her intent clear.

That was where she was. Waiting for him in bed, in an equally arousing pose. He forced himself not to rush to the bedchamber, but to move slowly so he could fully appreciate what was on offer. He entered the room. His smile died. She was not there either.

Had she returned home? That's where she would be. He forced down his irrational sense of foreboding, raced up the driveway and around to the stables to summon the carriage driver to take him to her house.

He found the man about to unharness the horses, but his attention was taken by the two other carriages in the stables. He did not need to ask the driver to whom they belonged. One bore the crest of the Earl of Musgrove, the other that of Viscount Meriwell.

It seemed he had guests, but he could not deal with that now. He wanted to see Irene. To that end he ordered the driver to take him to what was still officially her residence. When he arrived, the footman greeted him formally, but informed him that Miss Fairfax was not at home.

'When do you expect her back?' he asked. She was likely to be out sketching so the man would probably have no idea when she would return, but Joshua would wait no matter how long it took. Either that, or he would comb the surrounding countryside until he found her.

'I'm afraid Miss Fairfax has returned to London and has asked us to pack up the house. Once that is done, all the servants will also return to London.'

Joshua stared at the man as if he was speaking a foreign language. 'What? Why? Did she leave me a note?' he asked, panic rising in his voice.

'I don't believe so, Your Grace.'

Joshua remained standing at the door then, realising there was nothing more this man could tell him, he retreated to his carriage, unsure what to do next.

Had she missed him so much that she had rushed up to London to join him? Joshua hoped that was what was behind her sudden departure. But why pack up the household? Or had a family member taken ill and she had been called to their bedside? He could think of no other reason why she would leave so suddenly without at the very least informing him of why she had done so.

He returned home, entered his house and the sound of breaking glass and a loud peal of female laughter greeted him.

'You have guests, Your Grace,' the footman said as he took Joshua's hat and coat. In his desperation to see Irene he had all but forgotten that Musgrove and Meriwell had arrived, and by the sound of the squealing coming from the drawing room, they had brought company.

'I believe they have moved to the green drawing room while the servants put the blue drawing room to rights,' the footman added.

Joshua hardly needed instructions on where to find his guests. All he need do was follow the sound of shrieking laughter. When he opened the door to the green drawing room he could see it was now another room the servants would need to put to rights.

Chairs were overturned, abandoned bottles had been left to spill their contents onto the rugs, one man was passed out on the settee and a young man was pouring wine into a young woman's mouth, while watched by another couple who seemed to find this behaviour to be hilariously funny.

'There you are, old man,' said Frederick, the Earl of Musgrove, swaying across the room towards Joshua.

'We thought we'd surprise you. You've been stuck down here so long we decided you'd need a bit of cheering up. You must be bored out of your damn mind with nothing to do all day but stare at all this damn countryside.' He gestured towards the windows with his brandy balloon, sending an arc of amber liquid spraying over the Turkish rug.

'You haven't by any chance seen my fiancée, Miss Fairfax, while you've been here?' Joshua hoped beyond hope that the answer would be no.

'Yes, you'll be pleased to know I formally introduced myself to her just after we arrived yesterday.' He nudged Joshua in the ribs. 'Not bad, not bad at all, old man. She's a bit uptight for my taste, but she's certainly a beauty, so doing the deed and getting an heir out of her won't be an arduous task,' he said with a lascivious wink.

Joshua was tempted to strike the man for his disrespectful attitude but he had more important things to do. Instead, he ran down to the servants' quarters to find the butler.

'James, do you know when Miss Fairfax departed and whether she left me a note?' he asked, holding out little hope that his butler could provide any enlightenment.

'Miss Fairfax left not long after your guests arrived. She did leave a note, which I placed in the top drawer of your study as I suspected it would be the one room your guests would not enter. I'm sorry I didn't greet you when you arrived, but I was unfortunately detained by the demands of your guests.'

'Thank you, James,' he called over his shoulder as

he raced out the servants' quarters and up the stairs to his study. He wrenched open the desk drawer and found a crisp white envelope bearing her feminine handwriting and addressed to the Duke of Redcliff. This return to formality was not a good sign.

He grabbed his letter opener, slit open the envelope and devoured the contents. The note was short and to the point.

> *I believe it best if we see no more of each other.*
> *I am returning to London. Please do not con-*
> *tact me.*

Joshua continued staring at the letter, as if by some will of his own he could make the words change. She could not possibly mean it. Only two days ago they were in each other's arms, whispering words of affection in each other's ears. When they had made love he had seen his own love reflected in her eyes. And now she was gone. How could she possibly change so much in a few days?

The sound of a woman's shrill laughter, and feet running along the hallway, resonated through the house and up to his study, answering all his questions.

He hated to think what Musgrove and Meriwell had said to Irene, what anecdotes of his decadent behaviour they had taken pleasure in shocking her with or what scenes of debauchery she had been confronted with.

He needed to put this right. He would find her, tell her he was not like his friends, not anymore. Nor was he the man he once was. He looked down at the note in his hand. Yes, that was what he should do.

Instead, he sank down into the leather chair and placed his head in his hands. Was he just like Meriwell and Musgrove? A few days ago he would have said yes, quite definitely, and said so without shame. He was a man who liked a good party as much as they did, a man who spent his days and his nights finding new and ever more entertaining ways to amuse himself.

He claimed that he was now a different man. But could a man really change that much in so short a time? He doubted it.

What a man was more than capable of doing though, was convincing himself he had changed, but how long would it take for him to revert to form? Perhaps his father had thought he was a changed man when he first married his mother. Would history repeat itself if he did marry Irene? Would he hurt her just as his father had hurt his mother? That was a risk Joshua was not prepared to take.

She was right. It was best if they never saw each other again. This could never work. All he would do was make that lovely woman miserable, just as his father had made his mother miserable. That was a fate Irene did not deserve. She deserved to be loved and cherished by a better man than he ever would be.

Like a defeated man, his shoulders slumped, he walked down the stairs towards the drawing room to join the party. A loud cheer greeted him when he entered and poured himself a large brandy as if he had done something admirable.

He was back. Back in the world in which he belonged.

Chapter Twenty-One

Irene was unsure of a lot of things, but when she arrived at Paddington Station, there was one thing she was most definitely sure of. She could not face her mother. Not yet.

Despite going over and over what had happened between herself and the Duke, Irene still did not know what to think or what to feel, but she knew exactly what her mother would think and how she would react to the news that Irene wanted no more to do with him.

She would be horrified that her daughter had rejected a duke and run away back to London. Her mother would probably put her on the next train back to Devon, insisting that she do whatever it took to save their engagement and get herself up the aisle as quickly as possible.

And that was something Irene would never do. She did not want marriage. She did not want the engagement and she did not want the Duke. That was not entirely true. She did want the Duke, but the Duke she wanted was a man she had created; he was the man she wanted him to be, not the man he really was.

As if in a dream she boarded a hansom cab waiting outside the station, and instead of asking the driver to take her to her family's town house, she instructed him to take her to the home of her good friend Amelia. There she was sure to find a supportive listener, one who would hopefully help her sort out her confusion.

On arrival, while the footman was announcing her, Irene told her lady's maid she could go down to the kitchen and have a cup of tea with the servants. Irene could never be entirely sure that Mabel did not report back to her mother, and she did not want anything she discussed with Amelia to leave this house.

'Irene, this is a lovely surprise,' Amelia said as Irene entered the drawing room. Rising from her chair, she crossed the room, her arms outstretched. She stopped walking. Her smile fading. 'Oh, dear, what's wrong?'

'I needed to see you, because…it's just—'

Amelia's arms encircled her and all pretence was lost. The tears that she had been holding back since she left that dissolute scene in the Duke's drawing room streamed down her face in what she knew to be a most unbecoming manner. Still holding her in an embrace, Amelia led her to the settee, gently lowered her down and handed her a linen handkerchief.

Eventually her sobbing came to an end and Irene had to admit she did feel ever so slightly better for her outburst.

'So, tell me what happened,' Amelia said gently.

'I've fallen in love with the Duke.' Irene knew how foolish that sounded. She had fallen in love with a man she was engaged to, a man her parents wanted her to marry. That did not sound like a problem. Under usual circumstances the problem would be if she was not in love with him.

Amelia tilted her head in question but said nothing.

Irene clutched her sodden handkerchief tightly in a ball and tried to order her jumbled thoughts. 'I should never have let myself fall in love with him, and now I'm going to have to find a way to fall out of love with him.'

'Hmm,' her friend said with a frown, which did not fill Irene with optimism. 'I believe that is even harder than falling in love. I wish I could give you some advice on how to achieve that, but instead, why don't you tell me why you shouldn't be in love with him.'

'Because he's a rake. Because he's had more women than he can remember. Because we had agreed to get engaged but to never marry, and to give each other complete freedom.' She looked at Amelia, hoping she would understand. 'But I made that promise when we first became engaged. It seemed like the perfect solution for both of us. But I don't want him to have his freedom. Not now. If I hadn't fallen in love with him, it wouldn't matter, but I have.' More tears sprang to her eyes. 'It was such a perfect plan and now I've ruined everything.'

'Unfortunately, we can't help who we fall in love with,' Amelia said, once again placing her arm around Irene's shoulders.

'I'm so stupid,' Irene mumbled.

'You're not stupid, but unfortunately love can make fools of all of us at times.'

'But I'm the biggest fool of all. I knew exactly what he was like from the moment I met him. After all, what sort of man goes home with a complete stranger then takes his clothes off? A rake, that's who. I knew that, and I should have known better than to fall for him. I did know better.' She looked around as if to reassure herself that no one was listening and lowered her voice. 'After what happened with Edward Fitzgibbon you would think I'd be immune to the seductive appeal of a handsome, charming man.'

Amelia tensed, her face pinched. 'Did the Duke seduce you? If he did, then the man is worse than just a rake, he's a...a... I don't know what he is, but he does not deserve your tears.'

Irene sat up straight. 'No, no, no. It was nothing like that. He's not like Fitzgibbon in that way.' Once again she lowered her voice. 'If anything, I seduced him,' she said as tears coursed down her cheeks. 'After he kissed me I knew he wanted me but something was making him hold back. I wanted him so badly that I—' A sob cut her off.

Amelia patted her hand. 'You can't blame yourself for that either, and believe me, I know how love can make one act out of character and what it's like to want a man so badly that you lose all ability to reason, that all you can do is react to your feelings and ignore your rational thoughts.'

'Exactly,' Irene said and gave a small hiccup. 'So how do I get my sense of reason back? How do I stop reacting to my feelings and regain my willpower?'

'You're perhaps asking the wrong person. From the moment Leo first kissed me I lost all ability to think straight, and he still has the power to make me addlebrained.' She gave a little laugh, then pulled her face into a more serious expression. 'Sorry, that's no help to you. Perhaps you've done the sensible thing by leaving and putting distance between the two of you. Time apart might help cool things down.'

Amelia's words might be reassuring but the disbelieving expression on her face wasn't.

'And you're welcome to stay here for as long as you like,' she added.

'Thank you, Amelia, but I'm going to have to face Mother at some time. I might as well get it over and done with. I just needed some time and a chance to talk to someone who would not judge me harshly.'

'Well, you always know you can come back here, at any time, if things with your mother get too difficult.'

Irene kissed her friend on the cheek in thanks before she departed and prepared herself for what was inevitably going to be a fraught conversation with her mother.

Joshua's friends whirled around him. He heard laughter, the breaking of glass as yet another drink slipped from an inebriated hand, the ripping of fabric, even grunting and sighing from the drunken couples who cared little for discretion.

Usually, he would take an active part in the revels, but now it all seemed rather pointless and, he had to admit, intensely boring.

When a young lady approached him and made some open suggestions on how she could cheer him up he politely declined. He did, however, take her offer of a drink, hoping another brandy would either provide him with the anaesthetic he craved or give him the enthusiasm to partake in his friends' revels. It did neither.

Eventually, his low mood refusing to rise, he slipped away and walked down the driveway. He wasn't sure what drew him to the gatehouse. Was it because he wanted to sense her presence again, or try to relive their time together? Whatever it was, it was as ineffective as the brandy in dulling the pain in his chest. He slowly walked up the stairs into the bedchamber, picked up the pillow where her head had once lain and inhaled deeply, her feminine scent only intensifying the pain gripping his body.

He should leave the gatehouse, go back to his friends, put all this behind him and return to his pointless, frivolous life. It was foolish to stay here, torturing himself. He ignored his own advice and wandered through to her studio. He picked up her paintbrush, ran his fingers over her tubes of paints, then forced himself to look at her artwork, lined up along the wall.

There was one painting he was most drawn to, the very one he should avoid. The one she had been working on when he had entered the studio to find her lying naked on the chaise longue. He released a groan as he picked up the canvas and gazed on her beautiful body. Whether it was a groan of desire or despair he did not know, but whatever it was, it hurt, more than Joshua thought it was possible to hurt.

A noise at the door caused his sluggish heart to start racing. She was back. He raced down the stairs to discover two footmen carrying a trunk.

'Good afternoon, Your Grace. We've come to pack up the last of Miss Fairfax's possessions so we can send them back to London.'

'Yes, of course,' Joshua mumbled, crushed by his disappointment. 'Leave the paintings though,' he shouted out as the men walked up the stairs.

He rushed up and overtook them, ran into the room and turned the painting of Irene and the one of him as David to the wall.

'Miss Fairfax is to have an exhibition in London and I'll need to get these paintings crated up and sent to the gallery.'

'Very good, Your Grace,' a footman said before busying himself with the work.

Once the men had finished, Joshua arranged for the carpenter to pack up the paintings, but not the one of Irene, nor the one of himself. The one of Irene he would keep as a memento of the woman he had lost; the other he would keep because Irene had said she did not want to see him again and he doubted she wanted to be reminded of how he had uncaringly crashed into her life.

Eventually, his friends left, leaving behind a disaster site for the servants to clear away. No one seemed to notice he had not been involved in their revelries. They had been too busy enjoying themselves to care about anyone else, just as Joshua had once been, just as he surely would be again, once he had shaken off this maudlin sense of loss that had possessed him.

In the meantime, he occupied himself with organising the transport of her paintings up to London. When he arrived back in the bustling city, he expected his old life to beckon. There were clubs he could visit, parties he could attend, women he was sure would be eager to show him how much he was missed.

He avoided all his old haunts. Instead, along with George and his assistants, he helped arrange the paintings on the gallery walls so they would be displayed to their most advantageous. For a brief moment he was able to forget about himself and his pain. It felt good to be doing something constructive and satisfying to know he was helping Irene one last time.

He was certain the exhibition would be a success and this would be the making of her career. She would then go on to be a celebrated painter, mixing with other artists, people with the same passions as herself, not useless men who thought of nothing except enjoying themselves.

As much as it pained him to know she would have all this without him in her life, it was what he wished for her, success, happiness. He could help in a small way to give her the first of these wishes, success, but he knew he would never be able to give her the second. Happiness. And she knew it as well. That was why she had left. He had always known she was a sensible woman, just as he had always known that he was a man no sensible woman would ever want to become involved with.

When all the works were mounted on the walls he looked around and pride welled up inside him. He had no right to feel that, but he did. If nothing else, he was proud that he had once known such a talented, wonderful woman.

'Marvellous,' the gallery owner said. 'So, Joshua, are you going to tell me more about this reclusive artist of yours?'

Joshua merely shook his head, still staring at the masterpieces on display.

'Well, if you find any other unknown artists as gifted as this one, let me know. I'm always on the lookout for undiscovered talent.'

'Perhaps you're just not looking in the right places,'

Joshua said, staring at the painting of the cove near his Devon estate.

Irene had said that it was almost impossible for people outside the established art world, such as herself, to get their works displayed, or to even gain entry to art schools. That was something that had to change, and it was some compensation for all his suffering that he had helped in a small way to make that change for one very talented woman.

Chapter Twenty-Two

Irene's mother's reaction was nothing if not predictable. There were tears, recriminations and accusations. She pleaded, begged, threatened and did everything she could to cajole Irene into contacting the Duke. Irene was instructed to throw herself on his mercy, to appeal to his better judgement, to do anything that would get him to forget all this nonsense and forgive her impetuous behaviour.

She bore this onslaught with as much dignity as she could. She had allowed her mother's histrionics to affect her once before. That had resulted in a sham of an engagement and spending a dangerous amount of time in the Duke's company. Now she had finally learned the lesson that Edwin Fitzgibbon should have taught her. Charming, handsome men had to be avoided, and that particularly charming, handsome man more than most. She now knew that charm and good looks always concealed a darker side, one that could break your heart. No, she most emphatically would not be contacting the

Duke ever again, and the more her mother argued the firmer Irene's resolve became.

As the weeks passed, mother and daughter descended into an uncomfortable silence. When her art equipment had arrived, Irene had been determined to resume work, but even that refuge was denied her. She hadn't even had the energy to unpack her paints and brushes, and her mother had instructed the servants to put them away in the attic.

That had never happened before. For as long as she could remember she had sketched and painted. It had always provided her with comfort, but not now. She could only hope and pray her desolate mood would pass. Without her art what was she? A small voice inside her also added, without Joshua what was she, but that voice was firmly quashed.

Her father provided no help in the feud between mother and daughter. Each morning he announced he was frightfully busy at the office. His early departures and late arrivals home meant Irene had seen little of him since her return. Instead, she had to spend each day with her increasingly fractious mother. Visits to her friends provided some solace, and she was tempted to take up Amelia's offer to move to her town house, but was reluctant to inflict her sadness on that happy household.

Instead, she stayed with her mother.

Seated across the breakfast table, she could see her mother had now decided she would not speak to Irene, perhaps believing that was the best way to bring her disobedient daughter to heel. Irene had to endure a series of icy stares, the silence broken only by the slamming down of the teapot and a series of harrumphing noises of disapproval.

When the footman brought in the first post of the day and placed a small package beside Irene's breakfast plate it was a welcome distraction from the increasingly strained atmosphere.

'What's that?' her mother snapped, leaning over the table and peering at the package. They were the first words she had addressed to Irene that day. As Irene removed the string and brown paper a smile crept over her mother's face. 'Is it from the Duke?

She reached over the table to snatch the parcel from Irene's hands, but Irene was too quick and pulled it out of her reach.

'Well, what is it?' she asked, her hand still grasping at the package. 'Is it a love token? A gift to tell you all is forgiven? What is it?'

'It's much better than that,' Irene said, staring down in wonder at the open package in her lap. 'It's invitations to an exhibition opening.'

'What?' Her mother frowned, and Irene could almost see her mind working, trying to decipher how this could be construed as a love token.

'The opening of an art exhibition at a gallery,' she repeated. With all that had happened between herself and the Duke, Irene had forgotten his reason for going up to London.

She placed one of the invitations in her mother's outstretched hand.

Still frowning at Irene, her mother placed her spectacles on the end of her nose. '"The Westwood Gallery invites you to the opening night of a gifted Devon artist.'" She peered at Irene above her reading glasses. 'Is this someone we know? Is it a friend of the Duke's?' She turned the card over as if the blank back would reveal further information.

'It's me, Mother. I'm the Devon artist.'

Her mother stared at her, her brow furrowed as if trying to decipher a foreign language. 'You?'

'Yes, me, Mother. The Duke contacted a gallery owner he went to school with and showed him some of my artwork.'

Her mother looked back down at the crisp card in her hand and once again smiled. 'If the Duke organised this opening thing, then he will most probably be there. Won't he?'

'I have absolutely no idea.' And she had even less idea regarding what she thought of that possibility.

'Well, we will need to get a new gown made for this opening event, just in case.' She waved the card at Irene and sent her a cunning smile. 'After all, you are the featured artist—you'll need to look your best for your opening night.'

Irene sighed. 'You'll notice my name is not on the card. That was intentional. We knew the gallery owner was unlikely to exhibit the works of a female artist.'

Her mother nodded and Irene braced herself for the usual lecture on why young, unmarried ladies should not waste their time in such pointless pursuits, which included anything that didn't involve finding a husband.

'That was very clever of the Duke,' she said instead. 'And doesn't this show how important you are to him. He will even go to all this trouble just to indulge you in your little hobby,' she added, waving the card in front of Irene's face.

Irene made no response. Yes, she was grateful to the Duke for arranging this for her, and it was certainly kind of him, but that did not mean she had changed her mind. All she had to do to stop her resolve from waning was to remember the sight that had greeted her when she had opened the drawing room door and seen the antics of his friends. A small shudder of disgust rippled through her. That was his world, a world of drunkenness and debauchery, and one she wished she had never been exposed to.

'After breakfast we must go straight to the dressmaker,' her mother continued. 'With the season now over she should not be too busy. Last time I visited I saw she had some beautiful pale salmon silk fabric in stock. That would look divine on you and highlight your colouring to its best advantage.'

She looked down at Irene's hands and tutted. 'And it would be best if we got some new silk gloves as well.' Her smile became decidedly wily. 'We wouldn't want anyone to know you're an artist and those hands are a sure giveaway.'

Irene gave a resigned shrug. She cared nothing for what she wore to the opening, but if arranging her gown kept her mother off her favourite topic of berating Irene for her rejection of the Duke, then she would gladly go along with it.

Dressed in a fashionable gown of soft salmon pink, Irene and her parents took a carriage to Grosvenor Square for her opening night. Irene was unsure what was causing the churning in her stomach: having her work on display for the first time for all to see, and to criticise, or the possibility of seeing the Duke again.

Her mother was equally anxious, but there was no question about what was causing her nerves. Throughout the journey she kept rearranging Irene's hair and gown as if she was a package about to be gifted to an important person, which, Irene decided, in her mother's world was exactly what Irene was.

'Stop fussing, dear,' her father whispered, removing his wife's hand from further lowering the lace straps of Irene's gown. 'You'll make her even more nervous and this is such an important night.'

'You're right,' her mother said, although Irene suspected they differed on what exactly was important to Irene.

The carriage pulled to a halt in front of the gallery, its lights spilling out into the dark street, and the sounds of a string quartet and chattering guests filling the otherwise quiet night.

The gallery owner greeted them as if they were merely guests, and her parents thankfully followed her instructions not to reveal that Irene was the artist. Irene suspected that would be no hardship for her mother, who would prefer to keep secret that particular flaw in her daughter's character.

A waiter handed them each a champagne flute and the gallery owner continued to wax lyrical about the talents of this new and exciting artist.

'I believe this exhibition was organised by the Duke of Redcliff,' her mother said, cutting the gallery owner off in midflow about the artist's interesting technique. 'Is he here tonight?'

'You are correct madam, but I'm afraid he is not.'

'Are you expecting him? When do you think he will arrive?'

Irene took her mother's arm and tried to pull her away from grilling the poor man.

'I'm sure he will be in attendance, won't he?' her mother added, looking around at the elegantly dressed men and women, as if one of them would suddenly reveal themselves to be the Duke.

The owner nodded his agreement. 'I am sure you are right, madam. He did not say if or when he would be in attendance, but as the Duke is the one promoting this unknown talent I expect we will see him tonight. After all, how could he stay away?'

'Excellent,' her mother said, causing the gallery owner to raise his eyebrows slightly in question.

'When he does, make sure—'

'Mother, I believe the gallery owner has more guests to welcome,' Irene said, pulling on her mother's arm. Her mother looked over her shoulder and saw a line of patrons eager to get inside and reluctantly moved away.

Along with her parents, Irene circulated around the gallery. In this unfamiliar setting it was as if she was seeing her framed paintings for the first time.

'These are actually quite good,' her mother said, sipping her champagne and looking at a painting of men working in the field, with Seaton village in the background.

Irene stared at her mother. It was the first time she had complimented her work, the first time she had said anything that came close to being encouraging. Perhaps seeing them in the unfamiliar setting had affected her as well, and she was now seeing them as works of art, and not the source of constant conflict between mother and daughter.

'I'm so proud of you,' her father whispered, as they moved on to a painting of Hetty, her cheeks flushed as she stirred a pot of broth. 'You really are gifted and I'm so sorry we tried to stop you from painting. But this exhibition shows that a true talent can never be stifled.'

Irene took her father's arm. 'Oh, Father, thank you. But your talent was also stifled. You too should have been allowed to paint. You should not have been forced to focus solely on business.'

'Perhaps,' he said, looking wistfully at the painting. 'But I don't have your talent and am happy for it to be just a hobby, whereas you, Irene, you are truly gifted.'

Irene reached up and gave her father a kiss on the cheek, just as her chattering friends flocked around her.

'These are marvellous, Irene.'

'You're so clever.'

'And you should hear what people are saying about them. They love them.'

Irene was unsure who had said what as she waved her hands, patting the air downwards to indicate that they should lower their voices. 'No one knows I'm the artist and we want to keep it that way,' she whispered.

'Oh, yes, right, sorry, I forgot,' Amelia said quietly, while the other two nodded, then continued chatting in such subdued voices you would think they were in a church service.

'I just overheard a couple of critics discussing your work,' Georgina whispered. 'I could hardly understand what they were saying, something about the contextualised significance of the landscape revealing a sublime… oh, I don't know what. It made no real sense to me, but their meaning was obvious. They were in raptures.'

While her three friends squealed with delight, Irene looked around the room, wondering which critic Georgina was talking about. The gallery was filling up and she was pleased to see the owner had invited members of the art community, including many critics from leading publications and several well-known artists.

Her gaze continued to scan the guests. Only one person wasn't there. The Duke, but that was surely a good thing. Tonight was too important. She could not allow herself to become distracted by him. Although that, it appeared, was proving to be an impossible task.

How could she not think of him, particularly tonight? He was responsible for all this. It had been his idea. She had been against it at first but he had convinced her it would be a success, and he was right.

Was he staying away because she had said she did not want to see him again, or because he didn't want to attend? Had he moved on already? To the next woman?

She released a slow sigh, causing her friends to stop their chatter and gaze at her, their faces no longer excited, but filled with worry. She lifted the edges of her lips into a forced smile. She would try very, very hard to not think of the Duke tonight.

'If you'll excuse me, I think I'll do my own eavesdropping on a couple of those critics,' she said, wishing she was as excited as she was pretending to be.

Her friends continued to watch her, wearing matching looks of concern as she moved to where a group of critics had congregated around her painting of the Devon cove. It had begun as a quick sketch, the one she had been doing when the Duke had swum into view, but she had turned it into a painting. The Duke was depicted as a small figure in a vast ocean, moving towards the shore as storm clouds gathered above.

'It's not just the technique,' one man said in response to something a fellow critic had said. 'Which I agree is superb, but it's the emotion. He's captured so much feeling, the turmoil of the clouds, the swell of the water, and that figure appears unaware of the tempest coming his way. One could see it as a metaphor for life, how we are oblivious to what is on the horizon and one never knows how things could at any moment change irrevocably.' The other critics nodded their agreement. 'I believe I might use that in the review,' he said as they moved on to the next work.

Irene was tempted to call out to them that they were wrong. It was not a 'he' who they were praising, but a 'she,' and that *she* was standing right beside them. But they were right. The painting did signal a change was on the horizon. Irene hadn't known at the time that things were about to change irrevocably, but for the artist, not the subject.

She moved around the room and saw red dots denoting a sale had already appeared on numerous works. The fact that people were buying her work to hang in their homes was an even greater compliment than the critics' flattering words.

She also noticed that two paintings were conspicuously absent. The painting of David, and the one of her, lying in the pose of Velázquez's Venus. Irene was pleased. They were two paintings that meant so much to her, she would have hated for anyone else to buy them. Had the gallery owner decided not to display them because of their risqué subject matter? But if he thought the artist was a man it was unlikely he would care about such things.

Or, had the Duke kept them? That seemed more likely. And if he did, what did he think when he looked at them? Did he remember their times together? Did he think about how they met, or the first time they made love? Or did he just see them as trophies of yet another woman he'd had in his bed, one of those countless women whose names the servants didn't bother to remember as they would soon be replaced as part of the never-ending stream of lovers.

Her good mood crushed by melancholy, Irene continued to wander around the room, each painting now reminding her of the Duke. There was no denying that the paintings she completed after he came into her life held a greater intensity, a greater depth of emotion. And when he was in her life she did feel things more acutely: her senses had seemed heightened, scents were more intense, food tasted better, her skin reacted to even a feather-light touch.

And now he was gone, and the once vibrant, colourful world was suddenly so bland.

This gallery opening would once have been everything she wanted in life. It was wonderful, and it seemed she was on the cusp of becoming a successful artist, and yet, damn it all, without the Duke in her life, without him here to share it with her, it all felt like such a hollow victory.

Chapter Twenty-Three

Joshua never lurked in the shadows, but that was exactly what he was doing tonight. Standing across the road from the Westwood Gallery, where the light could not reach him, he leaned against the brick wall and stared at Irene, like a peasant gazing at a princess. In her pink gown she appeared to shimmer in the light of the gallery, the other guests melting into a swirl of colour around her.

It was so easy to see why he was bewitched by her. It was as if she glowed with an inner beauty that was translucent. He just wished she would smile more. Tonight was her night. She should be revelling in her success. And he could see that the opening was indeed a success. When his gaze strayed reluctantly away from her, he could see the smiling patrons and the look of delight on George Westwood's face as his assistants placed a red dot on yet another painting.

The exhibition was a triumph, as he knew it would be. Now that he had reassured himself of that fact, he should slink away. She did not need him ruining her big night. And yet he stayed, as if trapped, unable to pull himself away, knowing that this might be the last time he saw her.

He wished he knew why she looked so melancholy. Was it because of him, or was that wishful thinking on his part? And if it was because of him, then that was something else for which he should be ashamed. He had never wanted to cause her pain, and the only way that inevitable outcome could have been avoided was for him to have stayed out of her life. He had known that, and yet he had selfishly ignored his own vow. He knew that men like him should never, ever become involved with women like Irene, because it would always end in the innocent young woman getting hurt. Although this time there was some justice in the world, because he too had been hurt, deeper than he had ever thought possible.

So deeply, he wondered whether he would ever recover. But he wasn't going to recover by skulking in the shadows, staring at the woman who didn't want him. He should leave. That was what he should do, but he didn't. He didn't move from the wall. His eyes didn't leave Irene.

If his friends hadn't descended on his estate, perhaps right now he would be in the gallery, by her side, sharing her success. He released a long, slow sigh. If his friends hadn't turned up, he would still be deceiving her, pretending he was someone he wasn't, a good man who could be faithful to one woman. He should be grateful to his friends for opening Irene's eyes to the type of man he was, for reminding him that men like him would only ever cause pain to women like her.

The gallery owner tapped the edge of his wineglass

to call for silence and everyone gathered expectantly around him, including Irene. They all had their backs to him so perhaps he could sneak in, just for a few seconds, to hear what George had to say. As quietly as possible he slipped in through the gallery's door and placed himself discreetly in a corner as far from Irene as possible.

'I think we can all agree that tonight we have had the honour of being the first to be introduced to the works of a new and important artistic voice.' George's statement elicited murmurs of agreement from the assembled guests.

'Not only does his work show originality and technical proficiency, but his paintings evoke a depth of emotion in the viewer, which shows him to be a rare and exciting new talent.'

'She,' Joshua muttered under his breath.

'So who is he?' a guest called out.

'Why all this secrecy?' another added. 'Why can't you tell us who he is?'

'All I can tell you is he is an artist from Devon and he was discovered by the Duke of Redcliff.' George looked over the heads of the other guests and stared straight at Joshua.

Cursing his height, Joshua bent his knees slightly to disappear behind the crowd, and looked towards the door, wondering if it was too late to make a hasty exit.

'Your Grace, is there anything you can share with us about this artist?' George said.

As one the crowd turned in his direction, including Irene. But unlike the other guests, she wasn't looking at him with expectation, but with wide eyes and her hand over her mouth.

'All I can say is the artist is someone I admire very much.' He stared straight at Irene as he said these words, hoping she would understand just how true they were. 'Admire more than I have admired anyone I have ever met before.'

This was greeted with a murmur of approval, although the guests were surely assuming he was talking about the artwork. He just hoped Irene knew he was talking about her.

'Tonight you have all experienced the beauty of the artist's work, but these paintings are more than just masterful works of art,' he continued. 'They reflect the artist's good heart and passionate nature. They are a reflection of a truly beautiful soul.'

This caused a shuffling among the crowd, but Joshua didn't care what effect his words had on them. There was only one person in the room whose opinion he cared about. This would undoubtably be the last time he saw Irene and even though he respected her wish for him to stay out of her life, he wanted her to know how much she had meant to him.

'A beautiful soul that deserves to flourish, to be happy, to be a success.'

The crowd, including George, continued to frown at him, but he cared not. All he cared about was Irene. More than cared about. Loved.

'Meeting this artist was a transformative experience for me. Having the privilege of being near them, knowing them, made me realise what an unworthy, frivolous man I am.'

The shuffling increased, along with the murmur of surprised conversation, but Joshua did not care. Irene had lowered her hand from her mouth and was gazing at him, not in disapproval, but with a look of curiosity that spurred him on.

'I am eternally grateful that this artist came into my life, even though I was so undeserving of them.' He drew in a deep breath and exhaled slowly. 'What I really want to say is, the artist is someone I don't just admire, but someone I adore, someone I have fallen deeply, profoundly in love with, someone whom I wish was deserving of their love in return.'

A collective gasp of horror rose from the crowd, and the murmur of voices turned into a babbling cacophony.

'Oh, for goodness' sake,' a woman's voice called out above the hubbub. 'The Duke is talking about my daughter, Irene Fairfax. He is in love with her, and she did all these paintings.'

This did not still the voices but led to heads turning in all directions to find the source of this statement, and the woman Mrs Fairfax was talking about.

While the chatter grew louder and louder, Irene broke through the crowd, crossed the room, took his hand and led him out of the gallery.

'I'm so sorry,' he said as soon as they were outside in the darkened street. 'I never meant to reveal that you were the artist.'

Irene kissed him to stop his talking and because she could think of no words to express what she was feeling.

His surprise at her action quickly disappeared and he kissed her back, as if to do so was the most natural thing in the world.

Tasting his lips again, feeling his strong arms around

her, holding her close, all other thoughts left her head. This was what she had been missing; this was what she wanted, what she needed. To be held by him, to lose herself in him. She kissed him with a fervour that expressed all the tumult and yearning that had been boiling within since they parted. She kissed him with an intensity that reflected the depth of her feelings for him. She kissed him as an expression of her love for him. Her simple love, her complicated love, the love that consumed her.

When they finally parted, they stared into each other's eyes as if neither could believe what had just happened.

'I think that was what I was meaning to say in there,' he said, pointing towards the gallery window. 'But your way of saying it is so much better.'

She gave a small laugh, but there was so much she *did* want to say. She needed to get her thoughts in order. 'I'm so sorry, Joshua,' were the first words that cut through the confusion.

'Sorry? You? You have nothing to be sorry about. It's me who should be saying—'

'I'm sorry I judged you as harshly as I did. I'm sorry I ran off like a coward without even giving you a chance to explain.'

'No. You were right to leave. The way my friends behaved, of course you would leave. It was the only sensible thing to do.'

She shook her head, as much in denial as in a way to order the thoughts spinning around in her head. 'They were your friends, not you. Nothing you had done since the time I met you led me to believe that you were anything like them.'

But—'

'I ran away because I think I was looking for an excuse to leave you.'

He took a step backwards. 'I understand.'

She stepped towards him. 'No, I don't think you do. I hardly understood it myself at the time, but now it is all starting to make sense. I told you what happened between me and Edwin Fitzgibbon.'

His jaw hardened, and she placed her hand on his arm. 'None of that matters anymore, except that I want to explain to you why I ran away, why I told you I never wanted to see you again.'

He nodded, his face solemn. What she really wanted to do was kiss him again, to stop him from looking so forlorn, but she needed to tell him, to be honest with him, to finally be honest with herself.

'After what happened with Edwin, I no longer trusted men, all men. I told you I never wanted any man to touch me again. That was true, but it was more than that. I also never wanted to open my heart to a man ever again. But with you I couldn't help myself.'

'I'm sorry.'

'No, it wasn't your fault that I fell in love with you. And it was wonderful to do so, but it was also frightening. I was frightened of being hurt, frightened of losing myself, frightened of my feelings, frightened of how intense they were.'

He took hold of her hand, held it softly to his chest, but said nothing.

'When I saw your friends, I decided that you were

no different from Edwin and I fled back to London, but what I was really running from was my feelings, my love, a love so strong it was overwhelming. In a strange, perverse manner, when I saw your friends, I think I was pleased I had been proved right, that you were like Edwin so then I wouldn't have to love you.'

'Oh, Irene.'

She squeezed his hand. 'And I do love you.'

'And I love you, but I know you deserve a man so much better than me.'

She shook her head. 'No, you—' He placed his fingers lightly on her lips to still her words.

'I knew from the moment I met you that you were too good for me. I also knew that I most certainly should not fall in love with you, but I did. When you left, I thought the pain I was feeling was a punishment no less than I deserved for not keeping my distance from you. And I was in pain, deep, anguished pain, unlike anything I'd ever experienced, or ever thought I could endure.'

He lowered his hand from her lips and took hold of both her hands. 'But I also know that despite the pain, I would not change a thing. You coming into my life was the best thing that ever happened to me. You changed me in a fundamental way that I can hardly understand myself. Knowing you, loving you has changed me. Until I met you I had no purpose in life, other than pretending to enjoy myself, but I didn't know what pleasure and happiness really were until I met you.'

He looked down at the ground, then back up at Irene. 'Seeing my friends again made me realise that I am no longer the man I once was. I'm not sure if I ever really was that man, or whether I was pretending because I didn't know how else I could be. I don't want that life anymore. I want a life with purpose.' He paused, his face pained. 'I want a life with you, if you will have me, if you can trust me.'

She reached up and touched his face, wanting to take away his anguish. 'Yes, I trust you and yes, I want to be in your life.'

She could have added that she also wanted to be back in his arms, but that was unnecessary as before she could form the words his arms were around her, her lips on hers. Irene sank into the kiss, sure that her happiness was complete. But it ended too soon. He broke from her, leaving her disappointed, but when he took her hand and dropped to one knee on the hard cobblestones her disappointment evaporated.

'Irene Fairfax, will you do me the honour of being my wife? If you agree, I promise to love you with all my heart, to dedicate my life to your happiness, to worship you in the way you deserve to be worshipped. If you don't wish to marry me, I will understand, I will still love you but I will expect nothing from you. I will—'

'Yes, yes. I will marry you.'

'You will?' He gazed up at her, as if surprised that it was that easy.

'Yes, I will. Now kiss me again, for goodness' sake.'

And he did. As she melted into his embrace, Irene knew she was loved, knew she was safe with a man who loved her, a man she trusted and loved in return.

When their kiss finally ended, she opened her eyes to see her smiling friends standing in the door of the gallery, while the rest of the surprised guests stared at them out of the window. It seemed tonight Irene and

Joshua had provided an even greater exhibition than her paintings.

In the middle of the crowd was her mother. Irene expected to see that look of victory; instead, what she saw was affection. Standing beside her mother was her beaming father, who was surreptitiously wiping away tears from his eyes.

Amelia, Georgina and Emily rushed out, wearing matching smiles, followed by Amelia's husband, Leo. As Leo shook Joshua's hand in congratulations, her three friends surrounded her, their chatter and excitement so much she could hardly understand what they were saying.

As the hubbub whirled around them she looked at Joshua, the man she loved, the man she was to marry. Her heart swelled, and she knew this was just the start of their happy life together.

Epilogue

A quiet wedding would have suited Irene. She imagined slipping away and eloping, but her mother had other plans. She reminded Irene in no uncertain terms and on more than one occasion that she only had one daughter and it wasn't every day a young lady married a duke, so she wanted to make the most of this special event. For once, Irene gave in to her mother's wishes without a fight, and on the day of the wedding she was pleased she had.

Her mother had promised the day would be sublime, and she was right. The wedding service was held at the country church close to the Duke's Devon estate. Irene's mother was happy to break with protocol on this point and host the wedding at the groom's home. As Irene pointed out to her, it was not every day a mother got to see her daughter married at a duke's estate.

But that was not Irene's reason for wanting to marry in Devon. She wanted to celebrate her love in the place where it had all begun. Her mother had agreed that was a lovely, romantic idea, although Irene had her suspicions that her mother had given in so easily because she could take pleasure in showing off Redcliff Estate to all her friends, and especially her husband's brother and his wife, the Earl and Countess of Lanbourne.

Lady Prudence, who now insisted that Irene call her Aunt Prudence, was also in her element, and never failed to drop a hint or two that she hoped for an heir in the not too distant future. Joshua and Irene thought it wisest to not mention that the longed-for heir, or perhaps a daughter, was already on the way. They knew that no one in their family would object when they finally heard the news. After all, Irene and Aunt Prudence had already informed them that a scandal was not a scandal unless society knew about it. But for now, Joshua and Irene had decided to keep it as their own little, but growing, secret.

The entire village turned out and crowded around the church, wanting to see the previously notorious Duke marry his duchess. Irene ensured a pew was reserved for Hetty, her maid of all works, and her family. She had also invited her friend Madeline and her brother Joshua, although neither were aware how they had inadvertently brought Irene and Joshua together.

If the right Joshua—or was that now the wrong Joshua?—had been on the train from London to Devon when he was supposed to be, they would never have met. If the right Joshua had not been dressed in workman's clothing, the reason for which he was yet to explain to her, then she would never have taken him back to her cottage. She would not have asked him to take his clothes off for her, and set in motion a chaotic chain of events that had led to them pledging to stay together until death do them part.

When they had been faking an engagement, one of Irene's delaying tactics had been to insist that a gown be made by French couturier, the House of Worth, and she had claimed that the famous fashion house was extremely busy. At the time she had suspected that they would make time to create the wedding gown for a duchess, and she had been right. She walked down the aisle dressed in an exquisite white silk gown, hand embroidered in silver thread, with a flowing train that floated behind her like a dream.

And the entire day went by like a glorious dream. With her three closest friends as bridesmaids, and on her father's arm, she walked up the aisle towards Joshua, knowing that this memory would be something she would treasure for a lifetime and one day tell her children and maybe even her grandchildren about.

Once the ceremony was over, the rest of the wedding day passed in a whirl. All Irene could remember was the feeling of happiness and loving being able to share her happiness with so many friends and family.

They honeymooned in France and on the few occasions when they did leave their hotel bed they took in as many art galleries as they could. Although, it was never long before the desire to return to their love nest became too much for them and they left the galleries behind.

When they returned to London, they were a couple on a mission. While on honeymoon, lying in their bed, surrounded by crumpled sheets, they had discussed their future together, and had decided they would open an art school to provide tuition for underrepresented groups, and a gallery where their works could be displayed.

This was a project they would work on together, and Joshua's passion and enthusiasm for the project was as great, if not greater, than Irene's.

Following on from her successful exhibition, Irene now had quite the reputation in the art world. While that was heartening in itself, it also meant they would have no difficulty attracting students and tutors to their school.

Her exhibition had been reported in most of the leading newspapers and had generated heated debates in the letters-to-the-editor pages on women and art. This had extended to a debate on the role of women in general, and Irene found she had also excited a great deal of interest among women's groups. Countless invitations to speak on women in art followed.

The critics who had attended the gallery opening saw themselves as serious writers, so none of the publications mentioned how Irene and Joshua had inadvertently put on their own exhibition when they had declared their love to each other. But knowledge of that event spread just as quickly as if it had appeared in banner headlines. It meant the notorious duke now had notoriety for a completely different quality, that as a hopeless romantic. A quality Irene was reminded of every day, when in words or gestures he never failed to display his love to her.

Occasionally, Irene had to step back and take a breath, look around in amazement at the way her life had changed since Joshua Huntingdon burst into her life, took off his clothes and posed as David, about to sling his rock at Goliath. Since that day, they had truly overcome the odds, managed to slay their own personal monsters and learned how to love and trust themselves and each other.

* * * * *

If you enjoyed this story,
make sure to read the first book in
Eva Shepherd's
Rebellious Young Ladies miniseries
Lady Amelia's Scandalous Secret

And why not check out her
Those Roguish Rosemonts miniseries?

A Dance to Save the Debutante
Tempting the Sensible Lady Violet
Falling for the Forbidden Duke

Get 3 FREE REWARDS!

We'll send you 2 FREE Books _plus_ a FREE Mystery Gift.

FREE Value Over **$20**

Both the **Harlequin® Desire** and **Harlequin Presents®** series feature compelling novels filled with passion, sensuality and intriguing scandals.

Get 3 FREE REWARDS!

We'll send you 2 FREE Books plus a FREE Mystery Gift.

FREE
Value Over
$20

Both the **Harlequin® Historical** and **Harlequin® Romance** series feature compelling novels filled with emotion and simmering romance.

Get 3 FREE REWARDS!

We'll send you 2 FREE Books plus a FREE Mystery Gift.

FREE
Value Over
$20

Both the **Romance** and **Suspense** collections feature compelling novels written by many of today's bestselling authors.

HARLEQUIN
PLUS

Try the best multimedia subscription service for romance readers like you!

Read, Watch and Play.

Experience the easiest way to get the romance content you crave.

Start your **FREE TRIAL** at
www.harlequinplus.com/freetrial.